W9-ABT-756

Jennifer had been totally unprepared for the sight in front of her: Rich Larsen, bare-chested, wearing camouflage pants and holding a baby

Her breath caught in her throat. The vision was so sweet she almost wanted to weep. That innocent little boy with a halo of red peach fuzz snuggled against that hard, wide chest. The baby's eyes were half-closed and he sucked on one finger.

This was, by far, one of the most tantalizing, sexy sights she could ever have imagined. Jennifer swallowed, moistened her lips and swallowed again. What was wrong with her? How could she be lusting after the man as if he were a hunk-of-the-month calendar?

She just didn't do stuff like that.

Then again, there was a first time for everything.

Dear Reader,

May is *"Get Caught Reading"* month, and there's no better way for Harlequin American Romance to show our support of literacy than by offering you an exhilarating month of must-read romances.

Tina Leonard delivers the next installment of the exciting Harlequin American Romance in-line continuity series TEXAS SHEIKHS with *His Arranged Marriage*. A handsome playboy poses as his identical twin and mistakenly exchanges "I do's" with a bewitching princess bride.

A beautiful rancher's search for a hired hand leads to more than she bargained for when she finds a baby on her doorstep and a *Cowboy with a Secret*, the newest title from Pamela Browning. 2001 WAYS TO WED concludes with *Kiss a Handsome Stranger* by Jacqueline Diamond. Daisy Redford's biological clock had been ticking...until a night of passion with her best friend's brother left her with a baby on the way! And in *Uncle Sarge*, a military man does diaper duty...and learns about fatherhood, family and forever-after love. Don't miss this heartwarming romance by Bonnie Gardner.

It's a terrific month for Harlequin American Romance, and we hope you'll "get caught reading" one of our great books.

Wishing you happy reading,

Melissa Jeglinski
Associate Senior Editor
Harlequin American Romance

UNCLE SARGE
Bonnie Gardner

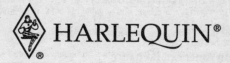

HARLEQUIN®

TORONTO • NEW YORK • LONDON
AMSTERDAM • PARIS • SYDNEY • HAMBURG
STOCKHOLM • ATHENS • TOKYO • MILAN • MADRID
PRAGUE • WARSAW • BUDAPEST • AUCKLAND

If you purchased this book without a cover you should be aware
that this book is stolen property. It was reported as "unsold and
destroyed" to the publisher, and neither the author nor the
publisher has received any payment for this "stripped book."

As always, to "Mud."
To the best critique group ever: Lyn, Pat,
Kathy, Dianne, Debby and Ellen.
To Sue and Donna. You know why.

To all the air force combat controllers I have known
and loved and sometimes hated. And to all the women
who love them in spite of it all.

ISBN 0-373-16876-4

UNCLE SARGE

Copyright © 2001 by Bonnie Gardner.

All rights reserved. Except for use in any review, the reproduction or
utilization of this work in whole or in part in any form by any electronic,
mechanical or other means, now known or hereafter invented, including
xerography, photocopying and recording, or in any information storage
or retrieval system, is forbidden without the written permission of the
publisher, Harlequin Enterprises Limited, 225 Duncan Mill Road,
Don Mills, Ontario, Canada M3B 3K9.

All characters in this book have no existence outside the imagination of
the author and have no relation whatsoever to anyone bearing the same
name or names. They are not even distantly inspired by any individual
known or unknown to the author, and all incidents are pure invention.

This edition published by arrangement with Harlequin Books S.A.

® and TM are trademarks of the publisher. Trademarks indicated with
® are registered in the United States Patent and Trademark Office, the
Canadian Trade Marks Office and in other countries.

Visit us at www.eHarlequin.com

Printed in U.S.A.

ABOUT THE AUTHOR

Bonnie Gardner has finally figured out what she wants to do when she grows up. After a varied career that included such jobs as switchboard operator, draftsman and exercise instructor, she went back to college and became an English teacher. As a teacher, she took a course on how to teach writing to high school students and caught the bug herself.

She lives in northern Alabama with her husband of over thirty years, her own military hero. After following him around from air force base to air force base, she has finally gotten to settle down. They have two grown sons, one of which is now serving in the air force. She loves to read, cook, garden and, of course, write.

She would love to hear from her readers. You can write to her at P.O. Box 442, Meridianville, AL 35759.

Books by Bonnie Gardner

HARLEQUIN AMERICAN ROMANCE
876—UNCLE SARGE

Don't miss any of our special offers. Write to us at the following address for information on our newest releases.

Harlequin Reader Service
U.S.: 3010 Walden Ave., P.O. Box 1325, Buffalo, NY 14269
Canadian: P.O. Box 609, Fort Erie, Ont. L2A 5X3

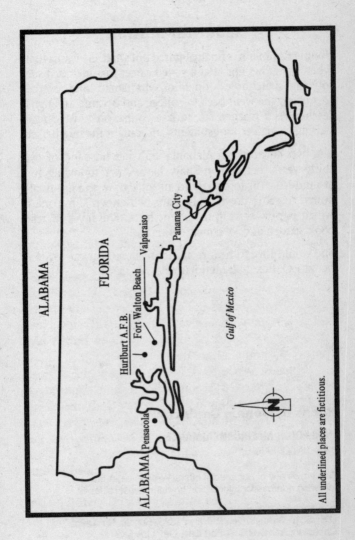

ALABAMA

FLORIDA

Hurlburt A.F.B.

Fort Walton Beach — Valparaiso

Panama City

Gulf of Mexico

ALABAMA Pensacola

N

All underlined places are fictitious.

Chapter One

Looking at the grimy storefront window of the Checkmate Detective Agency in Fort Walton Beach, Florida, Rich Larsen shivered in spite of the humid, ninety-degree August heat. He wondered if he should have called first, but shook that idea away.

He was a technical sergeant in the United States Air Force and a member of the Special Tactics Wing, Silver Team, one of the air force's most elite units. He could deal with a private detective on a side street in a military town. He drew in a deep breath and pushed open the glass door.

A rush of blessedly cold air hit him as he stepped inside and looked around. The office could have passed for something out of Mickey Spillane except for a profusion of houseplants cluttering every surface. The anteroom appeared to be empty, but the door to the rear was open.

"I'll be with you in a minute," a decidedly feminine voice said from somewhere. The floor?

"Okay, fine," Rich said, for lack of anything else, as a woman with long, dark brown hair peeked up from behind the reception desk.

This must be the secretary, he presumed, and as

the woman rose, Rich decided that she definitely did not look like someone out of Mickey Spillane. Her face was perfectly ordinary, like the girl next door. Her shape was anything but, in spite of the fact that she hid it behind a demure, cotton dress.

"May I help you?" she asked as she smoothed out the dress that did nothing to disguise curves that would make a showgirl proud.

"I'm looking for a woman," Rich said.

"This is a detective agency, not an escort service," the receptionist replied primly, and Rich amended his original description. She looked like a Sunday school teacher.

Rich blew out an impatient breath. "My sister. I'm looking for my sister," he clarified. "Look, if you'll just let me speak to the detective, I'll explain what I want, and be out of your way." He wasn't sure what she'd been doing on the floor, but she was obviously annoyed at being interrupted and was taking it out on him.

"Mr. King's out. Go on in the office and wait."

Shrugging, Rich complied. There had been other detective agencies listed in the phone book, but this one had the smallest ad. He figured it meant that they were either really good, or really cheap. Considering a tech sergeant's pay scale, even with jump pay and his other hazard bonuses, he hoped they were both. And when he'd asked around, he'd learned it was run by a former member of his unit who was now retired. Any time he could give a former combat controller his business, he tried to do it.

JENNIFER BISHOP sank back to the floor and fanned her face with her hands. That hunk of man was hot enough to melt the iceberg that had sunk the *Titanic*. He had to be six-foot-six if he was an inch, and his broad chest stretched the knit fabric of his navy Polo shirt. His shoulders were so wide that he surely must have had to turn sideways to come through the door.

No, she told herself. She was here to work, not drool over a man. Even if he did look like someone off of...what? The cover of a romance novel? She'd just come out of a relationship that ought to have put her off men forever. So, why was she getting hot flashes over this stranger?

She brushed the rest of the potting soil she'd spilled into a pile, reached for her minivac and vacuumed it up. Maybe it didn't fit the normal image of a private detective's office to be cluttered with houseplants, but then she wasn't a normal private detective. And she always whiled away slow periods by tending her plants.

Jennifer dusted her hands off and put the vacuum away. Then she drew a couple of deep breaths for good measure. Al King, her boss, was on vacation, and she was holding down the fort. Al had a military retirement to augment his income, but hers depended on whatever work they could get. With Al gone, she hoped to drum up a client or two of her own.

She took another deep breath, pasted an efficient look on her face and stepped into the office she shared with Al.

The guy hadn't gotten any smaller in the ninety seconds since she'd last seen him. He seemed to fill the room, and she wondered if the spindly, ladderback chair that looked almost comical under his huge body would continue to hold him up. A vision of the chair shattering and dumping him to the floor flitted through her mind and pushed away some of her nervousness.

"Thank you for waiting," she said as she seated herself at Al's desk across from the Adonis. No, Adonis did not fit this incredible hulk. He looked more like a man from the fjords of Scandinavia than the isles of Greece. There was a lean hardness to his face, but with ice blue eyes, a golden tan and sunbleached hair, he needed only a name like Olaf Olsen to finish the picture.

"You? You're the detective?" The man sat up straighter, inhaled and seemed to suck the oxygen right out of the room.

"I'm one of them," she said, fudging the facts only a tiny bit. "Jennifer Bishop. As I said before, Al King is out." She didn't add that he'd be gone for the rest of the month on a fishing expedition to Alaska to escape the heat and humidity of August in Florida.

"Oh. I get it. Bishop and King. Checkmate."

Score one for him. Not many people took the two names and made the chess connection. She didn't tell him that Al had bought the business from a guy who did surveillance in divorce cases. Considering the way the name worked to his advantage, Al had kept it. "Yes," she said. "And you are...?"

The man offered his hand. "Rich Larsen."

So, she wasn't so far off with the Olsen thing. Then he closed his huge hand over hers, and her brain ceased to function.

He held her hand in his firm grip long enough for Jennifer to feel light-headed and to be certain his fingerprints were branded permanently on her hand. She drew in a sharp breath and let go.

"Pleased to meet you, Mr. Larsen," she said when her breath returned. "Now, how can we help you?" Jennifer could see that he had doubts about her, and she really couldn't blame him.

After all, until a few months ago, she'd merely been the receptionist helping with the computer research. But, she'd studied, taken the exam, and she was now a licensed investigator. Funny, she didn't feel any different.

"I'm trying to find my sister," he said again.

"And how did you lose her?" Maybe she was being flippant, but she had to lighten it up. Jennifer couldn't see how a brawny guy like him could lose track of anything. He looked too together, too... male. She shook that notion away.

His blue eyes clouded. "We were in foster care. When I turned eighteen, I left to join the air force. She still had to finish high school. We kept in touch for a year or two, but when I got stationed overseas she wanted to go with me. Nothing I could say would convince her that a two-stripe airman was not authorized to take dependents. She thought I didn't want her. I wrote to her, tried to explain, but she didn't write back, and finally my letters started coming back marked, 'Moved—no forwarding address.'" He drew in a deep breath.

"I called and found out that the number for the foster family we'd lived with had been changed, and I knew I'd pretty much reached a dead end. By that time, Sherry was old enough to have graduated. I guess she got a job and started taking care of herself, but I haven't heard from her since. That was seven years ago."

He'd made other attempts to locate her through the

years, but he'd never had the time or the resources to do it right. This time he was serious.

"Why look now?"

He had expected that question, and it was easy enough to answer. "This is the first time I've been close enough to do anything about it. And the first time in a long time that my life has slowed down enough to follow through."

With special tactics training and assignments in both Bosnia and Kosovo, he'd just not had the time to do it. But after he'd attended the funeral for Dave Krukshank, who had been killed in that training accident, Rich had begun to see how empty his life had been. And he'd begun to think about his own mortality. If he died, who would mourn for him?

He didn't think he'd ever have a family of his own, but maybe Sherry would. Rich looked too much like his abusive father, and he didn't want to put any other children through what he'd been through as a child. He was big, he was strong, he was well trained. He could use what he had to save the world. But, he didn't dare dream about a family of his own.

Rich had hopes that world events would not intrude for a while, or at least that he wouldn't be required to participate in them. He'd been on the fast track far too long. He needed time to breathe.

"You're from Fort Walton Beach, then?" She started to write on a yellow pad.

"No, Val-P," he said, referring to Valparaiso, a town just to the east of sprawling Eglin Air Force Base—the huge military installation that dwarfed Hurlburt, where he was assigned.

Jennifer looked up from the pad. "I sure don't want to send away a paying customer, but have you tried to find her yourself? Surely, you have friends in common. Other relatives?''

Rich shook his head. ''Sherry's my only family. I tried looking myself, but nothing panned out. Called the high school. Looked in the phone book. Directory assistance. Everything I could think of. Even found a listing for the Parkers, our foster family. They haven't heard from her in years.'' He blew out a long, tired breath. ''I came up with zip. That's why I'm here. Hell, I don't even know if she's still in the area.''

He slumped back into the uncomfortable, straight-backed chair, and it creaked with the added weight.

Jennifer smiled. ''It sounds like you've made a good start, but there are still some avenues I can try.''

He sat up straighter. ''Like what?''

''Mostly computer stuff. You'd be surprised what you can find online if you know where to look. If you can give me some basic information about your sister, I should be able to track her down.''

She asked several questions, jotted down the answers, took his address and phone number, then put down her pen. ''I'll start working on this right away, Mr. Larsen.''

''Tech Sergeant,'' he corrected, then smiled. ''Rich.'' He started to offer his hand again, then remembered the jolt he'd gotten the last time. He stuck it in his pocket, instead. ''I'll wait to hear from you.''

He got up and headed for the door. Turning and looking back over his shoulder, he smiled. She didn't look like much of a detective, but maybe she could do the computer search thing. Besides, she did have an ex-combat controller for a partner. "Thanks. I hope you'll have something for me soon."

JENNIFER couldn't believe her first case had been as easy as this. She'd spent an afternoon on the computer, searching through data bases, and had come up with the information Rich—Tech Sergeant Larsen, she reminded herself—wanted. She wavered between waiting a little longer to make it look as though she'd worked harder, or calling him right away.

She called.

She wouldn't have charged him for the extra time anyway, but she knew how much he'd wanted to find his sister. He hadn't said so, but she'd seen the wistful look in his blue eyes when he'd spoken about her.

Of course, she'd gotten his machine.

So, now she was whiling away her time working on her plants. If only another customer would walk in off the street. Just not one as potent as TSgt. Larsen. And, maybe with a slightly more challenging request.

She puttered in her indoor garden, losing herself in Zen-like meditation. Working with the plants soothed her. When life with her ex had been at its rockiest, her plants had been her salvation. She smiled as she loosened the soil around a split-leafed Philodendron she'd nursed back from near death.

The phone rang.

Jennifer jerked out of her trance-like state and dropped the cultivator on her foot. That brought her back to her senses, and she limped to the phone. "Yes? I mean, Checkmate Detective Agency," she said sharply as she sat down and massaged the red mark.

It was Rich Larsen returning her call.

"I've found an address for your sister," she said, ready to provide the details.

To her surprise, Rich uttered a too-familiar exclamation. "Hoo-ah!" Then he hung up.

Stunned by what that single two-syllable word, the all-purpose cry of exclamation that combat controllers used, meant, Jennifer stood, holding the receiver until the phone company off-the-hook signal chimed in.

Her ex-husband was a combat controller. Was Rich Larsen one of them?

RICH MADE the ten-minute drive from his apartment just outside Hurlburt AFB in five. Good thing the afternoon rush wasn't yet in full swing. He hadn't bothered to change from his camouflage battle dress uniform; he'd just rushed out. He wasn't supposed to be wearing BDUs on the street, but he didn't give a damn about the regulations. This was too important.

He was pulling into a parking spot across from the agency when he realized that Ms. Bishop could have told him over the phone. He shrugged. He was here now.

He grabbed his scarlet beret, jammed it on his head, then locked the truck. He had to know what Ms. Bishop had uncovered. God, he hadn't even thought to ask whether it was good news or bad.

Preparing for the worst, but hoping for the best, he shouldered open the door.

Ms. Bishop was waiting at the desk. Today she

had her hair pulled back from the sides and anchored at the nape of her neck with a large barrette. She had on another flowered dress, and until she stood, she again looked like a member of the church choir.

The dress did nothing to disguise the sinful curves below that angelic face, however, and when she rose to greet him, he drew in a short breath. He said nothing, just waited for the blood to rush back to his brain.

"I've typed everything up for you," she said, handing him a sheet of paper. "She's married now...." Ms. Bishop glanced down at her notes. "To Michael Connolly. They live in Pensacola. Here's the phone number," she said, tapping the spot on the sheet.

Rich took the paper from her and held it gingerly as if it were a live grenade. He looked down at the information, neatly typed, and wondered at the ordinariness of it. A name, a social security number, an address and phone number. Name, rank and serial number. Everything you needed to prove you were real.

Was it real? Had Ms. Bishop really located his sister so quickly? He looked up from the paper, and he swallowed. "Did you call?" Why was his voice so thick and husky?

She smiled. "I thought you'd like to do that yourself." She gestured toward the phone. "Be my guest."

Rich wondered if he ought to do this here. Would he be better off calling from the privacy of his own phone? But Ms. Bishop had been a part of it this far, she might as well be there for the grand finale. He reached for the phone, his hands remarkably unsteady, and dialed.

His breath caught as the number connected. Ms. Bishop smiled and gave him a thumbs-up sign. One ring. What if she wasn't home? Two rings. He held his breath. Then the unmistakable sound of a phone company recording dashed his hopes of speaking to Sherry today. *Out of service.*

He closed his eyes and drew a long breath. "The phone's disconnected. Now what?" he said as he returned the receiver to its cradle.

Jennifer's smile faltered. Why hadn't she thought to try the number first? "Are you sure it's disconnected?" She reached for the phone Sergeant Larsen had just put down, pushed the Redial button and waited. She pasted a smile back on her face as she listened. "It said, 'out of service,' not disconnected. It could be out of order or they were late paying their bill for this month. They're probably still there." She met his eyes. "You could go. Knock on the door." As soon as she said it, Jennifer knew it was a big mistake.

He grabbed her arm, and the touch of his large, strong hand set her heart fluttering like a butterfly in a glass jar. "Go with me. I've changed a lot since I last saw my sister. She might not recognize me."

He paused and dragged in a ragged breath. "I'm a big guy. It might frighten her to have somebody like me show up on her doorstep. If Sherry sees someone like you with me, she might be more willing to let me in. Besides, I'm not familiar with Pensacola, I might never find the place."

As Jennifer considered the foolhardiness of going off on this expedition, he threw in the final piece of bait. "I'll spring for burgers on the way and you can navigate."

Burgers from a fast-food place sounded a lot better than the tuna casserole she had planned. Jennifer glanced at the clock. Almost quitting time. "I—I guess so," she heard herself saying. "Just let me lock up."

"Hoo-ah. It's a date," he said, his face regaining the animation he'd lost when he'd heard that tone.

"No," she corrected. "Not a date. This is business." Then she glanced at the way the fabric of his drab olive T-shirt stretched across that broad chest. She knew all about the kind of man who wore those scarlet berets and shouted hoo-ah. She'd been married to one. Duke had been the best at everything except commitment. She figured they were all the same. At least, until they'd gotten old enough to settle down as Al had. It must have something to do with the training.

No, she had a feeling that this story was going to wind up with a happy ending, and maybe it was foolish of her, but she wanted to see it through. Typing bits of information into a computer and waiting for it to regurgitate the answers was a living, but she longed to see the human side of her job. She wanted to see the results of her efforts.

This is *business,* she reminded herself. So why was she thinking about anything else?

"I FIGURE once I've eaten with a person, they have the right to use my first name. That okay with you, Ms. Bishop?" Rich glanced sidewards and chuckled at the flustered look on her face. "You can call me

Rich. Tech Sergeant Larsen's a little long, wouldn't you say?''

"I—ah—er—yes. Sure." She paused. "And you may call me Jennifer." Then she added, "Rich."

"Jennifer. It's a pretty name. It suits you."

She smiled and blushed. "I hope not. I always felt it was such an ordinary name. After all, every other girl in my class all through school was a Jennifer. I'd rather be a Rosemund or a Victoria. At least there aren't fifty of them lurking around every corner." Her smile quirked to the right.

"At least everybody knows how to spell it," Rich said. "What if you really did have one of those unusual names that nobody knew. That could be a problem," Rich said as she looked everywhere but at him.

"Yeah," Jennifer murmured.

The litter from the take-out meal scattered in her lap seemed to be more important to Jennifer than continuing the conversation. Rich shrugged. After tonight, it wasn't likely they'd see each other again. He shouldn't be getting his feelings hurt because a woman—an ordinary-looking one, at that—didn't want to make conversation with him.

Once they found Sherry's house, Rich reasoned, and he'd assured himself that his sister was alive and well and living in Pensacola, he'd take Jennifer home, and he'd never see her again.

They rode on in awkward silence until they reached the bridge that crossed Pensacola Bay and led into the city. "I guess we should pick up a map." Rich pulled into a service station. "I need to gas up anyway."

"Good idea," Jennifer said. "I'll see if they have one while you pump."

Jennifer reappeared before he had filled the tank. She unfolded the map and pored over it while he settled the bill.

"Ah, here it is. Smith Street," she said as Rich started the engine. "It's on the other side of town." She directed him to the main artery and settled back against the seat.

Rich drew in a breath and steered the truck toward the northwest side of town.

Jennifer knew she should be breaking his tension by talking, but darn it, sitting this close to him, she could barely think. She'd thought he'd made her office feel small, but in the confines of his small pickup truck, separated only by the space between bucket seats, it was all she could do to breathe.

She would be so glad when they were done with this.

Jennifer glanced at his strong profile and his lean jaw starting to bristle with golden five o'clock shadow and wondered if she might just explore... No, she told herself, it was too soon. Besides, she knew about his kind of man. Those special tactics combat control operators were love 'em and leave 'em all the way. She'd already been left once. And once was more than enough.

She busied herself reading the map and watching the landmarks fly by. Finally, they pulled off the main road and into a neighborhood.

Only a few more blocks and Rich would reach his sister's address. Only a few more blocks and he'd be reunited with the only relative he had. She smiled at that.

Most of Checkmate's work was doing background checks for Okaloosa County businesses. She seldom saw the people she researched. She seldom reached out and touched the people whose lives she explored. It would be wonderful to experience something good and positive.

"Shouldn't we be turning now?"

Jennifer snapped out of her thoughts and ran a finger along the course she'd marked. "About two blocks. Then turn left."

The neighborhood was a relatively new one comprised of small houses, with small mortgages, for couples just starting out. Most of the yards were well tended, and most had one car in the carport and one in the drive. She and Duke had once lived in a neighborhood like this together. She sighed. Now, she lived there alone.

Finally, they came to the street. "Right turn," Jennifer said with less than full confidence.

Rich turned, and Jennifer began scanning for house numbers. "I think we're headed in the right direction," she said. "It should be right around this curve."

It was.

Rich pulled up to the curb and parked. He exhaled slowly as he assessed the appearance of the small, yellow bungalow. Sherry had always loved the color yellow, but she never would have let the lawn go so long without mowing.

He knew that from the way she'd loved to do the yard work when they were in foster care together. She'd always said she wanted to have a little yellow house with a white picket fence and lots of yard to putter in. There was no fence, but two out of three was pretty good.

The lawn looked as if it hadn't been mowed in several weeks, and children's toys were scattered throughout the tall grass. There was a very old minivan in the carport, but the second car, if there was one, was gone. A pile of newspapers filled the seat of a lawn chair on the tiny front porch. Though it was too early in the evening for lights to be on, the house looked dark and forlorn.

"Do you suppose they've gone on vacation?" Jennifer echoed exactly what Rich had been thinking.

He nodded. "You'd think they'd've canceled the paper, though."

"Let me check the mailbox," Jennifer said, pushing open the door. She came back in a minute. "Nothing there. Maybe, one of the neighbors is picking up their mail. But, if they were going on a trip, wouldn't they put away their kids' toys first?" she mused.

"Beats me," Rich said. "Now what?"

"We talk to the neighbors. We've come this far, we might as well see what they know."

The house to the right was as dark as Sherry's with no cars filling the carport or the drive. But the one on the other side seemed cheery and open, and cooking smells wafted from that direction. "Guess we start with that one."

Rich drew a deep breath. "Okay," he said. "Here goes nothing." He rang the doorbell.

A plump, middle-aged lady appeared, drying her hands on a dishtowel. "May I help you?" Her expression was pleasant, but cautious, as she pushed open the storm door a crack.

Rich cleared his throat, struggling to dislodge the industrial-size lump, as Jennifer stepped forward and smiled reassuringly.

"My name is Rich Larsen. I'm looking for my sister, Sherry. I haven't seen her in several years, but I think she lives next door."

"Oh, Mr. Larsen. It's so good that you've come," the lady dithered. "I'm just so sorry you couldn't have come sooner." She pushed her screen door open and beckoned them in. "It's too bad you couldn't have come before..." Her voice trailed off, then she sighed. "It's so sad."

Chapter Two

She might as well have walloped him with a rifle butt. Rich staggered backward. Before what? No, he couldn't have finally found her only to have...

Jennifer took charge. "I'm sorry, Ma'am. What's happened?"

"You mean you don't know?" The woman paled. "I am so sorry. I could have softened the blow some."

"What blow? Please. Tell me what's happened to my sister."

"It was terrible, just terrible," the lady said, wringing her hands. "They had gone out to celebrate their anniversary. Five years, I think it was. They didn't go out much. They were just starting out and their budget was stretched to the limit. I used to sit with the little ones so they could take in a bargain matinee from time to time."

"Please, Ma'am. My sister?" Rich didn't like the way she kept referring to the past.

"It was a terrible accident. It was raining really hard and they skidded right into oncoming traffic. Mike was killed. Sherry's in the hospital. Broke her neck. They tell me it's going to be a long road before she's back on her feet."

Jennifer squeezed his hand, then released it. "Thank you, Mrs.... Can you tell us which hospital?"

"Oh, I'm sorry. I'm June Benton. She's in Baptist Hospital. I think she's supposed to be transferred to a rehab facility soon." She wiped her hands on the dishtowel she was still holding. "Sherry often spoke of her big brother. I'm sure she'll be glad to have you visit. It'll help having family around at a time like this."

Rich had heard everything, but he wasn't sure he'd absorbed the content of what Mrs. Benton had said. He had still been thinking of the fifteen-year-old he'd last seen, and in one afternoon he'd learned she'd married, borne children and been widowed. Not to mention the injury from the accident. This was not the happy reunion he'd hoped for.

"Thank you, Mrs. Benton. We're sorry to have bothered you." Jennifer turned to Rich. "Come on, we'll go to the hospital. At least, you can see her."

"Yeah, sure."

They started for the door, then Jennifer turned back. "Do you know what's happened to the children?"

Kids. He hadn't even thought about that. Sherry had kids. Who was taking care of them?

"Sherry's friend, Rebecca, took them home with her." Mrs. Benton looked inside. "I have a phone number for her somewhere."

"That's all right, Mrs. Benton. We have to hurry to reach the hospital before visiting hours are over. I can get that number later." Jennifer was certain Rich would want to know once the shock wore off, but right now, it was better to let him see Sherry than find the location of the children he didn't know. She took a business card from her purse and handed it to Mrs. Benton. "When you find it, call me. You can leave a message on my voice mail if I'm not there."

Mrs. Benton took the card and studied it, then nodded.

"Thank you, again, for being so helpful."

Rich had begun to show the classic signs of shock, so Jennifer took him by the arm and urged him through the door.

She steered him toward the passenger side of the truck and waited for him to protest, but Rich barely murmured a word as she climbed into the driver's seat and adjusted it to accommodate her smaller frame. "I need the key."

Rich dug it out of his pocket and handed it to her.

"There's some cola left in the cup holder. I think if you drink some, you'll feel better." She wasn't sure it would help, but Rich needed to do something, or when they did reach the hospital, they'd be visiting the emergency room and not his sister.

He did as she suggested. Jennifer checked the map for the location of the hospital, then turned the key.

Rich just stared out the window.

He'd probably been assuming that Sherry was living a fairy-tale life, and that presumption had just been tossed into the garbage. He might be in shock tonight, but when he had time to assimilate everything, he'd have questions, doubts. But for now, she knew he just needed to see his sister.

THE LARGE, suburban hospital came into view. Rich's heart began to race, and his breath rushed to catch up with it. It might not have been the same hospital, but it was the same feeling all over again.

Rich tried to push away the memory of his mother's last days, tried to forget those tumultuous, confusing weeks when he and Sherry had had nowhere to go, no one to turn to before the state put them into foster care. His father had died in the veterans' hospital several years before from the after-effects of his tour in Vietnam and alcoholism. The ten years Rich had spent in the air force might as well not have happened the way one look at that large hospital brought it all back.

Hospitals scared the bejesus out of him.

His parents had gone into hospitals and not come out. That Rick Larsen had not come home was a good thing in the long run, but Rich still missed his mother every day of his life. *Please,* he prayed silently, *let this not be history repeating itself.* He clutched the edges of the passenger seat and held on for dear life. *Please,* he prayed again, *let Sherry leave this place. Let her go home to her kids.*

Jennifer turned into the parking lot and followed the signs that directed them to the main entrance. "Do you want me to drop you at the door, or can you wait till we park?"

That was the $64,000 question. Yes, he wanted to see Sherry so bad he could taste it, but to do it, he'd have to go inside the hospital. He drew in a long, shuddering breath. He could wait a long time for that. He gripped the seat tighter. "I'll wait," he said finally. If he had to do this, he'd rather do it with Jennifer.

He didn't need her to hold his hand, but he had no objection to it.

She found a parking space close to the front doors, and pulled in. "It's close to the end of visiting hours, I'd expect," she said as she turned off the engine. "We probably don't have much time."

The possibility that he might not get to see Sherry at all gave him the strength to release his death grip on the seat. "Okay," he said, his throat tight, his voice husky. He pushed open his door.

And couldn't move an inch.

Damn, had his apprehension affected him so much that he was paralyzed with fear? Then he looked down.

He hadn't unfastened his seat belt.

Hoping that Jennifer hadn't noticed, but certain she had, he released the mechanism and stepped to the ground.

The air was still and thick enough to slice. Clouds piled up in the distance, obscuring the sinking sun, and flickers of lightning occasionally brightened the dark gray sky. The storm must be far out over the Gulf because there was no sound of thunder, but its proximity added a feeling of foreboding to the sultry atmosphere.

Rich felt a hand on his arm, and looked away from the gathering clouds to Jennifer. "I guess we'd best go see what we can see."

Jennifer slid her fingers down his arm to squeeze his hand. "It'll be all right. Didn't Mrs. Benton say your sister was going to rehab soon? They don't send them there unless they're ready for physical therapy. And they don't give them therapy if…" She didn't finish, but Rich knew what she meant.

If they were at death's door, she hadn't said.

"Yeah." He scanned the aisle for cars. "Let's do it," he said as if he were readying himself to jump out of the rear of a C-130 over a hostile drop zone. He set off with Jennifer in tow.

The front doors swooshed open at the touch of their feet to the door pad, and chilled air blasted them as they stepped inside.

Rich steeled himself for the medicinal odor that he associated with hospitals and death and still smelled in his nightmares, but it wasn't there. Relieved, he hurried to the information desk, then peered through the glass partition. "I'm looking for my sister, Sherry Connolly. I just found out she's a patient here."

The receptionist typed the name into a computer and after an eternity, or so it seemed to Rich, the information came up on a screen. She jotted the floor, ward and room number onto a sheet of paper and pointed Rich in the general direction. "Just follow the green lines to the elevator, and when you reach the floor, turn left."

Rich nodded, grabbed Jennifer by the hand and followed the green line to a bank of elevators.

As the doors closed behind them, Jennifer drew in a deep breath. What was she doing here with a man she hardly knew, visiting a sister he hadn't seen in years? She didn't belong here. She didn't want to be here.

But when she glanced at Rich and caught his grim expression in the mirrored walls of the elevator, she knew she had to stay. She might have entered into this venture as a detective, but now she was emotionally involved. If not with Rich, at least with the case.

She had to know how it turned out. She had to know if there was a happy ending.

The elevator stopped at the appropriate floor with a gentle jerk, and the doors seemed to take forever to open. Finally, they stepped out and into a wide area that branched into three halls. "Left, the receptionist said." Jennifer urged him through a set of swinging doors and toward the nurses' station beyond. She didn't know why, but she could tell that Rich's state of anxiety had to do with more than just worry for his sister.

A pretty, young woman looked up and smiled. "Are you Sergeant Larsen?"

"Who to—? How…?" He wore the expression of a boy caught with his fingers in the cookie jar, and Jennifer loved the way it softened his hard face.

"A Mrs. Benton called and said you were on your way," the nurse said, putting down a chart and coming around the desk. "She wanted to be certain your visit wouldn't be too much of a shock."

"A shock?"

Jennifer hadn't thought of that, and Rich hadn't been thinking clearly at all. It hadn't occurred to her that this visit might be upsetting to Sherry. "Will she be able to handle seeing her brother?"

"It's probably the best medicine she could have other than having her children come see her, but you know the rules about children on the wards." She gestured toward some chairs in a small waiting area.

"I'd rather go see my sister," Rich said, holding his ground.

"And so you shall," the nurse said. "But I have to prepare you for what you're going to see."

"Prepare me? Is there more I don't know?" Rich

sat in the indicated chair though he looked like he wanted to get up and run.

The nurse sat across from him, her knees almost touching his. "No. I just want to assure you that your sister will probably make a complete recovery. She's not in that much pain, though she's obviously sad." The nurse placed a hand over Rich's, and Jennifer felt a slight finger of jealousy stab at her, but she shook that notion away. She barely knew the man.

"Your sister is wearing a rather complicated apparatus called a halo. It looks frightening, but it's serving to stabilize her neck, and it's actually relieving her of pain, rather than causing it." She described it, then waited for Rich's response.

"I don't care if she's in plaster from head to toe. It's been a long time, and I just want to see my sister."

"Then, let's go." The nurse rose and gestured toward a corridor behind the nurses' station.

Jennifer squeezed Rich's hand. "I'll just stay here. This is your reunion. I don't know your sister." She wouldn't tell him that she was a coward, that she was afraid of the intense emotions this moment was about to bring.

"No. Come with me. Wait out in the hall, or something. Just be nearby in case I need backup."

As much as Jennifer didn't want to go, the panic in Rich's eyes told her she had to.

Rich followed the nurse down the corridor feeling as though his feet were encased in concrete. He wanted to see Sherry, yet he dreaded what he might find. He'd had more than his share of shocks today.

"Wait here," the nurse said as they reached a door. There was a nameplate of sorts: a strip of masking tape with Connolly scrawled on it with a red marker. They waited outside for what seemed like the longest moment of his life while the nurse went in.

"Richie?"

It sounded like Sherry. Only softer, huskier. The lump returned with vengeance, and Rich's eyes burned. Had the change in the timbre of her voice come from her injuries or the passage of time?

The nurse beckoned, and Rich stepped inside.

"Richie. It is you," a pale apparition inside an Erector set project of braces and stainless steel said. She looked as if she were being tortured by something from the Spanish Inquisition, but the smile on her face was angelic. She reached through a maze of tubes and wires toward him.

"It's me. In the flesh," he said, taking her hand. That lump made it damned hard to talk.

"And so much more flesh than the last time I saw you," Sherry said. "I guess they feed you pretty well in the air force."

"They did. Now I feed myself. And I work out." As if two hours of hard PT every day would qualify as a workout. It was more like the Olympic Decathlon with the Bataan Death March combined.

"You look wonderful." Sherry smiled ruefully. "Don't feel you have to compliment me in return. I know what I must look like." She let go of him and waved, encumbered with tubes from a nearby intravenous setup, toward the halo apparatus. "I promise, I'm not into body piercing," she said, indicating the brace that appeared to be anchored directly into her skull.

"You look damned good to me. I didn't think I'd

ever see you ag—" He stopped, his throat too constricted to go on.

"I'm so sorry, Richie. It was so stupid of me to leave the Parkers after I graduated and not tell anybody where I was. I was so upset about you going overseas and leaving me behind, I wasn't thinking clearly. At the time, I really thought you didn't want to be bothered with me."

"You know that wasn't why I couldn't take you. I explained it." Rich's throat was still tight, his voice husky, but he swallowed and went on. "I was just an airman. We had to have orders just to pi—" Remembering where he was, he stopped.

"I know that now." She paused, her welcoming smile gone, replaced by one more melancholy. One that matched the dull blue of her eyes. "Mike explained it all to me."

Rich sucked in a deep breath. He had hoped they could avoid the topic of her husband. He wasn't sure he knew what to say to a woman who'd been hurt and bereaved all at the same time. Even if she was his sister. "I'm sorry...." It seemed so inadequate, but he didn't know what else to say.

"I wish you could have known him," Sherry said, her eyes misty, her voice thick. "He was the best thing that ever happened to me." She paused. "Him and the kids." She reached through the apparatus and wiped at her eyes.

"Yeah." Rich didn't know what else to say. His eyes burned like crazy and for a moment his world looked as though he were seeing it through rippled glass. He swallowed. He was supposed to be strong for Sherry.

He rubbed at his stinging eyes with the back of

his hand and looked away. When his vision finally cleared and the lump in his throat shrank from baseball to golf-ball size, he looked back. Sherry was looking at something on the tray table at the side of her bed and making no effort to disguise her streaming eyes.

"This is a picture of us," she said, her voice watery and thin. "We took it at Easter. It was one of the rare moments we were all dressed up at the same time."

Rich followed the direction of her gaze and focused on the framed picture of a happy family. The lump in his throat swelled once more. It was past tense. Sherry's husband would never pose with them again.

"Sometimes it doesn't seem real," Sherry said, her voice cracking. "But at night I get snatches of memory. I hear the rain. I feel the moisture on my face. I see Mike lying so impossibly still." She sniffed back more tears. "I remember the policeman muttering to his partner about the guy being a goner.

"I couldn't even go to the funeral." She broke down then, her sobs wracking and harsh.

He had no idea what to do, so he took her hand and held on. He squeezed it from time to time until she stopped weeping. "I'm so sorry, Sherry. I wish it had never happened. I wish I had been there for you." Rich paused. "Hell, I wish I could've taken you to Germany with me. Maybe, none of this would have happened."

"No," Sherry said, her tone emphatic. "My time with Mike was short, but I wouldn't give up a minute of it if it meant not knowing him at all." She smiled sadly. "I loved him, but I have the kids to keep me going. His kids. He's gone, but he left a big part of him in the world.''

Rich couldn't look at her. He didn't know how to act, how to respond. Instead, he stared at the picture and tried to get some sense of the brother-in-law he'd never know. Mike had been a big man. He had the tanned, fit appearance of someone who worked outside. Rich wondered if he worked with his hands.

He couldn't tell much about the baby—they all looked like Yoda to him. But the little girl, a pixie with a mop of curly red hair, had mugged for the camera like she didn't have a care in the world.

''I wish you could've met Mike,'' Sherry said softly.

''Yeah, me, too.''

Sherry opened her mouth to speak, but a commotion in the hall stopped her. She turned her gaze toward the door as a pretty young woman with a mane of chestnut hair came bursting in.

''I'm sorry I'm so late,'' she said breathlessly. ''But Mrs. Garrigan couldn't come to sit until her daughter picked up her ki—'' She stopped, apparently only just noticing Rich.

''It's okay, Rebecca. Catch your breath, then I have someone I'd like you to meet.''

Rebecca, still flushed from rushing, turned toward Rich. ''Are you...?''

''Yeah. I'm the long lost brother.'' He offered his hand.

''We've been trying to find you, since... How did you know Sherry was here?'' She stopped, obviously still flustered, and looked at his hand. ''Oh, I'm Rebecca Tucker. Sherry and I were roommates in college.'' She pushed her hand toward him.

"Rich Larsen," he said. "I guess I should thank you for stepping in with the kids."

"Thank you," she answered. "I love those kids as if they were my own. I couldn't imagine anyone else taking care of them."

"What about that lady next door?" Hadn't she said she'd been baby-sitting the night it happened?

"Mrs. B?" Sherry smiled, her face angelic in spite of the metal contraption surrounding it. "She'd love to, but she works nights to help put two kids through college, so she isn't available."

"We weren't about to let them go to strangers," Rebecca cut in. "They go to their regular day care in the daytime, and stay with me at night." She shrugged. "It works."

"And I will not let them become wards of the court," Sherry added emphatically, her voice breaking. "I've been there, and it won't happen to my kids."

Rich swallowed and wondered what to say. Had it been so bad for Sherry after he left? Should he have stayed around and looked out for her? He thought he'd made the right decision. After all, what better way to harness the brutal tendencies he'd surely inherited than to focus on using them for the good of his country?

"Richie is stationed at Hurlburt now," Sherry said, her voice watery, the tone falsely cheerful. "He hired a private detective to look for me."

"Sherry is the only person left in the world who calls me Richie," he said, noticing that he was still holding Rebecca's hand and also noticing that he didn't get the same electrical charge from Rebecca as he had when he'd shaken Jennifer's hand that first time. He released her. "I'd like to keep it that way."

Rebecca smiled. "I understand." She paused. "It's nice to meet you, Rich."

"Yeah. Sorry about the circumstances."

"Me, too."

"Well, if there's anything I can do to help, don't hesitate to call." He patted the many pockets of his BDU shirt and located a pen. "If you have a piece of paper I'll give you my phone number and address."

"In the drawer, I think," Sherry said, casting her gaze toward the bedside table.

Rich found a small notepad and scribbled the information. "This is my home number and that's the admin clerk for the unit. I'm gone a lot on temporary duty or TDY. When I'm on TDY, he'll be able to track me down." He placed the pad on the table.

He shoved the pen back in his pocket and worried about the awkward silence. He had a lot to say to Sherry, but it didn't seem right with Rebecca there. And he'd left Jennifer waiting for him out in the hall. He wouldn't be surprised if she got fed up and left. He wanted to stay, but he searched for an excuse to leave.

The phone rang.

"Guess that's my nightly 'good-night' from Caitlyn," Sherry said, her face glowing.

Rebecca handed the phone to Sherry. "Caitlyn calls every night so Sherry can listen to her prayers."

Rich nodded, touched by the idea. He swallowed and changed the subject. "Who's taking care of the kids now?" He should have asked that earlier, but this family stuff was still new to him.

"They're at my apartment. My landlady watches them at night when I come here."

The nurse who had shown Rich the room, stuck her head in. "I'm sorry, but visiting hours are over."

Rich reached for Sherry's hand. She was still listening to the phone, and she smiled at him. "Gotta go," he mouthed. "I'll try to get back tomorrow."

Sad that he had to leave Sherry, but relieved at the same time, Rich backed out the door.

He started to go, but turned back to Rebecca. "I meant what I said. Don't hesitate to call if you need anything."

"Sure."

Sherry waved and blew him a kiss. Startled, Rich returned it. Then with the unaccustomed burning back in his eyes, he looked for Jennifer.

Jennifer looked up from a dog-eared magazine as Rich approached. She must have slipped back to the waiting area once she saw that the visit was going well.

The storm that had been threatening had finally kept its promise. Thunder rumbled and the occasional flash of lightning streaked the sky. "How did it go?"

"Pretty good," he said, his voice thick with emotion as he took the hard, plastic seat beside her. "It was more difficult than I thought, but great seeing Sherry. I wish I could help her out, but she's got a friend who seems to have everything under control. The best I can do is offer moral support."

Jennifer took his hand, but a sudden jolt of electricity made her let go too quickly. Had lightning struck nearby? She caught her breath and swallowed. "Well, it'll get easier each time."

Thunder crashed even closer than before. Rich looked up. "It's raining?"

"It'll rain itself out soon. You know how these storms are this time of year." She paused. "But I don't think I'd want to drive in it. Do you want to find the cafeteria and get a cup of coffee and wait it out?"

"Coffee's the last thing I need this time of night, but I sure don't want to go out into that storm. Sherry doesn't need me winding up in the hospital, too." And truth be known, he kinda liked being around Jennifer. He didn't know why. She wasn't anything like the squared-away, military women he was used to.

They found the cafeteria and collected steaming cups of decaffeinated coffee. Rich described his visit with Sherry, Rebecca's rushed arrival and Sherry's nightly prayer sessions with Caitlyn. As he talked, he wondered at how he, a guy who could rappel up the side of a building in full combat gear with a K-bar knife between his teeth, could suddenly think such ordinary things were so cool, much less spend hours talking about it.

He glanced up at the clock over the cash register. It was pushing ten o'clock. He had to show up for PT at zero six-thirty, and it was still a long drive home.

He glanced at Jennifer, and wished there was a way he could contrive to keep seeing her. But now that Jennifer had found Sherry, his business with her was done. After tonight he'd never see her again.

Chapter Three

Rich was glad he'd asked Jennifer to come with him. The way his mind had wandered all the way home, he suspected he'd have more likely run off the rain-slick highway than gotten home safely. And, he liked the idea that Jennifer seemed to care about what happened to him.

In no time the trip was over.

They passed the brightly lit gate of Hurlburt Air Force Base and continued on toward Fort Walton Beach. With rush hour long over, most of the traffic was headed for the Island where the tourists stayed. The roads were nearly empty now, and the going was easy. A few more minutes and they'd reach Jennifer's office, she could pick up her car and he could go home.

Trouble was, he didn't want to. He didn't want to go home to that empty apartment. Ski, his roommate, was on temporary duty, and though he'd rejoiced at finally being eligible to live off base, there were times when he missed the noise and camaraderie of living in the dormitories.

"We're here," Jennifer said quietly and roused him from his introspection.

Rich looked around. The street was dark and desolate, and the only sign of life was a man of questionable sobriety lurching down the sidewalk. "Where's your car?" he asked, suddenly realizing that his truck was the only vehicle on the block.

"In the alley around back. We try to keep the spots in front free for customers," Jennifer replied matter-of-factly as she pulled up to the curb.

Rich eyed the drunk, then assessed the situation again. "No way in hell I'm letting you walk down that dark alley by yourself at this time of night." He pushed open his door as Jennifer opened hers.

She stopped halfway between the running board and the sidewalk, hovering above the curb like a butterfly in flight. "Excuse me." She lowered herself the rest of the way to the ground. "*You* won't let *me* walk down that alley? Who gave you the right to give me permission to do anything?"

Unprepared for the venom in Jennifer's voice, Rich stepped back. He hadn't meant anything by it. He'd just... Hell, he didn't know what he meant. He drew in a deep breath.

"No insult to your ability to take care of yourself intended, but I feel bad about bringing you out this late at night. At least, let me see you safely to your car." He nodded toward the drunk, who seemed more alert than before and was unabashedly watching them. "Maybe that guy is harmless, but I sure would hate to wake up in the morning and read that you'd been attacked."

Truth was, Jennifer had been too aware of Rich's potently masculine presence to notice the other man. This wasn't the safest part of town, especially this late at night, and now that she'd seen the drunk, she wouldn't feel comfortable in that alley. "Thank you," she finally said. "I'm just a little touchy about that 'little woman' thing. In most cases I can take care of myself, but I do appreciate the thought."

"Anytime," Rich muttered, and Jennifer couldn't help wondering if she'd threatened his manhood. Those special tactics guys were nothing if not macho. They took pride in their strength and toughness.

Too much pride, she thought, if her ex-husband was any example. They shoved every bit of anything they perceived as softness away. They might have seen all the posturing as an advantage, but Jennifer knew that if her ex had been slightly more sensitive to her feelings and needs, she wouldn't be scraping for a living in this seedy section of this military town.

On the other hand, she thought, as she allowed Rich to take her by the elbow and escort her across the street, she wouldn't be standing here with this man's man, now.

Her breath caught. How could she be thinking about that? Rich was no different than her ex: all muscle and macho and very little thought.

But as Rich stood watch while she fumbled in her purse for her keys, Jennifer couldn't help wishing this were a date. And, it had been a long time since she'd felt this way about any man.

Keys in hand, she looked up at him. What would it be like to close her eyes, press against that magnificent huge body and feel his mouth on hers? She moistened her lips, and her eyelids drifted downward.

Rich took her keys and broke the spell. He opened the car door and waited while she slid behind the wheel, then inserted the key into the ignition. He watched to be certain that she locked the doors and stood guard until she backed out of the alley toward the street.

She idled at the curb and watched through her rearview mirror as he strode purposefully out of the dark side street and across to his truck. Then, after he'd shut his door behind him, she steered her car toward home.

Jennifer sighed. She hadn't even thought about dating since her divorce, but something about Rich made her think about rumpled sheets and hot, sweaty sex.

No, she told herself firmly and shook her head. She had finished her business with Rich. Unless he decided to come in and pay his bill in person, she'd never see him again.

And, as far as her heart was concerned, that was probably just as well.

RICH STOOD in the middle of the parachute shop, cluttered with stacks of equipment and materiel unloaded from the C-130 transport plane that had brought him back to base. He wiped his sweating forehead with the back of his arm. He looked down with disgust at the dark, damp smear, but there was nothing he could do about it. He had to get all the stuff stowed in the equipment locker before he could even think about getting out of these stinking clothes and into a cool shower.

The last few weeks had been so busy that Rich had barely had a chance to think. He'd made several trips to Pensacola to see his sister and had finally begun to believe he was getting to know her again.

Then he'd had to fly off on a long exercise, and he was probably back at square one.

After the first couple of visits with Sherry, the reserve between them had lifted. She still appeared sad sometimes, but Rich had learned how to dash the sadness away. All he had to do was ask her about her children.

On her better days, the sense of humor Rich hadn't seen since they were kids would make an appearance. When he saw that, it was possible to believe that Sherry would get through it.

He hadn't met the kids yet, and frankly, that didn't bother him much. There was an ops saying that he subscribed to wholeheartedly. He loved kids: barbecued.

Maybe that wasn't really the truth, but the thought of dealing with such tiny little beings scared him spitless. He figured he'd rather parachute into a nest of rattlers than have to deal one-on-one with a four-year-old. He hadn't really known any kids since he'd stopped being one himself, and now they seemed so...so small. Someday, he'd like to meet his niece and nephew. That thought stopped him. Niece and nephew. He was an uncle. He swabbed at his eyes, stinging with sweat and grime from the long trip.

"Hey, Sarge."

Rich looked up and chuckled, relieved by the distraction. Uncle Sarge. That had a kinda nice ring to it. "Yeah. What?" he said to the peach-fuzzed, admin clerk only recently assigned to his unit.

"You going to the Labor Day picnic out by the Sound? We've got to win back the volleyball trophy from the *P J's.*"

Rich had to chuckle. Baker had been with the unit

all of two months. He had no bragging rights to win back from the pararescue jumpers. Rich did, but he had something else to do this weekend. Rebecca Tucker was getting married, and he'd been invited. It was to be Sherry's first excursion out of the hospital. And the kids would be there.

He shook his head. "Nope. I'll be out of town. Got a family thing to go to."

It was the first time since he'd joined the air force that he had a place to go to on a holiday.

"Too bad," said Baker.

"Yeah," Rich agreed, his throat suddenly tight. This was probably no big deal to anybody else, but for him it was something big. He'd spent too many holidays alone on the base pulling extra duty for someone who had someplace better to go, or feeling like an extra wheel butting in on somebody's holiday plans.

There had been a time when he'd have tried the bars along the Miracle Strip, but not tonight, and he'd never really enjoyed the feeling of being drunk. Maybe it was the specter of his father's alcoholism rearing its head, or maybe it was just good common sense. Anyway, he wasn't going to go out tonight.

He had an occasion to rest up for. He smiled to himself. He liked the idea of having family to go to, even if Rebecca Tucker wasn't technically family. It was the closest thing to it he'd had in years. And his family would be there. Sherry and the kids were his family.

Hell, he liked the idea of having family.

JENNIFER SAT at her computer terminal and shuffled among the neat stacks of paper, looking for something else to do. She wondered if she'd ever get to the point where she didn't mind being alone.

Al had returned from his Alaska trip, but he'd already left to spend the weekend with his wife and kids. She'd finished up the one project she'd had pending, and now she had nothing to look forward to other than the long holiday weekend.

Holidays were the worst.

That was, maybe, the only regret she had about divorcing Duke. Now that her parents were retired and traveling across the country in a rented RV, she had no home to go to. Even a husband who drank too hard and flirted too much was better than being alone.

No, she told herself, anything was better than putting up with Duke Bishop, his infidelities and lies. He might have thought he was God's gift to women, he might have thought that he'd done her a big favor by marrying her and taking her away from Scranton, Pennsylvania, but he'd done her a bigger favor by letting her see the real him before they'd had children.

She let out a long gusty sigh, exited her program, turned off the computer and wandered toward the front door. She had a couple of plants at home she could work on. They were probably rootbound. Repotting them would kill at least an hour.

Then she'd have the rest of the three-day weekend to fill with nothing left to do.

Spending a long weekend alone and not having anybody to be with was far more preferable than trying to make a marriage work with somebody who hadn't been interested in working it out with her.

She couldn't help thinking about Rich Larsen and

how he now had family to spend this weekend with. How lucky he was. She couldn't help wondering what it would be like for him.

Jennifer sighed again and let herself out, locking the door behind her. No, she wouldn't think about him. Their business was over. She'd never see him again.

RICH SHOULDERED open the door to his apartment and dropped the heavy, canvas A-3 bag just inside. The room smelled musty and dank, thanks to the pervasive Florida humidity and being closed up for a week. Ski, his roommate followed him in.

Ski dumped his bag next to Rich's, then let out an amazed whistle. "Whoa. One of us must be pretty popular."

Rich followed Ski's gaze to their answering machine which was lit up like a Christmas tree. "Hell, I don't know anybody here. They can't be for me. They must be yours."

Then he realized that they could be from his sister. He lunged for the machine, hit Play and listened.

A woman's voice he didn't recognize. Rich started to call Ski, but then he caught a name. "This is Rebecca Tucker. Please call me."

Ski stood by, waiting to see if any of the machine's blinks were for him.

That message for Rich was followed by six more, all placed since noon, and each seeming more desperate. None were for Ski, and he drifted off to unload his gear.

Heart lodged in his throat, Rich dialed the number. Someone answered, and he recognized the voice as the same one in the frantic messages. He started to identify himself, then realized he had reached her voice mail.

Muttering a curse, he slammed the phone back down and played the messages back, trying to glean an alternate number or some other useful information from the urgent messages. Nothing.

Rich let out the breath he hadn't realized he'd been holding. Now what? Maybe, he should call the hospital. But, hadn't Sherry told him that she was going to be transferred to the rehab facility? She'd told him where it was, and he probably had the number stuck away somewhere, but right now, he couldn't put a finger on it.

He started to dial Rebecca again, but as he reached for the phone, somebody rang the doorbell.

"I'll get that," Ski called. "You find out what's going on with your sister."

Rich glanced in the direction of the door as he pushed redial. The door opened out of his line of sight, but as he watched, Ski backed away. His hands were raised; a look of incredulity was on his face.

Ski glanced over his shoulder toward Rich. "Hey, good buddy. I think this one's for you. I never saw that woman before in my life. Much less those rug-rats."

Dropping the receiver back on the cradle, Rich hurried to the door.

There, in the doorway, was Rebecca Tucker wearing a look of utter panic. In her arms was a munchkin that looked like Yoda's first cousin, and at her side stood a very tired-looking little girl. What were they doing here? Surrounding them all was a pile of pastel-colored baggage that looked like, at least, three times as much of the stuff he'd off-loaded this afternoon.

"Oh, Rich. I am so glad to see you. You have to help me. I'm desperate," Rebecca said as she stepped inside. She turned to Ski. "Would you mind bringing all that in?"

Ski, a bewildered expression on his face, looked at Rich, and all Rich could do was nod.

"What's happened to Sherry?" he finally asked when it became clear that Rebecca was too flustered to explain.

She shifted Yoda to her other hip and shook her head. "Nothing. Sherry's fine. You'll see her tomorrow. She's out of the halo and in a neck brace. I'm sorry, I didn't think how it might sound when I left all those messages."

Ski strode in with a pastel contraption in either hand. "I guess I should introduce you to my roommate," Rich said. "Ski Warsinski, meet Rebecca Tucker. She's the friend of my sister's who's been taking care of her kids."

Ski nodded and went back for another load.

At least Rebecca had the decency to apologize for scaring him out of his mind, but she'd yet to explain why she was here. He remembered his promise to help out in whatever way he could, and hoped she wasn't calling that one in. He had a feeling she was. Why else would she have the kids and all their gear with her? "Okay," he said warily. "What do you need?"

Ski went into the kitchen.

The frantic look faded, and Rebecca managed a weak smile. "The lady I had lined up to keep the kids for the wedding and honeymoon stumbled down the stairs and broke her hip. So far, I haven't been able to find anybody to take over.'' She shrugged. ''It's a holiday weekend and the last minute, at that.'' She looked at him hopefully.

Rich didn't have to hear the rest to know what she was working herself up to, but how should he respond? He only had to look into the mirror to see his father's face reflected back at him. He shook his head vehemently. What if he'd inherited more than just his father's looks?

What if he harmed one of those kids?

Why hadn't she postponed the wedding? Of course, he knew the answer: Sherry had told him she'd insisted that Rebecca go on with it.

''Please, Rich. You have to help me out here.'' When Rich was slow to agree, Rebecca went on. ''I promise it'll only be for tonight. I've got feelers out everywhere, and I'll keep looking. Surely I'll have someone by the ceremony tomorrow.

''In the meantime, I have to run. I have to be at the rehearsal dinner in…'' She glanced at her watch. ''About an hour and a half.'' With that she handed Yoda to him. ''This is Carter, and this is Caitlyn,'' she said, urging the reluctant little girl toward Rich. ''This is your Uncle Rich. He's going to take care of you until Mrs. Dahlstrom is better.''

''But, Rebecca…'' Rich protested. ''They don't know me.''

''You're not a complete stranger to them, Rich. They've seen pictures of you that Sherry had.''

''I don't know anything about taking care of kids,'' Rich insisted. ''What if I…?'' He didn't dare think of the rest of that sentence.

''Carter is an easy baby,'' Rebecca told him.

"He'll be fine as long as Caitlyn is here, and she knows what to do. She'll be a big help to you." She blew a kiss toward the kids. "I'll see you tomorrow. Thanks." She dashed out the door.

Rich looked at the door closing behind Rebecca. She hadn't even given him a chance to say no. Then he looked down at Carter. His face was screwed up and turning red, and before Rich had a chance to try to calm him down, he let out an ear-splitting shriek guaranteed to blow a 100-amp stereo speaker at fifty paces.

"What the hell was that?" Ski asked, coming out of the kitchen, a sandwich of Dagwood proportions in his hands.

"I think Carter wants something to eat. It is supper time. I guess we should try to feed them. Is there any more sandwich stuff in there or did you use it all?" Rich noticed one of those pacifier things tangled in the baby's clothes and popped it into his open mouth. Carter continued to cry, and the pacifier dribbled onto the floor.

"There's plenty," Ski answered, his mouth full, as Rich scooped up the pacifier.

"Okay, Katie, let's go get some grub." Rich, gingerly holding Carter, headed toward the kitchen to wash off the pacifier. "Does your brother like ham sandwiches?" When Caitlyn didn't respond, he turned.

Caitlyn was still standing where he'd left her, her hands on her hips, her lips pursed, looking like a miniature schoolmarm. "You can't feed him sammiches. He don't got no teef." She rolled her eyes at him as if she were talking to an idiot. "And my name is not Katie. It's Caitlyn."

"Okay. Okay." Of course, the rugrat had no teeth. He knew that. "Did your Aunt Becky bring anything for me to feed him?"

Caitlyn rolled her eyes again. "He gots baby food inna diaper bag."

"Get it for me." He tried bouncing Yoda, but all it did was slow the wails down a notch. He ran water over the pacifier and stuck it back in, holding it there until he felt Carter latch on. Relieved, he let go. So did Carter, and the pacifier squirted out of his mouth as the kid let out a wail as shrill as an air-raid siren.

Caitlyn grimaced, but she did as he asked. "You gots to heat it up inna microwave," she said as she handed him two jars of revolting looking stuff.

"Okay. Do it." He had enough trouble just keeping the baby from squalling any louder.

"I'm not 'lowed to touch the microwave."

Rich sighed and looked at Ski.

Ski held up his hands, one still holding half a sandwich. "Hey, don't look at me. They're your niece and nephew." He crammed the rest of his sandwich into his mouth and chewed. "You got your hands full. I think I'll just go crash at Murphey's. He's still pretty messed up since Allison dumped him. He can use the company, and I sure as hell know more about how to handle that mess than the one you got here." He wiped his hands on his pants and headed for the door. "I'm outta here."

"Coward," Rich muttered, but he envied the man, too, for having Murphey to go to. Danny Murphey was another guy on the team and had been Ski's roommate before he'd set up house with Allison Adler, the woman he'd thought he was going to marry. He guessed Ski owed Danny just like he owed

Sherry. If he just hadn't gone and opened his mouth and volunteered to help.

No, he told himself sternly. He'd passed arctic, desert and jungle survival school, no sweat. He could surely handle two kids until tomorrow.

Famous last words, Rich couldn't help thinking when, two hours later, he'd scraped the last of the cereal and strained peaches out of the jars. He'd managed to put together a peanut butter sandwich for Caitlyn with his right hand while he'd attempted to shovel food into Carter's mouth with his left.

Rich wasn't sure how much had gone into Carter. He must have scraped most of it off the kid's face and the rest was splattered all over the kitchen. He sighed and looked around the filthy room. It looked as though somebody had fought a paint ball war in here. But, Carter was quiet for the time being, and that little piece of silence had to be worth all the mess. Rich slapped a couple of slices of ham between two pieces of bread and shoved them into his mouth. He guessed he'd have to hose down the kitchen, but for now he had to get the kids settled while he could. He didn't know how long the lull would last, but he wanted to make the most of it.

He glanced at the clock. It was almost seven. Didn't little kids go to bed by now? He didn't suppose Caitlyn could tell time. Maybe, he could fool her into thinking it was bedtime even if it wasn't. He looked down at Carter. His food-encrusted eyelids were definitely drooping.

"Okay. Time for bed. Go put on your pajamas."

Caitlyn started to say something, but then closed her mouth. She turned as if to do his bidding, then stopped, looking like she was ready to cry herself. "I dunno where I'm s'posta sleep."

Rich propped the baby over his shoulder, and felt a surge of an unfamiliar emotion when the kid snuggled up against him. "I guess you can sleep in Ski's room." He pointed toward Ski's closed bedroom door, then he remembered the extensive collection of Babe of the Month posters on the wall. "Oops," he said, yanking her back. "On the other hand, you can sleep in mine."

He pushed open the door and ushered her in, pointing to his queen-size bed. "See, it's big enough for both of you." He started to put the baby down, but Caitlyn shook her head. "You hafta get his portacwib. He'll fall off da bed."

Portacrib? He'd seen Rebecca with a couple of suitcases, but he didn't remember anything that looked like a crib. He looked back out into the living room to the pile of stuff Ski had dragged in before he left. There were more supplies there than he'd need for a two-week hike. He looked at the bewildering pile of kid paraphernalia and blew out a tired breath.

Caitlyn marched over to a flattened contraption of wood and mesh. "Tha's it. You gots to unfode it."

"Okay," he said slowly, wondering how he could accomplish that and hold on to Carter, too. This project was going to take both hands.

"Can you hold your brother for me?" he asked, already knowing it wasn't going to work.

Caitlyn shook her head. "Mommy says I might dwop him."

Rich was beginning to run out of options here. If he put Carter on the bed, he might roll off. If he tried to hold Carter and assemble the bed, he'd surely drop the kid flat on the floor. That's it. The floor.

He laid Carter down in the middle of the rug and held his breath to see if he repeated the siren routine. So far, so good.

The mechanism wasn't too complicated, and Rich had the bed set up in short order. Just a few minutes and he'd have the kids squared away. Then he could clean up and catch some *Z's* of his own. He reached for Carter to put him in the crib, but the prim expression on Caitlyn's face stopped him. "Now what?" he asked irritably.

"You gots to put a sheet on," she said as if he were the dumbest man in the world.

"You got one on you?" he snapped, his patience stretched as far as it would go.

"Huh?" Caitlyn had apparently not heard that expression before.

"Never mind." He went to the hall closet and grabbed a sheet. The one with the beer can design. Carter wouldn't know the difference. He'd thought they were cool when he bought them; now he was thinking otherwise. He clumsily covered the plastic mattress and looked at Caitlyn. She might only be four years old, but she was the expert in the room.

"Okay," she said, looking like a less-than-pleased drill sergeant.

He put Carter in. The baby fussed a little, but seemed ready to go to sleep. He turned toward Caitlyn.

"You gots to change his diaper."

He was afraid she'd say that. He turned back to the crib. Carter looked pretty cozy, and he was reluctant to disturb him, but he figured a kid with diaper rash would really be hard to deal with.

Rich managed to get the wet diaper off easy enough, but he didn't have a fresh one to put on. He looked at Caitlyn. She pointed to another diaper bag.

"Mommy always throws a diaper over him until she's done," Caitlyn said matter-of-factly.

Rich wondered if she was shielding her daughter from a close view of the male anatomy, and decided as long as he stayed between her and Carter, he could manage until he got the new diaper and put it on him.

He turned back and quickly learned why Sherry covered him with a diaper as a jet of liquid squirted nearly to the ceiling. "Whoa! How the he—heck does one kid hold so much?" He tossed the disposable diaper over the stream, startling Carter and making him cry. This parent thing was tough duty, he couldn't help thinking as he struggled to fasten the thing.

The diaper looked none-too secure, but it would have to do. He turned to Caitlyn. "Okay, young lady. Time for you to hit the sack."

"I can't go to bed until Mommy hears my prayers," she said. "We gots to call her up."

Rich rolled his eyes and blew out an impatient breath. "How 'bout I listen tonight?" he suggested, knowing instantly it wouldn't fly. He still wasn't sure what he'd done with the number, and if Rebecca had left him any, he didn't know where they were.

"No. Mommy. I gotta say 'em for Mommy." So far, Caitlyn had behaved like a trouper, but Rich had a sinking feeling he'd just run out of luck.

"I want my Mommy," she wailed. Carter, who had almost drifted off to sleep, joined the chorus.

Rich had the greatest urge to join in, too, but that would solve nothing. He needed a kid expert, and he needed one fast. He called directory assistance and dialed the home number of the only person he could think of who might be able to help.

When she answered, he blurted out a desperate plea. "Jennifer, can you come over to my place? I need your help. Fast."

Chapter Four

Jennifer switched the phone from one ear to the other as she listened to Rich's panicked request. For one brief moment, she'd thought he was asking her for a date, but her fluttering heart skidded to a halt when she heard the unmistakable sound of a child crying in the background.

"Okay," she said, tempering her disappointment. It was probably better this way anyway, she convinced herself. And her curiosity was running at full throttle. "Why don't you tell me just what's going on."

She was on the living room phone, tethered by an eight-foot wire, and she needed to be in the kitchen. The spaghetti was past done, and if it didn't get drained soon, all she'd have was mush. She stretched as far as the cord would allow her and turned off the stove and listened.

Rebecca Tucker had stuck Rich with Sherry's kids. The woman had to be truly desperate if she was entrusting them to him. The man might be able to hack his way through a jungle with one hand tied behind him, but she'd bet he was clueless when it came to child care. Another wailing voice followed the first one.

She would definitely win that bet.

"Tell you what," she finally said when Rich had finished his desperate explanation. The guy had to be at the end of his rope if he'd actually admitted that he needed her. Even if it was just to help with his niece and nephew. "I don't have that much experience with kids, and I don't know how much help I'll be, but I just got finished cooking up a batch of spaghetti sauce. I'll bring it over. Once we get the kids settled, we can eat." *If* they got the kids settled, she didn't say. Of course, that meant that the noodles she'd already cooked were toast, but that couldn't be helped. She had plenty more to cook later.

Jennifer could almost feel Rich's relief coming through the phone wires. She wanted to think it was because she was coming, not to help with the kids, not to bring the food, but for herself. But she was realistic enough to know that wasn't the case. Besides, she'd already learned her lesson about that kind of man. She didn't need that.

Rich needed a woman to help with the kids. Period. Any woman who'd passed Child Care 101 would do.

Her experience with kids was limited, at best. She didn't have many friends with children, and her siblings hadn't started having theirs when she'd married and moved away. She wasn't sure how much help she'd be, but she'd give it her best effort.

"Jennifer?"

She hadn't realized that she'd been woolgathering and found herself blushing even though she was alone in the room. "Yes, sorry. I was thinking about the logistics of getting this stuff over to you," she said. "I'll be there in about half an hour."

"Great! You don't know how glad I am to hear that. I'll be waiting."

Probably watching at the window, Jennifer thought. Too bad the cavalry wasn't going to be that much help. "Just one thing, Rich. Go ahead and let Caitlyn call her mother. I'm sure that will be the best thing for everybody."

Rich mumbled something about not knowing what the number was, but Jennifer didn't respond. She just hung up. She wasn't sure why she'd just agreed to do this. She just knew she had to.

For the kids, she told herself.

She almost believed it.

FEELING SOMEWHAT relieved, Rich hung up. Jennifer was coming. Finally, an expert in the house. If he could only survive till she got here. Half an hour. He could do it.

He hoped.

In the meantime, he had to find the number so Caitlyn could call Sherry. She should have known that he wouldn't make a satisfactory mom substitute, even if Rebecca didn't. Hell, he didn't even know that diaper thing.

He looked at Caitlyn, her pixie face puffy and wet with tears. She looked back, her eyes wide and questioning. For the moment, she wasn't wailing, but her small body shuddered violently with residual sobs.

Rich took a deep breath.

"Caitlyn, did your Aunt Becky leave me any phone numbers in all that stuff?" He gestured toward the mountain of kiddie gear he'd yet to explore.

"Inna diaper bag," she said, then wiped her nose with the back of her arm. "Mommy always puts a piece a paper inna diaper bag in case of a 'mergency."

Rich exhaled and headed for the bag. He just hoped that Rebecca did the same thing. She wasn't a mother, so she might not know.

That stopped him. Jennifer wasn't a mother either. What if she didn't know anymore about what to do with the kids than he did?

No, he wasn't going to think that.

Even if she didn't have real mother experience, surely mothering was a woman thing. Didn't they have instincts? Wasn't child care know-how part of the package?

He found a sheet of folded paper, with neat printing on it, tucked into a pocket on the outside of the diaper bag. The numbers.

Damn, it had every number imaginable on it. From Sherry's to Rebecca's home number—where Rebecca wouldn't even be—to the pediatrician and poison control. Poison control? What did she think he was going to do with the kids, feed them tranquilizers?

Then he looked at Caitlyn, still sniffling, and glanced at Carter, whining in the tiny crib. It was tempting, but he did know better than that.

"Okay, Short Stuff, let's go call your mom."

"'Kay," Caitlyn said, still gulping back an occasional sob. She edged closer to him as he reached for the phone and dialed.

Rich held his breath while the circuits connected and the phone started to ring. What if she wasn't there? Two rings. What if something had happened?

Three rings. What would Caitlyn do if Sherry didn't answer?

She did, and Rich exhaled with relief.

"Hey, Sis. There's a little girl who needs to speak to you." He listened while Caitlyn held out her hand for the receiver. "Yeah, they're fine. Everything's under control," he lied. "Yeah, Caitlyn really wants to talk to you. Here she is." He handed the phone to Caitlyn and hoped she wouldn't squeal on him.

He was doing the best he could under the circumstances. And, besides, Rebecca had no business dumping them on him without, at least, some warning. Then he glanced at Caitlyn's little face, her eyes bright and shining as she spoke to her mother, and his heart swelled with emotion. No, he was glad he could help. And Sherry would surely make allowances for his lack of experience.

Surely, she understood that Rich was a rank amateur in all this. Even if Caitlyn didn't.

WHEN JENNIFER reached Rich's apartment complex, she stopped to consider what she was getting herself into. She hardly knew Rich Larsen. In fact, prior to this moment, all they'd had was a business arrangement. Should she be here at all?

She thought of the two small children caught in the middle of it all and decided that she wasn't doing this for Rich. She was doing it for them. If Rich hadn't sounded so desperate, she surely would have told him to take a long walk off a short pier.

Or would she?

Jennifer stared up at the second floor of the building that Rich's apartment was on and wondered what kind of place it was. Was it one of those ultra-messy bachelor pads? A passion pit waiting for the next victim? What was she getting herself into?

Then she reminded herself of the kids. They would be there. They were the reason. It had nothing to do with Rich. She reached for the grocery sack containing the fixings for a spaghetti dinner, then stopped. Why was she even thinking about him?

No sense even thinking about anything more than baby-sitting, Bishop, she told herself as she climbed the stairs to the second floor. There were going to be two pint-size chaperons in attendance.

In spite of all her arguments against getting involved with another combat controller, she wasn't sure a family evening was what she really wanted.

Mentally chastising herself, Jennifer shifted the bag of groceries in her arms. Her hands were sweaty and her heart pounded. So much for appearing cool and confident, she thought as she raised her hand to knock.

What happened next would be up to Rich.

And the kids, she reminded herself.

RICH HAD NEVER been so glad to hear the doorbell ring in all his life. It had to be Jennifer. He hadn't ordered a pizza, and they weren't making enough noise for the downstairs neighbors to be complaining.

He hoped.

Caitlyn had settled down some after talking to Sherry, but it was obvious that she was in no frame of mind to sleep. And Carter had woken up, too, right after Rich had managed to clean up most of the baby's supper mess.

Rich successfully maneuvered another diaper off

and a fresh one on, but the baby didn't seem the least bit inclined to sleep. How did mothers do it?

Carter seemed happiest—translation, quietest—when Rich held him, so hold him he did. He shifted Carter in his arms and went to let in the reinforcements.

He flung the door open wide and thanked his lucky stars that it really was Jennifer who'd rung. She stood there in the open doorway, her long hair restrained with a blue ribbon that complemented the print of her summer dress. She looked like a guardian angel come to his rescue.

Her arms were laden with a brown sack that emitted an aroma that had his mouth watering and his stomach clamoring for a taste. Rich swallowed and beckoned her in.

"Hi," he said. "I'd offer to take your bag, but as you can see, my hands are full."

She just stood there and stared.

"Jennifer?"

Jennifer blinked and tried to force her eyes back into her head. She had been totally unprepared for the sight in front of her: Rich Larsen, bare-chested, wearing camouflage BDU pants, and holding a baby.

Her breath caught in her throat. The vision was so sweet she almost wanted to weep. That innocent little boy with a halo of red peach fuzz snuggled against that hard, wide, bare chest. The baby's eyes were half closed, and he sucked on one finger.

This was, by far, one of the most tantalizing, sexy sights she could ever have imagined. Any mother seeing that, would have to fall even deeper in love with her child's father. Jennifer swallowed, moistened her lips and swallowed again. "What happened to your shirt?" she finally managed.

Rich looked down at his bare chest, and Jennifer could have sworn he was blushing. "Oh," he said. "Carter thought it was fun to spray his dinner everywhere. I swear, he got more stuff on me and the walls than went in him. I took my shirt off to put in the wash, but I never made it to the bedroom for a clean one."

Bedroom was not the right thing to say, Jennifer thought as she nodded her understanding. How could she be lusting after the man as if he were Mr. September in a hunk-of-the-month calendar? She just didn't do stuff like that.

She shook herself out of her wandering thoughts. "If you'll tell me where to put this..." She indicated the grocery sack. "I'll put it away, then take the baby. So you can get a shirt on," she added pointedly.

"Kitchen's over there." Rich inclined his head toward an archway on the far side of the room.

Jennifer entered the kitchen expecting to find a disaster area of the first degree, but the room was surprisingly orderly. There was a pile of soggy towels in the corner, but other than that, it appeared reasonably clean. Apparently, he'd found some time to tidy up.

She set the bag on the counter, removed the salad fixings and a bottle of wine and stashed them in the fridge.

Maybe the wine was a little optimistic, she couldn't help thinking when she considered that the baby was still awake and there was no sign of the little girl. But she had planned to have a glass with her meal when she thought she would be eating it alone. Why not share it?

"Whatcha doin'?" a tiny voice asked.

Jennifer spun around to find a redheaded sprite gazing, wide-eyed, at her. She hastily stashed the wine in the refrigerator and turned back to the child. "Hello," she said, much too brightly. Gee, she thought, you'd think the girl had caught her trying to abscond with the family silver. "I'm just putting away some stuff for supper."

"I already had a sammich. My name's Caitlyn," the pixie said without missing a beat.

"My name is Jennifer. I'm a friend of your uncle."

Caitlyn looked puzzled as if she didn't understand. "Uncle Witch is new," she said gravely. "My daddy went to heaven, so now I gots a new uncle."

Jennifer didn't know how to respond to that. Did the child really believe that Rich had been sent as a daddy substitute? She looked down at the tiny girl, and decided it wasn't such a bad thing for a little girl to believe. If it gave her comfort, why not? "How do you like your new uncle?" she asked for lack of anything else to say.

"He's okay. But he isn't my daddy."

Wow! How did she respond to that?

"Jen'fer."

"Yes?" She had to get it together. Didn't kids need constant attention?

"Are you getting married wif my Uncle Witch?"

That one hit her like a speeding bus. Jennifer's head spun as the thought bounced around like it had a life of its own. But, no. She'd already tried life married to a man's man. It wasn't for her.

She shook her head. "No, sweetie, I'm just a friend."

"Oh. Aunt Rebecca's getting married tomorrow."

It sounded so simple when Caitlyn put it that way, but was it simple? Already, she could see it was not.

Jennifer turned away from the counter. The best thing she could do now was to help Rich settle the kids. Then she'd worry about what came next.

IT WAS SURPRISING how easy it was to settle two kids when two people were doing the settling. Rich stood outside his bedroom door and watched as Jennifer tucked Caitlyn in. Carter had already settled down to sleep with the comfort of his thumb, and Rich had high hopes that he'd stay down for the count.

It was only about eight-thirty but it seemed like midnight. If this was the way things were all the time, he had greatly underestimated the amount of work that mothers put in every day. And once she was back on her feet, Sherry would have to do it alone.

He thought about the brother-in-law he'd never met and wondered if he'd helped, or had he been one of those hands-off dads like his father had been? Rich hoped not. Then he shrugged. It didn't matter. The man was gone. Nothing would change that. And if he had been hands off, at least, Sherry would be used to doing it all.

Jennifer tiptoed out of the bedroom and switched off the overhead light. Caitlyn murmured something about being afraid of the dark, but Jennifer reassured her. "It's all right, sweetie. We'll leave the door open and the light from the living room will shine in. Uncle Rich and I will be in the next room."

That must have satisfied her, because Caitlyn snuggled in and made no further protests.

Jennifer put a finger to her lips. "Come on. Let's let them settle down. The last thing we want to do is wake them up again."

"Roger that," Rich agreed as he stepped away from the door. He felt something in his stomach. A tightness, a clenching that he didn't recognize. Had it been so long since he'd had a meal? No, it hadn't been that long since he'd wolfed down that sandwich. Then he remembered the spaghetti sauce that had smelled so good. Was it the sauce or the maker that had him so intrigued?

"How long will it take to finish up that spaghetti?" he asked, wondering if he'd just been rude. He wasn't sure he was that hungry, but he had to do something to keep Jennifer from packing up and going home.

"I can have it on the table in about fifteen minutes," Jennifer said, her eyes still fixed on the tiny figure curled up in the big bed. "Do you think you'll be able to last that long?"

"I will if you will," Rich said, wondering if his desire to keep Jennifer there had more to do with the curves he could only guess about and less to do with the two munchkins finally sleeping in the next room.

NOT FOR the first time, Jennifer wondered what she was doing—first in Rich's apartment helping with the kids, and now in his kitchen dishing up spaghetti with her secret-recipe sauce. Rich's body seemed so huge, and now that the kids were sleeping, she was all too aware of how attractive he really was.

Jennifer stirred the sauce and waited for the water

for the noodles to come to a boil. She lifted the spoon to her mouth to test the sauce, but Rich stepped up beside her, and Jennifer offered the taste to him. He accepted, and she caught her breath as he closed his hand over hers and guided the spoon to his mouth. Her knees almost turned to jelly as he closed his lips over the spoon and tasted. The water wasn't the only thing starting to boil.

She grabbed for the package of noodles and gauged the right amount in the circle of her thumb and forefinger. "Just let me get this into the water," she said, noting the breathlessness in her voice. Had Rich noticed?

"I can't wait," he said, his voice sounding as husky as hers. "I'll just set the table and stay out of your way. Maybe, that way you can get it ready faster."

On one hand, Jennifer was relieved the distraction was gone. On the other, she already missed the way Rich filled the room. Without him, the kitchen seemed larger, emptier.

She shook her head. Stop thinking this way, she told herself firmly. This is a one-time-only deal. You're helping the man out. That's all. Once you've eaten dinner, you'll pack up your stuff and go home. End of story.

RICH HELPED Jennifer carry the dishes from the table and stash them in the dishwasher. Dinner had been strained, the conversation limited to Sherry, the kids and the weather, but he was sorry it was over. He couldn't explain it, but he had enjoyed having Jennifer there. Not just because she'd helped him with the kids, but because... He didn't know why. He just liked the way he felt when he was around her.

Jennifer stood at the sink, watching as it filled and foamed with bubbles around the saucepan and pot she'd used to cook with. Rich wanted to go over and lift that luxurious, long hair off her neck and press his lips to the curve where it met her shoulder, but he didn't.

He didn't know why he wanted to. Didn't know what to make of these new sensations churning in his chest. He wished he could name it. Indigestion? Not likely. Still, it was a feeling he couldn't name.

She wasn't the kind of woman he was used to being around. He knew goal-oriented military women, and he knew good-time, party girls. He didn't know what to do with a woman like Jennifer.

"When is Rebecca coming to pick up the kids?" Jennifer asked suddenly.

"She's not. I have to bring them back with me."

Jennifer stopped, her hand poised in midair as she started to place the pot on the drainboard and turned to face him. "Do you have another vehicle besides the truck?"

Not certain he understood the point of the question, Rich looked at her. "No. Why?"

"You can't take those kids in that truck."

"Sure, I can," he said. He'd already worked it out. "I'll put all their stuff in the back, Caitlyn on the seat, and Carter on my lap."

Jennifer turned off the water and stared at him. "I...don't...think...so." She enunciated each word very clearly as if English were not his first language.

"Sure I can." What the hell was going on here?

Who was she to tell him what to do with his niece and nephew?

"You have no idea, do you?" she said, staring at him, her face a study in consternation.

"What?" He was beginning to be annoyed here. She was looking at him like he'd suddenly grown horns, or a tail. He resisted the urge to reach back and feel for one.

"They have to be in their car seats. By law, I think. And I think I heard something that says you should never put children in the front." Jennifer searched her brain for the reasons. "Something about being thrown through the windshield in case of an accident," she said, turning the water back on. "Or the air bags blowing up in their faces."

"I'm not going to have an accident."

"You don't know that. Even if you don't have an accident, you could get a ticket for not having the kids properly restrained."

"What do you expect me to do? I can't leave them here. I promised Sherry I'd be at the wedding. It's her first trip out since the accident. She hasn't seen her kids in a month."

"Well," Jennifer said. "You'll have to find a car that has a back seat where you can install their car seats."

Rich looked at her for a moment, then inspiration struck. He'd seen Jennifer's car. "You have a car with room for the seats. Go with me," he said.

"No," she answered much too quickly and shook her head for emphasis.

"Yes," he insisted. "It's the perfect answer. Rebecca said I could bring a date. I'll bring you."

Jennifer slumped. Every time she thought her business with Rich Larsen was over and done with, he would say or do something to drag her in deeper. He already had her drawn in, hook, line and sinker, and now he wanted her to go to this wedding.

"Rich, I don't know any of those people. Why would they want you to bring me?" she protested. What she was really doing was looking for an excuse to accept.

His expression was needy, earnest. "They wouldn't know anybody I'd bring. I hadn't invited anybody, so it might as well be you."

That was a backhanded compliment, but Jennifer got his point. And she couldn't let him transport the kids in the dangerous way he'd proposed. "All right," she found herself saying. "I'll go with you. But only to make sure the kids arrive safely." She wondered who she was trying to convince. Rich? Or herself?

"Yesss!" Rich cheered, pulling her into his arms in an exuberant hug. "You won't be sorry," he insisted, though Jennifer already sensed with a strong feeling of doom that she would be sorry. "It's a date."

No, it isn't, Jennifer told herself in no uncertain terms. She's just doing her good deed for the day. The month. The year. The millennium.

Rich swooped in for a quick kiss, and Jennifer's heart leapt as she wrapped her hands around the back of his neck. She reveled in the sensation of his lips on hers, his strong, firm body pressed so close against her. If it had been like this with Duke, maybe she'd have hung in there.

Who was she kidding? Just because the man was

a good kisser, it didn't follow that he would have anymore staying power than Duke.

She pushed herself out of Rich's arms, and out of reach. Drawing a deep, ragged breath, she tried to ignore the heat, the tingle, where his lips had ravaged hers. "So," she said slowly, all the time knowing she was making a huge mistake, "what time do you want me to pick you and the kids up tomorrow?"

Chapter Five

Still wondering why she was doing this, Jennifer arrived at Rich's place at ten-thirty the next morning. She knew she was early for a one o'clock wedding, but something told her that her help would be necessary.

She was right. Jennifer could hear Caitlyn wailing before she even had a chance to knock on the door. She rang the bell and waited. And waited.

She rang again, and knocked for good measure.

Finally, a harassed-looking Rich, with Carter on his arm, yanked the door open.

At least, this time, Rich had his shirt on.

Behind Rich, Caitlyn, wearing only her underwear, stood crying. "What's wrong, honey?" she said, brushing past Rich and stooping in front of the distressed little girl.

Caitlyn's lower lip trembled as she tried to explain. "He won't... He won't..." A racking sob interrupted. "Uncle Witch won't let me wear my weddy dwess."

Jennifer shot a questioning glance at Rich.

He shrugged. "I tried to get her to put on that, and she went ballistic." He pointed to a pastel pink jumper and white blouse. "Insisted she had to wear her 'weddy dress.'" He pointed to a ruffled, buttercup-yellow dress encased in a plastic garment bag that had been draped over a chair. "I didn't want to let her wear that in case she spilled something on it. It seems like an awful nice dress to put on a little girl."

Jennifer looked at the frothy concoction, then looked at Caitlyn. "Are you supposed to wear that dress to the wedding?" she asked carefully.

Caitlyn nodded, still sniffing.

"Are you supposed to be part of the wedding party?"

Caitlyn looked puzzled. "I din't know about no party," she sniffed. "I'm supposed to frow the flowers," she said.

"You're going to be the flower girl?" Jennifer asked, suddenly understanding.

Caitlyn nodded, her small face broadening with a smile. "Yes, I'm posed to frow the flowers for Aunt Webecca to walk on."

Jennifer smiled reassuringly at the upset child. "I think your Uncle Rich didn't know that. But, that's okay. I'll straighten him out." She glanced pointedly at Rich.

He shrugged and gestured with one hand, the other still encumbered by Carter, and said, "I give up. You know, it would help if somebody would tell a guy these things."

Jennifer stood and took Caitlyn's hand. "Caitlyn is going to be the flower girl. Her special dress probably matches the rest of the bridal party's gowns." She looked down at Caitlyn. "Uncle Rich meant well, but he didn't understand. Now that we've got him all straightened out, I'll help you get ready. You are going to be the prettiest flower girl in the whole wedding party."

Caitlyn smiled at that. "You're silly, Jen'fer. I'm gonna be the onliest flower girl in the weddy party."

Jennifer shot a glance over her shoulder as she took the plastic-encased dress and led Caitlyn to the bedroom. "You're in charge of Carter. I'm going to go and make Caitlyn beautiful."

Rich didn't say anything for a moment, then shook his head. "I don't suppose Carter is going to be best baby or anything, is he? I didn't see a pint-size tux anywhere."

"Uncle Witch, you're so funny. Carter's just a baby. He's gonna just watch," Caitlyn said.

"I knew that."

Jennifer suppressed a smile. "Uncle Rich was just making a joke, Caitlyn. He knows Carter can't be the best man." She sneaked a glance over her shoulder as she took Caitlyn to dress. She didn't know about the rest of the wedding party, but she'd bet that the best man was standing there holding one small, red-haired baby.

IT TOOK Jennifer no time at all to wash Caitlyn's face and help her into the yellow dress. It was a little girl's dream, full of flounces and ruffles, made of crisp organza. A long, satin sash went around Caitlyn's chubby middle and tied in a huge bow in the back. It was the kind of dress little girls got to wear to parties a long time ago, but that most modern girls had never seen except in picture books. No wonder Caitlyn had been so heartbroken when Rich had told her she couldn't wear it.

Jennifer stood back and looked her up and down. Dressed in the delicate little gown, she looked like a princess. "There you are, Caitlyn. You look beautiful," she said as she made a quick adjustment to Caitlyn's carroty curls.

Caitlyn looked down at herself, then up at Jennifer. She grinned broadly. "I feel like a fairy pwincess," she said, her voice filled with awe.

"You look like one, too, sweetie. Let's show Uncle Rich."

"Okay," Caitlyn said, all smiles.

Jennifer pushed open the door and announced, "I would like to introduce Miss Caitlyn Connolly."

Caitlyn stepped through the door and pirouetted, letting her full skirt swirl around her.

Rich let out an appropriate wolf whistle. "Wow. I'll have to fight all the boys off with a stick."

"Why?" Caitlyn said, looking confused.

"Never mind, honey. You'll understand when you're older." Jennifer looked at Rich. He was still wearing his jeans and white T-shirt. Carter was dressed and looked cute as a button in a pair of navy shorts with suspenders and a tiny red bow tie attached to the front of his white cotton shirt.

"Here let me take him," Jennifer said, holding her hands out for Carter. "If you don't hurry, we'll be late." She checked her watch. "It's already eleven-fifteen. We should probably leave in fifteen minutes to be sure we have enough time."

"It only takes an hour to get to Pensacola," Rich said, handing Carter over.

"Do you know how long it takes to get to the church?"

Rich shook his head. "No."

"Then we need extra time to navigate." Jennifer jiggled Carter, who'd started to fuss. "Go on. We have to get this show on the road or we'll be late." She glanced at Caitlyn. "Can't start the wedding without the flower girl."

"Yeah, I suppose," Rich said. Jennifer probably had a point about leaving early. The church could be on the far side of town, and neither of them had been there before. He wondered if there were directions in that miracle diaper bag. So far, every time he'd needed something, he'd found it in the magic bag.

"Look in the diaper bag and see if Rebecca thought to put in directions to the church or a map or something while I dress." He turned without waiting to see if Jennifer complied.

He'd already showered and shaved, so all he had to do was put on his mess dress uniform. He'd wondered whether he'd have many occasions to wear it when he'd bought it for his graduation from Noncommissioned Officer Leadership School, but he was glad he had. At least he wouldn't have to go out and rent a tuxedo. He'd feel out of place, as it was, in that church full of strangers.

Rich removed the dry-cleaning bag from his blue, formal dress suit and hooked the hanger over the closet door. He had to pin on his decorations, but that would only take a few seconds.

Medals attached and positioned, Rich stood back and checked from a distance. He probably could get away with them not being regulation straight. Nobody at the wedding would likely know, but he would. They were fine, but might need some adjusting when he put the jacket on.

He quickly slipped into the white, pleated dress

shirt and fastened the studs and cuff links. He didn't know why the pleats were necessary, seemed a little froufrou to him, but they were part of the uniform.

He reached for the black bow tie. He should have bought a clip-on, he thought as he drew in a deep breath and pulled it around his neck. He started the knot. Though his fingers seemed clumsy and thick, he managed to tie an acceptable bow.

He drew in a deep breath, ran a hand through his hair, exhaled, then glanced at his watch—11:27 a.m. Three minutes to spare.

Jennifer was pacing and jiggling Carter in her arms when Rich pushed open the bedroom door. Funny, he hadn't noticed what she looked like when she first came in, probably because of the crisis with Caitlyn, but he sure noticed now.

She had chosen something more sophisticated than he had seen her in before. Instead of the long, sacky dresses, she wore a pale blue suit. The skirt was knee-length, revealing the legs of a chorus girl, and the form-fitting jacket showed off her curves in a way Rich really appreciated. Her long, dark brown hair was done up in one of those funny braids that looked both sophisticated and girlish at the same time.

He liked what he saw.

Jennifer's back was to him as she walked the floor. Rich cleared his throat. ''Will I pass inspection?''

Jennifer turned quickly. She seemed to take a short breath or, maybe, she gasped. Her eyes grew wide, but she didn't speak.

Rich looked down, brushed at a speck of dust, then asked, ''What's wrong?''

Jennifer swallowed and shook her head. ''Nothing,'' she said, sounding positively strangled.

Caitlyn tugged at his jacket hem. "You look like a handsome pwince from a fairy tale, Uncle Witch."

"I couldn't have said it better, myself," Jennifer agreed. "You look…" She paused for a moment. "You look fantastic."

Fantastic was an understatement, Jennifer thought as she took in the man in his resplendent, military glory. Rich had looked great in his camouflage fatigues, civilian clothes, and Lord knows, he'd looked like the hero on the cover of a romance novel with his shirt off, but this… This was by far the best.

"I'm not used to getting this dressed up," Rich said.

"You look fine," Jennifer said. "Like you do it every day." And, she couldn't help thinking, he looked good every day. When he had been hesitantly asking her for help finding his sister, when he'd been confused and vulnerable after he'd found her, even when he'd been at his most "take charge," he'd looked great.

"Oh, yeah," Jennifer repeated, her voice breathy and low. "You look just fine."

THIRTY MINUTES and three false tries at getting all the kids' paraphernalia arranged in Jennifer's car later, they were finally on the way. Rich hoped that Jennifer had been right about them not being able to start without the flower girl, because they were going to be late unless a miracle happened.

And he hadn't witnessed any miracles lately.

Unless he counted finding Sherry so quickly. He glanced at Jennifer, concentrating on the Labor Day weekend traffic on the road ahead. Maybe, Jennifer was a miracle, too. She'd certainly come to his rescue this time. Twice, if he counted helping him figure out what had happened to Sherry.

Jennifer had, at first, seemed like the most unlikely of investigators when he'd marched into her office and made what he thought was an impossible request. But she hadn't batted an eyelash, just calmly took down the information and called back with the results in less than a day.

How could a guy like him get so lucky?

"Uncle Witch?"

He glanced at Caitlyn, strapped into her car booster seat in the back. "What, short stuff?"

She grimaced. "I am not short. I'm almost old enough to go to school," she informed him haughtily. "What happens at a weddy?"

Rich drew in a deep breath. "The two people who are getting married stand up in front of a minister. The minister asks them some questions, and they make some promises, then they kiss, and they're married."

"They have to kiss?"

Jennifer saved him. "They don't have to," she said matter-of-factly. "But they usually do. It's sort of the way they seal their promise."

"Why don't they just shake hands?"

Rich swallowed a chuckle, and he noted that Jennifer's lips twitched, too. "They like to kiss each other. They want to."

"Yuk," said Caitlyn. "When I get married I'm gonna just shake hands."

Jennifer trembled with suppressed laughter, but she didn't comment.

"You'll want to by the time you're old enough to

get married," Rich finally said, glancing over his shoulder at Caitlyn.

She made a skeptical face, but she didn't comment. And Rich was fine with that.

JENNIFER PULLED into the church parking lot with seven minutes to spare. Too close for comfort in her book, but at least they weren't late. The parking lot was jammed, but they found a spot not too far from the door.

Mrs. Benton, the next-door neighbor they had met that first night, was on the steps scanning the incoming traffic. "We'd better put Mrs. Benton out of her misery," Jennifer said as she turned off the engine.

"Who?" Apparently, Rich hadn't seen her.

"Mrs. Benton, Sherry's neighbor. We met her that first night when we were looking for Sherry. She's out front, probably waiting for us."

"They can't start wifout the flower girl," Caitlyn chimed, saving Jennifer from explaining. Sometimes, men were so clueless.

"Oh, yeah. I guess you're right," he said as he opened his door. He climbed out of the car, unfolding himself and arching.

Jennifer felt a twinge of pity, but he would have been in worse shape if he'd tried to drive her compact car. "Wave to Mrs. Benton so she knows we've arrived." She reached for her purse, and checked her makeup. Her lipstick needed a touch-up, but the rest was fine. "I'm sure Mrs. Benton and Rebecca need Caitlyn right away. I'll get Carter as soon as I'm done."

"It's okay, Jen'fer. I'm alweady unhooked," Caitlyn said, pushing the strap up over her head.

Rich bent over and lifted her out. "Don't want to wrinkle that pretty dress climbing down." He set her carefully on her feet on the oyster shell parking lot, executed a shallow bow, then straightened and crooked his arm. "Shall we go, Miss Connolly?"

Caitlyn giggled, and reached up to take his arm.

An unfamiliar rush of emotion made it difficult for Jennifer to swallow for a moment, and she blinked away tears. Rich was so patient with the child. Even last night when he'd been so obviously overwhelmed with everything, he hadn't lost his temper.

She wondered how long that would last.

She knew all too well what short fuses those macho men had. She'd seen it firsthand. Her ex would be patient up to a point, then he'd explode worse than Mount Saint Helens. Take it from her, it wasn't fun to be on the wrong side of those explosions.

No. Jennifer shook her head. That was in the past. It was over and done with. This was supposed to be a happy day.

Still, she wondered as she touched up her lipstick. How long would this calm before the storm hold?

RICH HERDED Caitlyn to the top of the steps and handed her off to Mrs. Benton.

"So glad you finally got here," Mrs. Benton said more to Caitlyn than to Rich. "Miss Rebecca is as nervous as a butterfly in a hurricane. Can't seem to light anywhere."

"I'm here now," Caitlyn said. "We can start the weddy now."

Mrs. Benton, nodded absently, then looked confused.

"Caitlyn has an overinflated view of her importance in the ceremony," Rich explained. "We were worried that we'd be late and they'd have to wait for the flower girl."

"Oh. I see." Mrs. Benton smiled, but she seemed distracted at the same time.

"Is something else wrong?"

"Ye—" Mrs. Benton cut herself off and shook her head. "No, I'll let Rebecca explain it." Then she took Caitlyn's hand. "The wedding's soon to start. You'd best get your friend and the baby inside and find your seats."

Rich turned to see Jennifer unfastening Carter from the car seat. She straightened, balanced the baby on her hip and turned. She'd said she didn't know anything about kids, but to him, she seemed a natural. It's a shame they didn't have a house full of their own kids.

He smiled as Jennifer produced a white lace handkerchief from a pocket and wiped Carter's face. Then Rich swallowed quickly and almost choked. What had he just been thinking?

No, he told himself. That was just a...a Freudian slip or something. He didn't want kids or a wife. He was too busy. Gone all the time. He wasn't ready to be married or settled down. Besides, he wasn't about to follow in his father's footsteps.

Jennifer joined him on the steps, and he dragged himself away from that disastrous line of thought. Maybe it was just that he was at a wedding, even if it hadn't started yet. Hadn't he heard somewhere that weddings triggered all kinds of mushy thoughts in people?

"Are you ready?" Jennifer asked as she handed Carter to him and brushed at her suit.

"Yeah," he said, his voice husky, his thoughts confused. He tried to shake the unfamiliar emotions away. "You look great, by the way. If I haven't told you already."

Jennifer gifted him with a brilliant smile. "Thanks."

Mrs. Benton pushed open the church door and beckoned frantically to them. "Come on," she said. "We're waiting for you."

Rich drew in a deep breath. "I guess this is it," he said, adjusting his grip on Carter and offering Jennifer his arm as he had to Caitlyn earlier. "We'd best find our seats."

Jennifer nodded. "Will your sister like me?" she asked unexpectedly as they stepped into the cool interior of the small church.

"Well, yeah," he answered for lack of anything else. "Why shouldn't she?"

Before Jennifer could answer, Rebecca Tucker peeked out of the bride's room. "Rich," she said, looking more nervous than a blushing bride should. "Be sure to stay for the reception. I have to talk to you."

Rich supposed Rebecca needed to set up the hand-off arrangements for the kids, but he didn't have a chance to think about it for long.

A teenage usher came up to them. "They're saving you seats up front," he said. "Follow me."

Rather than delay the ceremony any further, Rich followed the young man as he led them to the front of the church.

Rich spotted Sherry in a wheelchair parked at the end of the front pew. The torturous-looking halo was gone, though angry, red marks showed where it had been attached, and she still wore a cumbersome neck brace. Her chair was set at an angle, so that she wouldn't have to turn her head too far to see the flower girl, the bride or the ceremony.

Her face lit up with a brilliant smile when she saw them. Carter must have seen her at the same time, for he lurched in Rich's arms and leaned, arms outstretched like an animated divining rod, toward his mother.

Carter started to cry as Rich lowered him into his mother's lap.

"Oh, I have missed you so much, you sweet thing," Sherry murmured, her voice sounding thick and husky as she pulled her son close and kissed the top of his fuzzy head, soothing him. Then she looked up, her eyes misty and bright with tears.

"I missed you, too," she said to Rich. She smiled though her eyes were still shining and watery and reached out to squeeze his hand. "Now sit down so we can get this show on the road."

RICH ROSE and stood, hip to hip, with Jennifer by his side in the front row of the bride's side of the church. Though he should have paid more attention to the way Caitlyn marched down the aisle performing her flower girl duties, all he could think about was the woman by his side. The beaming flower girl reached the end of the aisle, dumped the remaining flower petals on the floor in a heap, and flounced onto the seat between Rich and Sherry. She gave her mother a loud kiss on the cheek.

"Mommy," she announced in a stage whisper. "Didn't I do a gweat job?"

There was a quiet titter of amusement from the

congregation, then a collective sigh as everyone turned to look at Rebecca as she and her father marched slowly down the aisle.

Sherry smiled indulgently, squeezed her daughter in a quiet hug, making a sandwich with Carter in the middle. "Shh," she said. "We have to be quiet now." She raised a finger to her lips. "You can tell me about being a flower girl later."

"Okay," Caitlyn said in another stage whisper, then settled onto the hard surface of the pew, taking up more space on the seat than was her fair share.

Caitlyn's position on the pew pushed Rich closer to Jennifer as they took their seats. The place where he brushed against her, though separated by layers of clothing, tingled with awareness.

Rich shot a quick glance sideways and wondered if Jennifer felt the same. She seemed so calm, so serene as she sat quietly beside him, her eyes on the couple at the altar.

Yet, when his gaze settled on her, Rich sensed a flicker of interest in Jennifer's dark brown eyes. Her hands were folded primly on her lap, clutching her small, summer purse, and Rich couldn't resist the urge. He covered her slender fingers with his and squeezed. Then he held his breath until he was certain Jennifer wouldn't jerk her hand away.

Jennifer flexed her hand beneath his, and Rich dared another quick glance in her direction. A slight turning up of her lips told Rich it was all right.

That nearly imperceptible gesture of pleasure told him more than a thousand words. He drew in a sigh of satisfaction and settled back against the seat and tried to pay attention to what was supposed to be the main event. He enjoyed sitting there with Jennifer beside him like she belonged there. He enjoyed the possessive feeling of his hand on hers. As far as Rich was concerned, the rest of the ceremony was over much too soon.

"May I introduce Mr. and Mrs. Tom Williams," the minister announced, as Rebecca and her new husband turned to face the gathered well-wishers.

Rich felt a surge of envy for the man who'd just claimed Rebecca as his forever in a church filled with witnesses. How he could be jealous of a man he'd never met, Rich didn't know. But Tom seemed so happy, so proud. And Rich's life suddenly seemed so...so...empty.

Would he ever know what it was like to have one woman care enough to pledge herself to him forever?

He hadn't spent a lot of time thinking about marriage and family in his twenty-eight years. At least, not in the context of his own life. He'd wondered what had become of his long lost sister and what her life was like, but prior to today, marriage had been a distant, if not abstract, thought.

Now, sitting with Jennifer so near, he wondered if that faraway notion might be closer than he'd imagined.

JENNIFER SAT next to Sherry during the reception and smiled as she watched Rich dance with Caitlyn. The little girl waltzed with her patent leather shoes braced securely on top of her Uncle Rich's own spit-and-polished ones and held confidently on as if it were a given that he wouldn't let her down.

Sherry leaned across the sleeping form of Carter in her lap and whispered conspiratorially, "He's a natural, don't you think?"

Jennifer's breath caught in her throat. Had Sherry read her mind? "I hadn't really thought about it," she lied. Then her better judgment got to her. "Yes, he plays the favorite uncle very well," she said as she raised a cup of punch to her lips.

"How long have you and Rich been dating?"

That caught her so much by surprise that she almost choked. Using the resultant cough as cover, Jennifer took a moment to formulate an answer. They hadn't really been dating, but she felt she'd known him forever. "We're just friends," she said, too embarrassed to meet Sherry's eyes.

"Oh." Sherry blushed. "I'm sorry. I just assumed you... I don't know what I assumed."

"It's all right," Jennifer said, feeling heat rise to her own cheeks. "I don't really know how to describe our relationship. I met Rich the day he came into my office wanting to find you." She paused a moment to watch the man gliding across the floor with the little girl perched on his feet. "I didn't really expect to see him again once I gave him the information."

"Oh." The tone was knowing, challenging.

"Oh?" Jennifer slanted a glance at Sherry. "What do you mean by that?"

"Nothing. Except that for someone who's just in a business relationship, my big brother certainly has drawn you in deep."

Jennifer couldn't dispute that. Unlike her other clients, she hadn't forgotten him once the job was done.

And she surely wouldn't have come running to help with the children—or agreed to come to this wedding—if he'd been just a business acquaintance. And she'd never kissed a client before, much less experienced the overwhelming sexual attraction she'd felt in his arms.

"I probably won't see him again after today," she said too quickly. Then she crossed her fingers and hoped it wasn't true.

Sherry just smiled.

What did she know that Jennifer didn't?

Rich danced his niece back over to her mother and gestured to Jennifer. If he had to wear this monkey suit, he might as well get something out of it.

Jennifer colored prettily, then with a flustered look, excused herself and walked into his arms.

"Having a good time?" he asked as they began to sway to the music. Whoever invented dancing sure had got it right. It was the best excuse a guy could have to hold a woman in public.

"Yes," Jennifer answered, her voice husky. "I'm glad I got to meet your sister."

"Me, too," Rich replied.

As he wondered what to say next, someone tapped his shoulder. He turned and discovered Rebecca and her groom standing at his elbow.

"Mind if we cut in?" they asked in unison.

Rich did mind, but it was their wedding so he didn't say so. He simply relinquished his claim on Jennifer and watched as another man swept her away.

Slowly, he stepped back into the sway of the music with Rebecca in his arms. He supposed this was one of those duty dances, something he was supposed to do at a family wedding, but he'd much rather dance with the woman he'd come with.

"I want to thank you for helping with the kids," Rebecca said.

Rich nodded, still watching Jennifer glide away.

"And…" she said slowly. "I have an even bigger favor to ask."

Chapter Six

Rich wondered what kind of favor could possibly be bigger than the one he'd just done. Hell, dropping two little kids he didn't even know on him with no notice was pretty damned huge. "Sure. What?" Maybe she needed him to help with Sherry. He could do that.

"I spent all night on the phone and half the morning trying to get someone to take Mrs. Dahlstrom's place, but..." Her voice trailed off, and wearing a sheepish look on her face, she shrugged.

The impact of what Rebecca was leading up to hit him with the force of a mortar round at close range, and Rich stopped dancing and stood motionless in the middle of the dance floor. Still, he waited, holding his breath. He had a rapidly sinking feeling he knew what was coming next, and he fervently hoped he was wrong.

"It's a holiday weekend. Most of the people who know the kids have already made plans. Even the employment agencies had closed by the time I realized I couldn't find anyone." She took a quick breath, then charged on. "I don't have any family in Pensacola, so you're the only person left I can call on.'' She glanced toward the table where Sherry sat with Carter on her lap and Caitlyn leaned over the arm of the wheelchair. ''I hate going on my honeymoon now, but all along, Sherry has insisted that I not change my plans on her account.''

Rich exhaled slowly, then drew in a deep, long breath while he tried to formulate his answer. He didn't know whether he was stalling till he could come up with a good excuse or just postponing the inevitable.

What did he know about kids? He was a busy man. He was trained to kill, he wanted to protest. He really did want to say no, but the truth was, in the short time he'd spent with Caitlyn and Carter, he'd come to like the kids. Maybe even love them. They had given him a taste of the family life he hadn't realized he'd missed growing up in foster care.

Sure, there had been problems last night, but they'd been nothing he couldn't handle. At least, with Jennifer's help, he'd done fine. He looked around for Jennifer who was still dancing with Tom Williams, and experienced a twinge of unfounded jealousy. With the responsibility of the kids there, maybe he'd still have a reason to keep Jennifer coming around.

Why he wanted to keep her coming around, he still didn't know. Or maybe he did know, but he couldn't admit it. He knew there was no point in pursuing a relationship with any woman. Marriage was just not for him. Not after the royal mess his own parents had made of theirs. He might be able to handle these kids for a few days, but he had no confidence at all that he could manage it for the long haul. No, he wasn't going to take any chances with anybody else's future.

"Rich?" Rebecca's voice trembled, the tone uncertain.

Still, he couldn't force himself to answer. Not until he'd weighed all the options, examined every side of the issue. He had just come in from a weeklong exercise, so he wouldn't be going out again soon, he reminded himself. He had leave coming if he needed to take it. Yeah, he guessed he could do it. He drew in a deep breath, and started to answer, but Rebecca spoke first.

"Tom and I have already agreed that we'll take the kids when we get back from the honeymoon. And we'll work something out for Sherry after she's out of rehab and keep things going until she's back on her feet." She looked at him, her big green eyes wide and pleading. "We are newlyweds, Rich. Let us have our honeymoon."

How could he deny that request? Rebecca had done so much for Sherry already, and he had done so little. Hell, she wasn't even family. Sure, he would have taken Sherry and the kids in if it had come to that, but she needed to be close to her doctors, and it would be far easier on everyone involved if she didn't have to move from Pensacola to Fort Walton Beach.

The music stopped and the pregnant silence seemed to demand an answer even more than Rebecca's questioning green eyes. "If we don't do something, the kids might end up with Child Protective Services."

She had to hit him with the big gun. Rebecca surely had to know how he and Sherry felt about that. They'd do anything and everything to keep those kids out of the system. It might have served them well enough, but it wasn't a choice he'd willingly make for any child. Especially, not his own niece and nephew. He'd have to tell Rebecca yes.

He knew he wouldn't regret it, but he wasn't sure how he was going to do it. Rich closed his eyes, issued a silent prayer to whatever deities might be listening and answered. "Yes," he told her. "I'll do my best."

Rebecca threw her arms around him and squeezed him in a hug so tight, he wondered how long it would take to fill his lungs again. "Yess," she breathed. "Yess. Oh, thank you, Rich. Thank you, thank you, thank you."

Maybe it was damned stupid of him to feel so good about his decision, but Rich did. Maybe he didn't know squat about taking care of kids, but he hadn't harmed them so far. Maybe they'd all survive the next week. And, considering his crash course in child care—mostly on-the-job training—it could only get easier.

Rich nodded toward where Jennifer stood with Tom. "Was Tom supposed to work on Jennifer while you were sweet-talking me?"

Rebecca looked puzzled for a minute. "What? Oh, you mean try to convince your girlfriend? No. It just seemed polite to exchange partners."

He should have corrected her about the girlfriend thing, but Rich didn't. After all, though it wasn't exactly true, he'd like it to be if things were different and he were the right kind of man. "Well, let me be the one to tell her."

The music began again, and Rebecca stepped out of Rich's arms. "Sure." She started to leave, then stopped and looked back. "Thanks again, Rich."

Rich sighed. Come Tuesday morning he was going to have to go into the section and convince Captain Thibodeaux that he was going to need some time off. He hadn't been assigned to this unit for very long, and he didn't know Thibodeaux that well, but he'd seemed like a fair man. And, if he remembered correctly, he had a kid of his own.

Maybe he'd understand.

And Thibodeaux would probably be easier to convince than Jennifer. Rich looked around for her. He was going to have to break the news to her somehow, and considering his own reaction to Rebecca's desperate request, he figured he had his work cut out for him.

He looked around for Jennifer, but didn't see her in the crowd. Tom had already reclaimed his bride, and Jennifer wasn't dancing with anyone else. Nor was she sitting with Sherry at their table.

For that matter, he didn't see Sherry or the kids.

Where had they gone?

JENNIFER FINISHED changing Carter's diaper, expertly fastening it around his chubby middle and pulling his navy shorts back up over his well-padded behind. She hadn't thought much about the problems associated with Sherry's condition, but seeing the way the woman watched so longingly as Jennifer took care of Sherry's child, she began to understand. Confined to the chair, Sherry hadn't been able to reach the changing table in the ladies' room, and Jennifer could see that it hurt her not to be able to give her child even that most basic care.

It was going to be a long time before Sherry would be able to cope with the children on her own. Jennifer wondered what kind of arrangements Rebecca had worked out, and she wondered what Sherry thought about strangers taking care of her kids.

"You do that like a pro," Sherry commented as Jennifer stashed the baby wipes back in the bag and tossed the soiled diaper in the can. "Rich is so lucky to have your help."

Jennifer picked Carter up and placed him back in Sherry's arms. She could see that the excitement of the day had begun to catch up with Sherry. Her face was pale and gray shadows surrounded her blue eyes. She smiled and took a seat on the couch in the ladies' lounge across from Sherry's wheelchair. "It was just a case of the blind leading the blind, I suppose," she said, smiling as Caitlyn came out of a stall and washed her hands like a big girl.

"Rich seems to think that knowing what to do is part of the standard female package. Prior to yesterday, I might have argued with him." She bent down to tweak Carter's chubby cheek. "But maybe he was closer to the mark than I thought."

Sherry smiled, her wan face seeming to brighten with it. "My big brother might not be as dumb as he looks." She drew in a deep breath and smiled again, this one softer. "Seriously, I think more people are born with the right instincts than not. The bad behavior is learned, not inborn."

Jennifer wondered why she had said that, but didn't get a chance to question it.

"You know, Rich and I didn't have the best childhood. We were raised in foster care after our mother died. Our foster parents were nice people, and life was pretty comfortable with them, but Rich wasn't with them long enough to really know a normal fam-

ily life.'' Sherry paused a moment, a faraway look
in her eyes. ''Daddy abused alcohol, he abused our
mother and he abused us. He was a pretty good guy
when he was dry and sober, but when...'' She swallowed and looked off into the distance. Then she
cleared her throat. ''Life was pretty bad around our
house until he went into a veterans' hospital.'' She
paused again and blinked at brightness in her eyes.
''He died there,'' she finished, her voice thick with
emotion.

Sherry shook her head and forced a brittle smile.
''Mama tried, but she was sick herself.'' She sighed
and looked away.

''Sherry, you don't have to—''

But Sherry cut her off with a wave of her hand.
''Yes, I do. I think Rich's way of seeing life and the
world has been colored by it. He looks a lot like
Daddy...before he got so out of control. I think Rich
is afraid that he's going to turn out like him.''

Jennifer's breath caught.

Sherry continued. ''But Rich has been so good
with the kids. So patient. I don't think he has anything to worry about,'' she said.

Jennifer wondered why Sherry felt she had to tell
her that. Was she trying to convince her to hang in
there? Or was she warning her away?

She'd already had a taste of life with a man who
couldn't control his baser instincts. Did she want to
risk a repeat of the same thing with Rich?

''Come on,'' said Sherry. ''We've been hiding in
here long enough. Surely, somebody's been wondering where we are.''

''Yeah, sure,'' Jennifer answered absently, her
mind churning with troubled thoughts. For a few

brief hours she'd hoped that maybe something was starting to develop between her and Rich Larsen. Now, maybe it wasn't such a good thing. Jennifer pushed the door to the rest room open, then wheeled Sherry through.

Maybe it was good that somebody else was going to be taking care of the kids. Maybe it was a good thing that she and Rich wouldn't have an excuse to see each other after today.

RICH COULDN'T HELP thinking that Rebecca had put her honeymoon on the line by trusting that he'd make the right decision. What if he had said no? Would she have had to cancel her wedding trip? He knew she wouldn't have let the kids become wards of the state.

Maybe it was cynical, but he'd bet Rebecca had counted on him not being able to turn her down, not after she'd thrown in the bit about putting the kids in foster care. He smiled wryly as he helped himself to a plate of hors d'oeuvres and scanned the room again for Jennifer and his family.

He took a bite from a mini-egg roll and thought while he chewed.

Okay, maybe Rebecca had banked a lot on him not being able to turn down her request at the wedding reception, but she hadn't been devious. He didn't know Rebecca well, but he was pretty sure that she'd exhausted every possibility before she'd come to him again. She might have been able to find somebody to stay with the kids if she paid them enough, but just thinking about it bothered Rich. He didn't like the idea of his niece and nephew—his family—being taken care of by strangers.

His family. He liked the sound of that. It had been a very long time since he'd thought of himself in the context of a familial group. It felt good to know that he belonged to people who were bound to him by blood. He had formed some strong ties while in the air force, especially among the combat control operators he worked with, but it wasn't the same. Those guys could walk out of his life at any time and never look back.

It pleased him to know that Sherry had been thinking about him all that time. Even if it had taken her too long to get over her hurt feelings about being left behind and start to look for him.

"Uncle Witch, Uncle Witch." Caitlyn's clear, treble voice brought him out of his thoughts.

"Yeah, short stuff?" He turned, to see the entire gang returning to the table they'd deserted earlier. Where had they been?

"Mommy says that Aunt Webecca is gonna frow her bokay, and whoever gets it is gonna get married next. Did you know about that?"

Jennifer's mouth twitched at Caitlyn's simplistic assessment of the tradition, and Rich arched an eyebrow. It almost sounded as if his niece thought that the next wedding would occur immediately. Rich chuckled and placed his plate on the table. "It doesn't quite happen that quick," he explained to the child as he swung her up into his arms. "Do you need to be first in line?"

Caitlyn's little face puckered up with a confused look. "Huh?"

Rich grinned. "Just thought maybe you had a guy all picked out and you were just waiting for a chance to snag him."

"Oh, Uncle Witch. You are so silly. I'm only four. I have to go to high school first." She lowered her voice conspiratorially. "I think Jen'fer needsa get it. She doesn't have a daddy she's married wif."

Caitlyn's remark hit too close to home, and Rich didn't know how to respond. He wasn't sure how he felt about marriage, but he was definitely interested in Jennifer. On the other hand, he didn't know how she felt about him.

Rich glanced over at Jennifer and Sherry and shot them a "can-you-help-me-out-here?" look, but Jennifer just produced a weak smile and shrugged. Sherry's reaction was much the same. He wouldn't be getting any help from that quarter.

His best defense was a good offense. "How about another piece of cake?" he suggested, hoping the diversion would get Caitlyn's—and his—mind off that subject.

"'Kay," Caitlyn answered happily. "Can we get some for Mommy, too?"

"Of course, we can," he said. After all, getting cake was a lot easier than having to answer all the questions that Caitlyn kept coming up with.

Sherry leaned over to Jennifer and whispered softly, "You'd better watch out. It looks like Caitlyn is horning in on your territory."

Jennifer could see that Caitlyn was clearly besotted with her newfound uncle—"weddy dress" episode notwithstanding—but she wasn't sure what Sherry meant by her statement. Rich wasn't her possession. She had no claim on Rich. After the wedding, she'd go back to doing computer research with Checkmate, and he'd be flying off to exotic places at a moment's notice and jumping out of perfectly good airplanes.

She'd been there with a man who'd done that. Had nothing but divorce papers and a wounded heart to show for it. She didn't need it again.

She wanted stability. A nice, steady guy who made a comfortable living and came home at five-thirty every night and loved only her. Somebody like an accountant. Yeah, an accountant. Maybe, he'd be busy during tax season, but there were still nine or ten other months of the year when she could depend on him. Yeah, that was it.

Then she looked at Rich and wondered how many accountants could fill a mess dress uniform or a tux—and a room, she couldn't help thinking—like Rich did. She shrugged mentally. It was a trade-off she'd just have to live with.

Of course, she'd have to meet an accountant first.

"Okay, everybody. It's time for Rebecca to throw the bouquet," Mrs. Benton announced, clapping her hands to gain attention. "Single girls need to line up over here."

Jennifer watched with amused interest as an elderly lady, a couple of teenage girls and the maid of honor gathered near the side door of the banquet hall. She hoped the maid of honor got it, and she hoped the woman knew what she was getting into. Jennifer wasn't interested in a husband, nor was she interested in some silly ritual that didn't mean anything in the scheme of things.

Rich returned with Caitlyn, and a stack of paper plates with a jumble of cake slices on the top plate. He dealt them out like a Las Vegas card dealer and distributed cake all around. After he had doled it all out, he leaned toward Jennifer. "I need to talk to you," he said.

"Sure." Jennifer arched a brow. She supposed it had something to do with the plans for getting the kids to the sitter Rebecca had arranged. "Go ahead."

"Not here." Rich jerked his head toward an empty corner of the room. "Over there."

She couldn't help wondering why, but Jennifer followed Rich away from the table. "What's up?"

"There's been a slight change of plans," he said, sucking in a deep breath.

"Okay," she said slowly. "What kind of change?"

The drummer from the five-piece combo that had provided the music for the party executed a drumroll, and Jennifer glanced over her shoulder. At least, she'd be safe from that spectacle over here in the corner.

"No, wait!" Mrs. Benton held up her hand like a cop stopping traffic, causing Jennifer and Rich to turn. "We don't have all the single girls over here yet." She came barreling across the room toward them, and Jennifer had a sinking feeling she was going to have to participate whether she wanted to or not.

"Rich Larsen. Go wheel your sister over to where she can see what's going on." She turned to Jennifer and leveled a pointed glare at her. "The rest of the single ladies are waiting for you, missy," Mrs. Benton said to Jennifer, her hands planted authoritatively on her hips. When Jennifer didn't move, she motioned with her hands. "Shoo. Go on. Rebecca and Tom have a plane to catch. They're going to be late."

"Yes, Ma'am," Rich said, saluting.

Jennifer blew out an exasperated breath and followed Rich over to his sister. "What were you going to tell me about?" she asked as Rich unlatched the wheel locks on Sherry's chair and pushed her toward the rest of the gathered wedding guests.

Rich started to speak, but Mrs. Benton grabbed his arm and steered him toward a knot of men huddled on the other side of the women. Rebecca and Tom stood just to the front of both groups. Mrs. Benton pushed Jennifer toward the cluster of unmarried women.

Seeming to be satisfied with the arrangements, Mrs. Benton nodded toward the drummer. "Okay. Now."

He began the drumroll again.

Tom leaned in and kissed his bride, and Rebecca blushed prettily. She bent over, pulled her dress up slightly, and proceeded to roll a lacy, blue garter down her leg.

Jennifer had forgotten about the garter tradition. The groom tossed it to the single men, and whichever one caught it was supposed to be the next to marry. She couldn't help a derisive snort.

The drumroll stopped. The room was expectantly quiet as Tom pulled the garter past Rebecca's trim ankle and over her shoe. Rich glanced toward Jennifer and mouthed something to her again. *We still have to talk,* she thought he said.

Then Tom tossed the garter. Several laughing men and boys lunged for it, but Rich reached up and snagged it effortlessly out of the air. Then he looked at it as if he didn't know what it was.

"Congratulations," Mrs. Benton announced. "Rich Larsen, you're next."

"Next what?"

"The next man to marry."

Rich looked at the piece of blue ribbon and lace in his hand, then tossed it away like it was a live grenade. He held both hands up. "No, no. Not me," he protested.

Mrs. Benton tut-tutted and shook her head. "It's only a tradition, not a disease." She scooped up the garter and pressed it into his hand.

Rich scowled, shoved it into his pocket and looked toward Jennifer. She shrugged as he turned and, ignoring the rest of the gathered people, made his way toward her.

"We have to talk," he insisted as he worked his way around behind Jennifer. The drums began again, and Rebecca faced away from the crowd.

"One," the women chanted.

"We have a problem," Rich said.

"Yes," Jennifer answered absently, her eyes drawn, like someone trying not to look at a car wreck, to the spectacle in front of her.

"A big problem," he insisted.

"Two," the single ladies went on.

Jennifer sighed. She was beginning to think that Rich was stalling. "Do you think you could get to the point?" she finally asked, turning her head toward him, but still keeping one eye on what was happening.

Rich drew in a deep, long breath. "Rebecca called everyone she could think of to keep the kids."

"Good," Jennifer said.

"Three."

Rebecca bent low and then let the bouquet fly up over her head.

It seemed to soar toward Jennifer at the speed of light while Rich's next words seemed to come in slow motion.

"I told her I'd take them for the rest of the week."

Jennifer turned her head around so fast, she almost lost her balance. "What?"

"I said I'd keep the kids."

Something in her peripheral vision caught her eye, and Jennifer instinctively reached for it.

She felt her fingers connect and realized that she, in spite of all her efforts not to, had caught the bouquet. The instant she knew what it was, she flung it away, and it bounced into Sherry's hands.

Jennifer stepped back, surprised, or horrified, or both.

She looked at Rich, she looked at Sherry raising the bouquet to her nose to sniff the fragrant blooms, then she looked at Rebecca.

Rebecca smiled, waved, then dashed toward the changing room with Tom.

"No," Jennifer protested. "No. We can't take the kids back with us. You can't take care of them."

Mrs. Benton spoke up again. "Well, I never. It's the first time I've ever seen that happen."

Jennifer looked at the woman. How could she be worrying about something as trivial as the bouquet when Rich had just volunteered himself—and her, she'd bet—for another week of child-care duty?

She looked at Rich as if he'd lost his mind.

Chapter Seven

"What do you mean by saying that you'd take care of those kids for another week?" Jennifer demanded.

Rich looked into her wide brown eyes. Did she seriously think that he'd had a choice? He steered Jennifer away from the knot of people surrounding Sherry and the bouquet. He felt Jennifer's muscles tense under the smooth, blue fabric of her sleeve. "They're my family, Jennifer. What else could I do? I didn't want them to go to strangers."

She jerked her arm out of his grasp and looked at him with an expression that appeared more like disgust than Rich would have cared for. "Almost any stranger has more knowledge about children than you do," she said through clenched teeth. She nodded toward Mrs. Benton and directed as phony a smile as Rich had ever seen her way.

Then she turned back to Rich. "I sincerely hope you don't expect me to bail you out this time. I have a job that is important to me. I can't take time off to take care of those children."

"Well, fine," Rich answered. "And, for the record, I didn't ask you to. I'll work something out. They do have a day-care center on the base."

"That has a waiting list a year long," Jennifer retorted.

Rich hadn't known that. But then, why would he? And why would *she*? Was it something women automatically knew? "Well, maybe I can find somebody to come to the apartment during the day."

"Good luck," Jennifer replied sweetly. "Rebecca hasn't been able to find anyone, and she knows people."

Expelling a long, tired breath, Rich shook his head. "I don't know what I'll do, Jennifer. If I have to throw myself on Captain Thibodeaux's mercy and beg for leave, then I'll do it. Those kids are my family, and I know what it's like to be all alone," he said tiredly. "Maybe you don't, but I do, and I'm not going to let that happen to those kids."

Jennifer jerked her head away as if he'd started to strike her. She blinked and looked at him again. Then her eyes misted with tears.

Rich reached toward her, but she shrugged him off, blinking her eyes frantically. "Don't touch me, Rich Larsen," she said, her voice decidedly wobbly.

She turned her back to him for a moment, her shoulders shaking. Rich wanted to hold her, but something told him that that wasn't what she needed right now. Jennifer turned to face him. "I do know what it's like to be alone and lost," she said slowly and evenly. "I might not have been a child when it happened, but I do know," she said, her stubborn chin thrust high and forward. "So don't come at me with anything like that ever again." Jennifer's voice broke, and she walked away.

Rich watched her leave and wondered if she was walking out of his life. He drew in another deep, long breath. Maybe this was for the best. He had enough to worry about right now without being distracted by Jennifer.

Sure, he had hoped he could count on Jennifer's help, but he hadn't really considered the ramifications. He barely knew the woman, they weren't dating, he had no hold on her. Hell, she'd done him an enormous favor just by agreeing to come with him to this wedding.

Then, he realized, he'd been counting on a lot of things. He'd counted on Captain Thibodeaux's support, and he'd counted on the day-care center on base.

He hadn't counted on Jennifer turning on him.

Now what was he going to do?

JENNIFER HATED that she'd had to speak to Rich that way, but she couldn't, she wouldn't, be sucked any deeper into his life. It was better this way, she tried to convince herself as she kept as much distance as she could between them until she could go home.

The more time she spent with Rich, the harder it would be to get away safely. Oh, she knew he wasn't about to hurt her. At least, not physically or intentionally. But she knew all too well about those kinds of guys. They were excitement junkies. They liked the chase, but they didn't hang around for the long haul. They weren't good husband material.

She tried to convince herself that the only reason she'd thought of him in the context of husbands was because she was standing in the middle of a wedding reception. After all, didn't everybody get sentimental and dreamy at a wedding? She drew in a deep breath and glanced over her shoulder at the man standing ramrod straight in the tailored blue uniform. Even as angry as she was, the sight of him made her breath catch and her heart flutter.

She would bet that he'd be an excellent lover, she thought as she looked at the angular lines of his face and the way those well-trained muscles filled out that dark blue uniform. She remembered all too well what those muscles looked like, and the sight of him bare-chested, holding that baby was something she wasn't likely to forget even if she lived to be a hundred.

Good lover, yeah. She glanced again toward where Rich still stood, looking perplexed and confounded. He'd all but knocked her socks off just with his kisses. It wouldn't take much time or effort on his part to talk her out of the rest of her clothes. And, she didn't need to get involved in anything like that at this stage of her life. She was still getting over Duke.

She had too much to do, she thought as she settled in a chair in a safe corner.

Though she had managed to leave Rich on the other side of the room, he hadn't left her. No matter what she did, he wasn't far from her thoughts.

Yeah, he was surely a good lover, but a lover wasn't what she wanted. Or needed. She needed somebody she could count on, and she knew from hard experience that she could never count on him. Those military guys could be depended on in a pinch, in an emergency, but it was during the ordinary times that they fell down on the job.

She'd love having someone like Rich around during a crisis, but she also knew that she wouldn't be able to depend on him when times were good.

At least, when she thought times were good.

She wanted an ordinary, happy-ever-after kind of life, and just like her ex, Rich wanted adventure and excitement. They were oil and water. They wouldn't mix. What they wanted was just too different.

Caitlyn came running up and distracted Jennifer from her churning thoughts. "Hey, Jen'fer, we hafta frow some birdseed at Aunt Webecca and Uncle Tom so they can go on their hummymoo."

Saved by the child, Jennifer couldn't help thinking. She loved the way Caitlyn seemed to put everything into the simplest of terms. Caitlyn didn't spend a lot of time pondering and analyzing things. She just accepted life at face value.

Jennifer risked another glance over her shoulder toward Rich as she followed Caitlyn toward the door where the maid of honor stood holding a basket full of little net bundles tied with white satin ribbons.

Rich wasn't there.

And for a brief second, Jennifer felt vindicated. See, she knew he wasn't a stay-around kind of guy.

Rich TRIED to make himself comfortable in the front seat of Jennifer's little car, but the silent treatment from the driver's side was harder to take than the cramped conditions. The trip back to Fort Walton Beach was long enough, and the fact that the kids were upset about not being able to stay with their mother didn't help the strain between him and Jennifer.

Caitlyn had been uncharacteristically quiet, but Carter had cried for almost half an hour. He had finally stopped whimpering about thirty miles out of Pensacola. He had petered out, sounding like a mechanical toy slowly winding down. Rich glanced behind him and noted that the baby had fallen asleep, his body limp against the car seat and his fuzzy pink head lolling to one side.

"He'll be all right like that, won't he?" Rich asked, not realizing that he'd spoken out loud.

Jennifer glanced into the rearview mirror, twisting her body to get Carter into view. "He'll be fine," she said. "I think babies fall asleep like that all the time."

Rich shrugged. "You're the expert."

Jennifer muttered a derisive snort. "I hardly think so. I just know more than you." She glanced back over her shoulder. "Looks like Caitlyn's given up the ghost, too." Then she clamped her mouth shut like she'd said too much, and focused again on the road ahead.

Rich still didn't know what Jennifer was so upset about. He hadn't asked her to help with the kids. And, now that he knew her opinion of what he was doing, asking her was the last thing he'd resort to. He'd show her.

He'd show Jennifer he could handle two kids without help from anyone of the female persuasion.

Or die trying.

Jennifer kept her face carefully pointed ahead, her eyes on the road, as the miles ticked away on her odometer. She really didn't know why she was so upset. It wasn't as if Rich had volunteered her to do anything with those kids. In fact, it bothered her that he hadn't.

Of course, she'd all but ordered him not to. And now, she didn't know how to take it back.

But then, that wasn't really what she was so mad about, she realized. She wasn't angry at Rich. In fact, his agreeing to take the kids had actually elevated him a notch in her mind. She sighed.

She was upset with herself.

In spite of everything she knew from past experience about military men in the particular specialty field that Rich belonged to, she was beginning to fall for him. That's what really bothered her. In spite of her fears that Rich wouldn't stay around for the long haul, he was stealing her heart.

And she didn't know what to do about it.

RICH HAD SENT Jennifer inside with the kids so he could quickly unload their paraphernalia from the compact car and send her on her way. Trouble was, he didn't want to send her on.

If he had known that they wouldn't be leaving the stuff back in Pensacola he might have been spared this chore, but he welcomed the physical activity.

He picked up the economy-size package of disposable diapers and grinned. Before this week, he'd never diapered a baby in his life. Now he could change a diaper like a pro.

He had left his jacket inside the apartment, so he rolled up the sleeves of the white dress shirt as he surveyed the jumble of stuff packed into the trunk of the tiny car. The quicker he got it unloaded, the sooner he'd be done and the sooner Jennifer could go.

It was almost enough to make him sit down on the curb and...and what? Pout?

No, just postpone getting the stuff unloaded as long as he could. Even if Jennifer wasn't in his sight, it was good to know that she was there.

He expelled a long, frustrated breath. He had to

get a move on. After all, Carter needed a place to sleep, and Caitlyn needed to change out of her "weddy" dress. He put the diaper bag aside in favor of something bigger. Until he brought all the baby furniture back in, they couldn't do either.

Of course, he suspected that Caitlyn would be just as happy to wear that dress all day, all night and the next day, too. Rich smiled, in spite of the weight of the responsibility pushing down on him, and grabbed the portable crib. That was one battle he would have to win this time. Caitlyn would have to put on play clothes.

The wedding was over. It was time to get back to reality. Still, as he hoisted the folded crib up on his shoulder and grabbed another pastel-colored bundle, he realized that real life—family life—wasn't exactly something he was used to living.

JENNIFER PRESSED a kiss to the top of Carter's peach-fuzzed little head and carefully laid him down in the crib. He was still sleeping, and she hoped he'd stay down until she could help Rich get the rest of the kids' things put away and she could make her escape.

She had to admire Rich for agreeing to take on the task of caring for these children, but she didn't envy him. She knew he was going to have to do some serious juggling, and she knew he was probably poorly equipped for it. Sure, he could scale a bare cliff face with a forty-pound rucksack on his back, but she wasn't sure he could handle a forty-pound girl. Not for the long haul, anyway.

"I'm going to take some of my stuff out of the drawers and move into Ski's room," Rich said from somewhere behind her.

Jennifer jerked around, startled by the sudden intrusion of Rich's voice into her thoughts. Why did the man set her heart to fluttering so? She pressed a hand to her chest to try to still the racing. "Don't sneak up on me," she snapped to cover the breathlessness in her voice.

He shrugged. "Sorry. The rugrat still asleep?"

"Yes, and he'll stay that way if you'll stop tromping in and out of here."

Rich scooped up an armful of T-shirts and underwear and backed out of the room. "I called Ski," he said when they were both outside and Jennifer had pulled the door shut. "He's going to bunk at Murphey's for the duration."

Jennifer had halfway hoped that Rich would have Ski Warsinski's help to take care of the kids, but then she knew Ski from when she was still married, and she was probably being overly optimistic to hope that he'd be any help whatsoever. He was probably even more clueless about a child's needs than Rich.

She looked up to see Rich setting up Carter's playpen. He'd already settled Caitlyn in front of the television set with a Strawberry Shortcake video that he'd found somewhere among the piles of stuff Rebecca had packed. Jennifer couldn't help smiling.

Rich really wanted to take care of those kids, she reminded herself. He didn't know what to do or how to go about it, but he had an emotional connection to them. Rich was part of their family.

Jennifer sighed. In spite of all her protestations to the contrary, she was going to have to help. She just wasn't going to let Rich know it.

Just yet.

She wanted to see what he would do, how much he would be willing to sacrifice for those kids.

Judging from what she had seen so far, it would be quite a lot.

RICH LUGGED the last of the kids' stuff up the single flight of stairs to his apartment and paused outside his door. As much stuff as he'd already carried in—Rebecca had told him she'd already packed for a week with Mrs. Dahlstrom when she'd heard the bad news—he wished there were more because once he was done, Jennifer would be free to go home.

He reached for the doorknob, but he couldn't make his hand close over it. Once he stepped inside, Jennifer would go. Then he'd be all alone.

All alone with the kids. All alone without Jennifer to help him muddle through.

He sucked in a deep breath.

All alone without Jennifer.

He couldn't help thinking that when she was gone, that would be the end of it. The end of something that hadn't yet begun, but had shown some promise.

Or had he been reading more into it than he should have?

Had he only been reacting to her because of gratitude for her finding Sherry and helping with the kids? Or had it been something more? A real connection?

No, he shook that thought away. What did he know about connecting with someone? All he knew was that he wanted Jennifer.

Rich adjusted the armload of stuff and reached for the door again, but it swung inward before his fingers closed over the knob.

"I thought maybe your hands were too full and you couldn't get the door open," Jennifer said as she stepped aside and held the door wide.

Apparently, she couldn't wait to make her escape, Rich couldn't help thinking. He put the remaining bags by the door and turned to her. He wasn't about to prolong this, so he'd just as well send her on her way.

"Thanks," he said, offering his hand. "I couldn't have made it through the day without you."

Jennifer looked up at him, then down at his hand. She started to reach out, then closed her fingers and snatched them away. She blinked and looked up at him again. "Yeah, sure," she said. Her hand stayed clenched at her side. "I'll just get my purse, and I'll be out of your way." She scurried into the room like a frightened mouse, then returned to the door the same way. "Thank you for letting me meet your sister," she said as she edged past him. "I liked her."

"Yeah. I like her, too," Rich said, wondering at this stupid, awkward conversation. Jennifer had to get the hell out of Dodge, or stay, but she needed to do it quick.

Jennifer raised a hand to wave goodbye.

Rich couldn't stand it. He had to have one last kiss. It might be the last time he saw her, and he wanted to be sure she wouldn't forget him. He sure wouldn't forget her. Jennifer might want to walk away, but he wanted to make it damned hard.

He grabbed her hand and pulled her to him. She didn't resist, Rich noted as he felt her soft breasts flatten against his chest. He looked into her eyes and she up into his. She swallowed, her throat contracting, her chest rising and falling. She moistened her lips.

She must have known what was coming as well as he did, maybe better, and satisfaction surged through Rich. He was going to win this battle.

He slanted his mouth over hers and tried to tell her with his kiss how he felt. How much he needed her.

And not just to help him take care of his sister's kids.

He'd meant to deliver just a simple kiss, just long enough to convey his feelings, his gratitude, for the way Jennifer had helped him out, but as soon as it started, he knew he was lost. One taste of her tender lips, and he wanted more.

Rich didn't know what he was thinking. Hell, maybe he wasn't thinking at all, just feeling, but he forced his fingers into that loose braid and pulled her hair free of its restraints. He plowed through her silken tresses and cupped her head, drawing her closer. It was almost as if he wanted to crawl inside her. He wanted to...

He stopped himself and pulled away. He couldn't be thinking that. He barely knew the woman. If he kept this up, he'd send her running from him and he'd never get to know her better.

HEART RACING and gasping like she'd just run a marathon, Jennifer wriggled out of Rich's arms, pulled the door shut behind her and stood, her body pressed against the other side. She raised her trembling hand and touched her lips, swollen and sore from Rich's sensuous assault against them. She didn't have to touch them to feel how he had bruised them and brought them alive. How could the man keep setting her so off balance?

How could a simple handshake have come to this?

She leaned against the door and willed her heart rate to return to normal. Apparently, she had as much ability to control that as she had to control herself around him. As much as she wanted to stay, Jennifer knew that the only way her heart would be safe would be if she stayed away.

Because every time she found herself in the same room with Richard A. Larsen, she found it more and more difficult to resist him.

He was fairly unsophisticated in his interactions with her. No, he wasn't flirty and smooth like Ski, but Ski didn't draw her to him like Rich did. There was something elemental within the man that dragged her helplessly toward him like a scrap of metal to a magnet. That's what scared her to death.

She wasn't scared of Rich, but of the way he almost compelled her to go to him. And he didn't even have to ask.

Jennifer gasped and that simple realization propelled her away from the door. She had to get away, and she had to stay away....

But she had to help him, too. She might not want to get involved with their uncle, but she cared about those children and they needed her help. If she was unwilling to do it herself, she'd have to find a stand-in.

And she thought she knew just who to call.

She stumbled down the stairs, twisting her ankle as she hit the bottom step. Jennifer limped to her car and yanked the door open and slid in. Fingers still clumsy with fear, or maybe need, she managed to insert the key and start the car to make her escape.

Yes, she would do everything she could to help him, but she would stay as far out of his reach as she could until she figured it all out. But even from afar, she could help.

As soon as she got home she'd call Beverly Wilson, the one combat control wife she'd stayed in touch with after her marriage to Duke had ended. She'd severed all her other ties with the air force and the combat control squadron in particular, but not with Bev.

Beverly would know what to do. Jennifer certainly didn't.

THE KIDDIE VIDEO ended, and Caitlyn sighed and pushed herself up off the floor. "I'm hungry, Uncle Witch. Are we gonna have supper soon?"

Rich dragged his thoughts away from the woman who'd all but fled through his door and focused them on the little girl. Caitlyn was his main concern right now, he reminded himself sternly, not Jennifer Bishop. However, he was equally perplexed about what to do with either of them.

"I don't suppose there's something for you to eat in one of those bags your Aunt Rebecca packed yesterday, is there?" he said, peering into the diaper bag. It had saved him before.

Caitlyn rolled her eyes. "That's silly. Stuff in the diaper bag is for Carter. It's baby stuff. I'm a big girl. I eat grown-up food," she said indignantly and managed to make Rich feel stupid.

"Grown-up food, huh?" Rich looked down at her. She was hardly wasting away, and he remembered how much cake she'd eaten at the wedding reception, but now that she'd mentioned dinner, he couldn't help noticing that his own stomach was signaling that it was hungry. And not for Jennifer Bishop like the rest of him.

"Well, short stuff, let's go look in the kitchen and see what we've got." Rich and Ski had been away on that exercise for the last week and hadn't had a chance to go to the commissary since they'd been back, so the pickings were undoubtedly slim. He could probably find something for himself, but he wasn't sure it was anything Caitlyn would like. He and Ski ate a lot of frozen dinners when they were at home.

Caitlyn made a face upon hearing him call her short stuff, but she didn't say anything. She just pursed her lips in a gesture that reminded him, surprisingly, of Jennifer. Maybe it was a gesture every woman made. Hell, he didn't know.

Rich yanked open the refrigerator door and scanned the contents. Caitlyn stood at his elbow, her hands on her hips, and perused them, too.

There were a couple of shriveled apples, a limp bunch of celery and a package of baby carrots. There was some milk, but he didn't have to smell it to know it was probably sour. According to the date stamped on it, it had expired almost a month ago. There was a plate with something green covered with plastic wrap, but Rich didn't think it had started out that color.

"What happened to that lunch meat?" he said to himself more than to Caitlyn as he tossed the green stuff into the garbage can, plate and all.

"We ate that yesterday," Caitlyn said, then

sighed. She looked hopefully toward the cupboard. "Don't you gots any pisgetti?"

Of course! The spaghetti that Jennifer had brought yesterday. Rich thought there had been some left, but what had he done with it? He pushed the dead milk aside and spotted the bowl covered with plastic and looking like a red oasis in a barren desert. He snatched the bowl and showed it to Caitlyn. "We have spaghetti," he announced with triumph.

Caitlyn looked skeptical, but apparently hunger won her over. "You gots to heat it up."

"That I can do," Rich muttered through clenched teeth as he opened the microwave and stuck it in. The kid was going to need milk and cereal and...who knew what else? How was he going to shop for the right kind of food if he couldn't take both of the kids with him in the truck?

He was getting a crick in his neck. Tension, he supposed. He flexed his shoulders to try to relieve it.

How do parents do it all?

How was Sherry going to manage on her own?

Now he was certain he didn't have the right stuff to be a father, he couldn't help thinking. He'd barely been in charge of these kids for twenty-four hours, and he already felt like a failure. He couldn't even provide food for them.

Even Jennifer, who had claimed to know nothing about taking care of children, had more common sense about the creatures than he did. Maybe it came naturally to some people like Sherry, Rebecca and even Jennifer.

But, he sure didn't have it. Maybe, he was too much like his father.

No, he protested as he watched the plastic wrap

on the spaghetti fill with steam and rise above the heating noodles and sauce. He would never follow in his father's footsteps. He would keep these children safe. He'd promised Sherry. He'd promised Rebecca.

The timer dinged, and Rich snatched the dish out of the machine, burning his hand on the superheated steam. He started to mutter a curse, but, remembering Caitlyn standing behind him, censored himself. "Ow, that's hot."

"You're posta use a poffhoder," Caitlyn said, her mouth pursed disapprovingly.

"I knew that," Rich muttered as he grabbed a dishtowel and carried the dish to the table. "I just forgot." But he wouldn't forget his pledge to Sherry.

He would take care of her children as if they were his own.

He had no idea how he'd manage, but he would. He had promised.

Chapter Eight

Rich paced the living room as he waited for the Wilsons to come. He'd tried to sit, but he'd been too antsy for that. He still couldn't believe the luck that was bringing them to him. He'd expected to get a lecture when he'd called the captain. Instead, he'd gotten an answer to his prayers. Well, it would have been if he'd been a praying man.

Captain Thibodeaux had listened to his problem without interrupting, had thought for what had seemed like hours, then come up with the answer. Nick Wilson's wife was looking for some temporary work to tide her over till her baby arrived. Maybe she'd like to baby-sit.

Rich had called her as soon as he hung up.

He worked with Nick every day, but he'd only met Nick's wife once. He didn't remember much about her, but at work Nick went on and on about how wonderful she was until Rich sometimes wanted to clobber him. Now, he hoped she really was as great as Nick seemed to think.

Caitlyn was watching another video involving that purple dinosaur, and Carter was playing quietly in his playpen. All was well for now, but he'd be in big trouble as soon as lunchtime arrived. It had been hard enough to come up with something for breakfast. Caitlyn had been satisfied with jelly toast, and Carter had eaten the last of the stuff in the diaper bag.

As Caitlyn sang along with the dinosaur, Rich wondered how parents could stand it. But, if Sherry could, so could he. Reinforcements would be along any time now.

Caitlyn broke into another chorus, and Rich desperately tried to figure out how to go about converting his niece to appreciating his type of music. Fortunately, someone rang the doorbell.

"Saved by the bell," Rich muttered as he let them in.

Beverly Wilson wasn't a pretty woman, but she had that serene look that pregnant women had. Glowing pink or purple like the dinosaur, she was a sight for Rich's eyes.

"Hey, man." Nick stuck out his hand and ushered his wife inside. "Do you know Beverly?"

Trying very hard not to grab her into his arms and hug her senseless, Rich nodded. "We met at that beach barbecue right after I signed in on base." He nodded at Beverly and wondered what to say.

Beverly seemed to know. She lowered herself to the ground next to Caitlyn and introduced herself. "Hi, I'm Beverly. Are you Caitlyn?"

Rich watched, amazed, as Beverly made instant friends with his niece. Of course, Caitlyn was a great kid and she made friends with everyone. After all, she'd taken to him with a minimum of fuss. Carter had been a different matter. He wondered how Beverly would do with him.

"I think Caitlyn and I will be just fine," Beverly

said as she straightened slowly and rubbed the small of her back. She turned to Carter. "Just let me get acquainted with this big fellow, and then we'll come up with a plan."

Well, this is going to work out great, Rich thought as he watched Beverly reach into the playpen and pick Carter up. Why hadn't he thought of it himself?

JENNIFER ACCEPTED an invitation to join Beverly and Nick for dinner, but only after she'd insisted on contributing to the meal. As a single woman, she didn't get many invitations from married friends, but she'd always been welcome at their place. She glanced over as a cardboard box containing her homemade potato salad and a store-bought, banana nut bread slid around on the floorboards as she turned onto Bev and Nick's street in Hurlburt Base housing.

Nick was out front moving a lawn sprinkler when she drove up. "You didn't have to bring a care package," he said, grinning as he opened the door and took the box of food. He peeled back the foil from the potato salad.

Jennifer smacked his hand before he could scoop up a taste. "Just wait. Beverly said we'd eat soon, and I went to a lot of trouble to make it pretty."

"Ex-cu-use me," Nick said, feigning offense. "I wouldn't want to ruin the presentation."

"Oh, shut up, Nick. Just take me to your leader. I have a surprise for the baby," she said, drawing a pastel-wrapped parcel from behind her.

"Hey, I'm the leader," he protested.

"I'm sure Beverly lets you think that," Jennifer said sweetly as she followed Nick inside.

"I do not," Beverly said from the darkened living

room. "He knows perfectly well that he's not the boss of me," she said, pushing up from the couch. "He can order guys around as much as he wants at work, but at home, I'm in charge."

"Anything you say, dear," Nick said. "I'll just take this into the kitchen."

"Don't eat any till the chicken's cooked." Beverly turned toward Jennifer and gestured toward the couch. "Sit. And explain to me exactly why you feel it necessary to stay away from gorgeous Rich Larsen. Are you out of your mind?"

RICH STOOD in the kitchen and surveyed the contents of the cupboards. Satisfaction surged through him as he looked at the rows of boxes and cans. He had to admit, it felt good to have all that bounty at his fingertips. He liked the idea of being able to open the fridge and look inside and find something good.

He opened the refrigerator and reached for a crisp, shiny apple. Not one of those withered things that had been there the day before. He closed the door and took a bite.

He'd learned long ago that his life wasn't the kick it had been cracked up to be. Now that he'd met Jennifer Bishop and his sister's kids, he couldn't help thinking it was time for a change.

If he hadn't been so hung up on his own dysfunctional family and his unpleasant childhood, he might have thought about it sooner.

No. He shook his head. He wouldn't have thought about it sooner because he hadn't found his family, and he hadn't yet met Jennifer Bishop. Besides, his parents had thought they were doing the right thing by marrying and having kids, and look what had happened to them.

He still had a long road to go from realizing his bachelor life wasn't right for him anymore to actually settling down. He still had to get his head straight. He still had to prove to himself, if no one else, that he was capable of taking on the kind of life he craved.

After all, wanting was one thing. Having it was something else.

JENNIFER STARED at Beverly, the baby gift in her lap momentarily less important than the discussion forced upon her. "What do you mean, 'Am I crazy?' I'd be crazy to hook up with another Duke," Jennifer said.

Beverly snorted and shook her head, the gesture seeming to be an indictment of Jennifer's statement.

"You were there, Bev, when my marriage was falling apart. You saw what I went through those last few months when Duke only came home long enough to get clean clothes, if he came home at all. I'd be crazy to do it again."

"Jennifer, Jennifer, Jennifer." Beverly sighed and shook her head. "What makes you think Rich would put you through the same stuff? Just because Duke was a jerk, it doesn't follow that everyone else is."

"I didn't say everyone else is. Just every special tactics combat control operator. Nick excepted," she amended quickly.

"They're all excitement junkies. They can't be happy unless they're doing something dangerous. And if the world situation doesn't provide them with a fix, they go out and contrive something to keep them from withdrawal till the next 'situation'..." She etched quotation marks in the air with her hands. Jennifer thought she'd nailed it, and there was no way for Beverly to refute it.

Beverly started to say something, but snapped her mouth shut before she could. She seemed to sputter and splutter, trying to formulate words. "Yes, Duke was an adrenaline junkie, but they aren't all like that. Maybe some of the guys start out that way, but once they've been through it for real a couple of times, the thrill is gone."

Nick had come in from the backyard grill and stood in the kitchen doorway. He said nothing, but it was obvious that he was interested in the conversation.

"Well," Jennifer said, feeling like anything she said in her defense would be lame. Still, she wasn't willing to let it go. "How do I know Rich isn't just like Duke?"

Crossing his arms over his chest, Nick let out a long, gusty sigh. He shook his head. "It sure must feel good to be able to categorize all men just by their occupations. I guess, if I believe your theory, then all used-car salesmen are crooks, and all doctors are good providers. And we won't *even* get into what we think about politicians or detectives—computer or otherwise."

Jennifer winced. "Touché." She had a strong feeling she was going to lose this argument, but she didn't want to give up yet. "Yeah, Nick, I know I can't judge every book by its cover, but I haven't had the happiest experience with military men."

Beverly stopped her. "Man. Singular. Just one. Don't judge the rest by Duke's sorry self. I've gotten to know the guys on the team here, and from my observation, most of them do not fit into the same category as your ex. I've made a point of inviting them over and giving them a taste of the real world from time to time, and most of them are good, honest men who want to serve their country.

"Sure, some of them start out doing it for the kicks, but most of them want to make a genuine contribution to world peace." Beverly paused.

"Did you ever notice how young most of them are?" Nick interjected.

Jennifer sat back. No, she hadn't. But now that she thought about it, she didn't remember meeting many who were in their thirties. She floundered for a rebuttal, but she couldn't find one.

Nick went on. "Being a combat control operator is a young man's game. It's hard work. It's physically hard on the men and just as mentally draining. Sure, they let loose now and then, but it's only a release. I know it's hard on their wives, and it's hard on families. It takes a special type of man to do the job, and it takes a special woman to love him."

Jennifer wanted to say something, to argue, but she couldn't come up with anything that made sense.

"Don't blame your problems with Duke on the job, and don't indict us all because of one man." Nick pushed away from the doorjamb. "I've got to get back to the grill."

Was he telling her it was her fault that she hadn't been able to make Duke act like a married man who loved her? Jennifer sat back against the couch and drew in a deep breath. She hoped not, but it was something to think about.

"Okay," Beverly said, "I can see those cogs turning in your head. Before you go putting all the blame on yourself, remember this—Duke was a jerk. He wanted to have his cake and eat it, too. Duke wasn't one of the guys we've been defending. You did everything you could to make it work.

"I'm sure Duke loved you when he married you. Or thought he did. But he didn't know how to be married. He wanted to have a wife and all the perks that came with, but he didn't know how—or want—to make it fifty-fifty." Beverly took Jennifer by the upper arms and pulled her around to look squarely in her eyes.

"Listen to me, Jennifer."

Jennifer blinked, then nodded.

"Duke was a jerk. He made none of the compromises necessary to make a marriage work. You tried—he didn't. So, don't blame yourself, and do not blame an entire group of men for Duke's failure. It wasn't their fault." Beverly shook her. "Do you get what I'm saying?"

Jennifer nodded. "I think so." She forced a weak smile. "Thank you, but I still can't help wondering if I could have made it work if I'd just been a better wife."

"You couldn't have been a better wife if you'd taken lessons, Jen. The problem was his, not yours." Beverly sighed and leaned back against the sofa cushion. She placed her hand over her huge stomach and drew a deep breath. "I think it's time to change the subject. This little guy tells me when I need to calm down." She smiled. "You think about it and come to your own conclusions.

"Now." Beverly rubbed her hands together. "Let's see what's in the pretty package."

WITH THE APARTMENT appropriately stocked with supplies, Rich had a relatively easy two days with the kids. He'd kept them fed and happy and had even managed a couple of short excursions to a park a few blocks from his apartment.

This Uncle Rich stuff was a piece of cake, he told himself. And better yet, with Beverly Wilson's help, he'd gone back to his regular routine. Of course, he'd only survived one day of work, he reminded himself. He still had Wednesday, Thursday and Friday to get through.

Still, he couldn't help thinking he'd managed it all. He could do this stuff. Feeling pleased with himself and looking forward to the next day, Rich drifted to sleep.

It seemed he had been sleeping only a few minutes when something roused him. He pushed himself up and rubbed his eyes while he waited for a repeat of the sound. The walls were thin in the apartment complex, and he was used to the many noises that disturbed sleep. This was different. This was one he hadn't heard before and couldn't identify.

Rich listened again, but it had gone. He hoped. He'd have a hard enough time getting back to sleep without having to worry about unidentified night noises, and he had the kids in the next room to think about.

He would have thought a guy who could sleep most anywhere would be able to in his own apartment, but Rich had a hard time settling down in Ski's bed. Maybe it was the calendar girl posters on the wall, or the streetlight sneaking in through a missing slat in the blinds, or maybe it was just knowing that somebody in the next room depended on him that had him on edge.

How Ski could sleep with those women staring down at him, he didn't know. Rich rolled over and tried to shut his eyes, but a finger of light from outside seemed to point directly toward the poster above him.

He didn't know why, but that particular model reminded him too much of Jennifer. She didn't really look that much like her, but something about her made him think of the prim woman who was far sexier clothed than that pinup.

This woman had long mahogany-colored hair and legs that went on for miles, just like Jennifer. He could only guess at this, but that body had to be just like the one Jennifer tried so hard to hide.

Comparing the model to Jennifer Bishop was probably not the smartest move he'd ever made. Not if he was going to get any sleep tonight. He pulled the pillow over his head to block out the image and the light.

The pillow did nothing at all to block out thoughts of Jennifer. Now that Rich had seen that near-nude poster girl, he had no trouble imagining what it would be like to unwrap Jennifer layer by layer like a warm, sexy Christmas present.

Rich groaned and threw the pillow across the room. This wasn't working.

He got up. He could do something about the posters, even if he couldn't do anything about Jennifer Bishop. At least, not tonight.

He tried to take each picture down without tearing it so he could put it back up when Ski regained possession, but his fingers weren't used to that kind of delicate operation. After several attempts to be careful, frustration, both sexual and physical, made Rich impatient. He gave up all pretense and ripped the pinups off the wall. He'd gladly buy Ski a new set later.

Rich wadded the posters up and jammed them into the trash can. He yawned. He had to get some *Z's*.

He sank back down to the bed and tried to block out the light sneaking through the broken venetian blinds. Even if the kids weren't in the next room, he had to get up at the crack of dawn for PT.

He'd begun to debate whether the penalties for shooting out a streetlight were worth a good night's sleep when he heard it again. He held his breath and didn't move for fear that the rustle of sheets or the creak of the mattress might cover the sound.

Just when he thought he'd imagined it, the noise, nothing more than a soft whimper, returned. This time it was louder, more distinct.

This time he realized what it was.

Carter.

Rich threw off the covers and leapt to his feet. All thoughts of sleep forgotten, he yanked open the door and hurried into the other room. What could be wrong? Carter had slept the last few nights, so Rich had assumed he would again. Weren't babies supposed to sleep all night by the time they were Carter's age?

By the glow of the nightlight, Rich could see Carter. He had pushed himself into a sitting position, and his face was contorted with...pain? His little fist was balled up tight, and he alternately sucked on it and wailed.

Caitlyn appeared to be sound asleep in the big bed,

oblivious to Carter's apparent distress. This time Rich wouldn't have minded some of Caitlyn's big sister experience and expertise. But Caitlyn wasn't the problem.

As soon as Rich had entered the room, Carter zeroed in on Rich like a homing device. He reached out with chubby arms and whimpered louder.

Not knowing what else to do, Rich picked him up.

A quick check showed that Carter's diaper wasn't wet, but he obviously needed something. He kept putting his fist into his mouth, and his face and the top of his pajamas were soaked. From what, Rich didn't know.

Rich felt the baby's head, but didn't know what he was looking for. He just remembered his own mother doing it to him when he was a kid. Carter's forehead felt cool, so Rich guessed he wasn't sick.

Maybe he was just hungry.

At least, once they were out of the bedroom, he could turn on a light. Carter's face was red from crying and the moisture appeared to be drool. Rich wondered briefly if there was some sort of foaming-at-the-mouth disease that babies got that he should know about. He dismissed the idea. Carter wasn't a dog, and he didn't have rabies.

Rich hoped.

He warmed a bottle of formula. Rich would have liked to put the baby back in bed as he'd done before, but something told him that Carter needed to be held. Truth be told, Rich needed to hold Carter. There was something very comforting about holding a little person in his arms.

Maybe, once Carter settled back down, Rich could get back to sleep, too.

Carter sucked greedily on the bottle and emptied it in no time, then rewarded Rich with a resounding burp. Carter snuggled close, and Rich was loathe to put him down. But he did have to get to sleep.

He glanced at the clock on the VCR. It read 2:00 a.m. He had to be at PT in four hours.

"Okay, kiddo. Midnight snack's over. Time to hit the sack." Rich pushed himself up off the couch and headed for the kids' room. If his luck held, he'd have Carter changed and tucked in and be back in bed in a few minutes.

He should have known, he thought as he tossed the diaper into the can and tried to tiptoe out. Carter resumed whimpering as soon as Rich's back was turned. Rich stumbled back in desperation. The last thing he needed was for Caitlyn to wake up, too. Carter should be fine now and settled deep into dreamland. After all, his diaper was dry, his stomach was full. What else could he possibly need?

The baby had already pushed himself into a sitting position and held his arms out to be picked up.

Rich had a fleeting urge to call Beverly Wilson, but he couldn't do that. Beverly was sleeping for two, and she'd be there soon enough in the morning. No sense depriving anybody else of sleep.

Bouncing Carter gently, Rich walked the floor. Carter had been quiet enough while he'd been taking his bottle, but now he just whined and whimpered and chewed on his fist. He was no closer to knowing just what was wrong than before.

The hours seemed to drag on. Rich walked, he paced, he bounced the baby on his knee. But every time he put Carter down, he cried again.

Finally, exhausted from walking and jiggling—

hell, he'd even tried humming—Rich sat down on the couch. He didn't know any lullabies, but he managed a ballad or two. Finally, Carter fell asleep in his arms. Too exhausted to get up, and afraid that any movement would wake him, Rich stayed where he was.

He'd slept sitting up before. If he could do it in the noisy bay of a loaded C-130 transport, he could do it in his own living room. He glanced over Carter's fuzzy head to the clock on the VCR. It was 4:00 a.m. If he stayed where he was he could get one good hour of sleep before he had to get up.

THE DOORBELL WOKE HIM.

Briefly disoriented, Rich pushed at the dead weight on his chest. The weight, he discovered, was Carter, who was, fortunately, still asleep. The light coming in through the slitted blinds was bright, and the clock said 6:00 a.m.

The doorbell rang again.

It was Beverly coming to his rescue. He hoped.

As he maneuvered himself and Carter up off the couch, he realized he had to be at PT in thirty minutes.

Balancing Carter on his shoulder, Rich yanked open the door without even looking to see who it was.

"Rough night?" Beverly stepped inside and dropped a totebag beside the door and took Carter.

"That's an understatement," Rich said, yawning. "I don't know what's wrong. He woke up crying after midnight. He wasn't wet, so I gave him a bottle, but that didn't help. He doesn't have a fever, I don't think, but he's drooling like a rabid dog, and he keeps putting his fist in his mouth."

"Well," Beverly said, settling onto the couch. "I'm no expert, but I'd say Carter is teething. Babies can get quite uncomfortable and fretful, and it's worse at night."

"Like a pain you can live with in the daytime bothers you at night, right?" Rich yawned again. He longed for a shower, but he didn't have time. And he'd just have to do it again after the workout, anyway. "I hate to run off when you just got here, but I do have to make it to PT."

Beverly dismissed him with a wave of her hand. "Don't worry about us. That's why I'm here."

Rich headed for his room to dress.

"Rich?"

He stopped and turned back. "Yeah?"

"Try splashing some cold water on your face."

Nodding, Rich hurried on. Like anything as simple as cold water would compensate for being up half the night.

JENNIFER HAD TRIED to keep from thinking about Rich and the kids all weekend, but now that Beverly was on duty, she couldn't stand not knowing. She had to see firsthand.

Rationalizing that Rich wouldn't interrupt his day to see the kids at lunch, Jennifer thought she just might drop by and see for herself how Beverly was getting along.

She had called Bev to make sure the coast was clear and had received an odd request. Beverly wanted her to stop at a store to pick up a couple of gel-filled teething rings and some numbing ointment to rub on the baby's gums.

Beverly didn't say why, but Jennifer guessed that Carter was cutting a tooth.

While she was running errands, Jennifer picked up a couple of premade lunch salads. Then, looking forward to a nice visit, Jennifer drove to Rich's apartment.

Beverly must have been watching for her, because she yanked the door open before Jennifer could ring the bell.

"Boy, am I glad to see you." Beverly shut the door and stood just inside wringing her hands. She must have spilled something, for the front of her maternity slacks was wet.

Caitlyn was sitting on the floor, raptly watching cartoons on television. She barely turned to acknowledge that anyone else had come into the room. Jennifer didn't see Carter.

"Have you discovered that taking care of two little kids isn't as easy as you thought?" Jennifer carried her purchases to the dinette table and put them down.

Beverly didn't follow, but bent over almost double and clutched at her stomach. Jennifer gasped as Bev's face contorted with what she could only describe as pain.

"What's wrong?" Alarm flashed through her.

Beverly gasped like a fish out of water, or maybe panted like a dog would be a more apt description. "Nothing's wrong, exactly," she said once the spasm had passed. "However, my water broke right after I spoke to you, and my contractions are about eight minutes apart."

Chapter Nine

Jennifer gasped. "But the baby isn't due for almost a month," she protested.

"Well, apparently Junior, here, didn't read the memo." Clutching the small of her back with one hand, Beverly stooped to pick up a tote she'd left by the door. "I called the doctor and Nick. He's on the way to take me. We couldn't reach Rich. He's out surveying a drop zone or something. You're going to have to hold the fort."

"Sure, Bev. Anything. You just go and have that baby." Jennifer tried to be sound reassuring, but her first instinct was to be alarmed. Beverly's baby wasn't due until the end of the month. It was too soon.

"I'll be fine, Jen." Beverly looked far calmer than Jennifer felt. "I've spoken to the doctor, and she said not to worry. The baby's nearly full term and plenty big enough, and it'll probably be hours before he makes it into the world."

"Are you sure?"

"No, I'm not sure, but I'm going to take the doctor's word for it." Beverly didn't seem to be taking this sudden turn of events as well as it had first appeared.

The doorbell rang.

A relieved expression flitted across Beverly's face, and Jennifer hurried to let Nick in.

He looked calm, concerned and excited all at the same time as he strode inside. "I left the motor running," Nick said, nodding at Jennifer, but going straight to his wife. "Can you walk?"

Beverly rolled her eyes. "I think I can manage. After all, in the old days women gave birth in the fields and went back to picking cotton as soon as they were done." She smiled; although, to Jennifer's mind, it seemed forced. "Now, do you think we could get going before I have another contraction?"

Panic replaced Nick's calm facade, and he hurried his wife toward the door.

"I'm sorry to put you on the spot, Jen," Beverly said as Nick ushered her out. "But, you're going to have to stay here till Rich gets back. Carter's napping so he's okay for now, and I already gave Caitlyn her lunch."

"Sure, anything." Jennifer closed the door, then watched through the window until Nick had settled his wife safely into the car.

Then, and only then, did she realize that she'd just been commandeered to take care of Rich's niece and nephew.

She had no objection to watching the kids, but that wasn't the problem. Staying with them meant she'd have to come face-to-face with their uncle, whom she'd been trying so hard to avoid.

Jennifer stayed by the window for a long time. What a startling turn of events. Here, she'd thought she had it all figured out, and this had to happen. Worry, and not a little guilt over the early delivery warred with the excitement of finally having Beverly's baby arrive. After all, if Jennifer hadn't suggested that Bev step in and take care of the kids, this might not have happened.

"Where did Beberly go?"

Had Caitlyn been so engrossed in what she was watching on television that she hadn't even noticed that Beverly was gone? Jennifer marveled at the power of concentration the child must have. She wished she possessed it. Maybe then, she could stop thinking about Rich Larsen.

Wondering how much of the situation Caitlyn had absorbed and how much she should tell her, Jennifer tried to come up with a simple explanation. She finally settled on the truth. She just hoped that Caitlyn wouldn't be alarmed. Jennifer swallowed and cleared her throat. "Um, Beverly went to the hospital to have her baby."

"Oh." Caitlyn turned back toward the television, but stopped in midturn. "I thought babies took a long time to get made."

"Sometimes babies are so excited about coming to meet their mommies and daddies that they come early."

Caitlyn thought about that for a moment. She seemed to be satisfied, and Jennifer hoped that it would be the end of the discussion. "My mom's in the hopsitle, but she isn't getting a baby."

"I know." What else could she say?

"She's coming home from the hopsitle in a few weeks."

"Won't you be glad?" Jennifer would be glad if they could drop the subject.

"I sawed her at Aunt Webecca's weddy. She hadda thing around her neck and hadda sit in a chair that gots wheels. She tode me she'd come home when she got outta the chair."

Caitlyn gave a big, exasperated sigh. "I tode her to get up, and we would go home right now, but she said she hadda wait till her legs weren't so tired."

"I remember that. I'm sure it won't be long until your mom can get up and go home with you."

"That's what Aunt Webecca said. I just wish my mom would hurry up."

Jennifer sighed. "Don't you like staying with your Uncle Rich?"

Caitlyn sighed again. "He's okay, but he gots too much grown-up stuff here. Alla time he keeps tolin' me don't touch." She drew in a deep breath. "I was only looking."

Jennifer looked around the room and was glad to note that a lot of the contraband had been removed from the area. Apparently, Rich learned quickly. She laughed. "My mom used to tell me to look with my eyes, not my hands."

"Yeah," Caitlyn said and expelled another long breath. "But I can't see as good with only my eyes."

"One day you'll grow up and be able to look with your hands, too." Jennifer gathered Caitlyn to her and squeezed her in a hug.

It was really sort of fun spending time with Caitlyn and Carter, even if Carter was still sleeping. Jennifer enjoyed the little girl's chatter and some of her insights were quite perceptive. Why was it only Jennifer who couldn't think clearly? At least, about Rich Larsen.

RICH DRAGGED himself in off Range 72 much later than he'd anticipated. The Humvee had gotten mired in the swampy muck in the low-lying range, and he and Radar had had a helluva time getting it out. Those tank-like vehicles were pretty good on dry land, no matter what the terrain, but they were damned heavy, and mud was not their best surface.

Ray Darling was pretty new to Silver Team, and this was the first time Rich had worked an op with him, but he seemed to be all right. Radar was sort of a computer geek, and Rich had had his doubts about how useful he'd be in the field. But the guy was smart, and he could think on his feet. He'd come up with the idea that worked.

They'd finally resorted to hooking the on-board winch to a pine tree and dragging the vehicle out through the scrubby brush and palmettos. Hot, dirty, sticky and hours late, they stashed their gear in the equipment locker.

Rich didn't think he'd ever get his boots clean enough to wear again. He exhaled a long, tired breath. The last thing he needed right now was to have to spring for a new pair of jungle boots.

"Wanna go by the Club for a tall, cool one before you head home?" Radar still lived in the dorm, and it wasn't an issue if he had too much to drink before he went home. He could walk.

"Boy, would I? I'm about as dry as the Sahara." Rich shook his head. "But, I'll have to pass this time." He shoved his survey kit into his locker, pushed the door shut and spun the combination lock.

"I've got my sister's kids with me, and I have to get home to them."

"Yeah. I forgot." Radar saluted with one finger and turned away. "I'm outta here."

"Later," Rich said.

He wondered if he should call Beverly to tell her that he'd be late, but she'd probably figured that out by now. And surely, Nick would have known about the problem with the Humvee. Rich drew in a deep breath. If he stopped to call, it would just delay him more.

He looked around the section, but didn't see anyone. He was too tired to check his box for messages. Anything anybody could want him for could surely wait. His clothes were muddy and damp with sweat from the ever-present Panhandle humidity. He didn't even want to think about the number of bug bites he must have. God, he could use a shower.

Anything on his desk that didn't involve all-out war could wait until morning.

JENNIFER PACED the living room. Rich should have been home hours ago. It was nearly seven o'clock. He should have been off before five.

Caitlyn's gaze was glued to the television screen, and Jennifer worried that she was letting the child get away with too much TV. Carter sat in the playpen and gnawed at a frozen teething ring like a dog with a bone.

"Damn," she muttered, as she looked out the window again. The sun was low in the sky, and soon it would be dark. She'd been through this too many times before with Duke not to know what was going on. He'd stop by the Club on his way from work for one drink with the guys, and he wouldn't leave until somebody had to peel him up off the floor and carry him out.

Jennifer had thought she'd seen the end of that when she'd ended her marriage.

She'd cooked a simple supper of macaroni and cheese and green beans for Caitlyn and fed Carter something from a jar. She'd even found time to eat the salad she'd bought for Beverly. Food wasn't the issue; Rich was. He should have been home hours ago.

He had responsibilities now.

She knew that sometimes circumstances would keep the men later than four-thirty when the bugler played "Retreat" and the flag on base was retired for the night, but he could have called. He was just like the rest of them. As long as he thought he had somebody there to take care of his niece and nephew, he apparently saw no need to hurry home.

It gave Jennifer no satisfaction to be able to report that she was right about Rich, and Beverly had been wrong.

She glanced at the clock on the VCR again. It was now officially late. She might as well get Caitlyn ready for bed before she got interested in another program. Jennifer had no instructions about bedtimes for either one of the kids, but surely it must be getting close.

She turned around and clapped her hands together authoritatively. "Come on, kiddo. It's bath time."

Caitlyn didn't move.

"Now, Caitlyn," Jennifer said firmly and hoped she wasn't overstepping her bounds. "You can show me how to get Carter ready for bed."

The girl pushed herself up and trudged, slump-shouldered, toward the bathroom. "It wasn't over. I didn't see the words." She heaved a big, weary sigh.

Jennifer bit back a smile. She remembered using the same stunt with her mom. When she was little she would milk her television hour for all it was worth, and if she didn't see the credits, her time wasn't up.

"You've had a long day. Let's get you guys cleaned up and bathed before your uncle gets home." If he comes home before midnight, Jennifer couldn't help thinking.

As the tub filled, Jennifer undressed Carter and Caitlyn undressed herself. Caitlyn seemed uncharacteristically quiet, and Jennifer wondered about that. She would have expected more of an argument about the bath and bed, but except for the brief mention of "the words," Caitlyn had said nothing else. Her face was flushed and her skin seemed warm. But it was Florida, Jennifer rationalized.

Other than the child's silence, Jennifer had nothing else to go on, and considering her limited experience with small children, she was probably mistaking normal fatigue for something more serious. Caitlyn hadn't complained, so she wouldn't worry until she had to.

She shrugged it off and quickly sponged Carter clean in the sink while Caitlyn bathed herself. Jennifer toweled Carter dry, dressed him and put him into his bed. Then she watched Caitlyn brush her teeth.

So far, so good.

Caitlyn crawled into bed without an argument, and despite her brief flash of concern, Jennifer couldn't help thinking she'd gotten off lightly. Maybe Caitlyn was just an obedient child, she thought as she warmed a bottle.

When she returned to the room, Caitlyn was curled up in a tight little ball and seemed to be sleeping peacefully. She handed the bottle to Carter and tiptoed away. That had just been too easy. Something was bound to happen.

Jennifer glanced out the front window. The sun was even lower in the sky, just minutes away from sinking below the horizon. Where was Rich?

She laughed bitterly. She knew where he was. Though she should have felt vindicated now that she'd been proved right, she felt no satisfaction. She wished she were wrong.

Well, at least the kids were settled. That way, they wouldn't see Rich when he staggered in. Jennifer bent to pick up some toys Carter had tossed from the playpen.

The front door flew open, and Jennifer straightened with a jerk and turned around. She clutched the rubber toy to her chest from the suddenness of it.

"What the hell are you doing here?" Rich, holding his boots in his hands, was grimy and dirty and damp with sweat. He eyed her suspiciously.

Jennifer moved toward him.

He held his hand up and backed away. "Stay away from me. I stink."

"What's the matter? You afraid I'll get close enough to smell the beer on you?"

"What?"

She had to hand it to him. Rich played innocent well.

"You stopped off at the Club, didn't you? Figured

that since you had the home front covered, you didn't have to hurry.'' Jennifer drew in a long, deep breath of air. "You are some piece of work.''

"I don't know what the hell you're talking about. I've been up to my ankles in swamp for most of the afternoon. I'm tired, and I need a shower. I don't need an argument from you.'' Rich pushed past her.

He only brushed her arm, but the touch was electric. Why did he do that to her? Along with that fleeting contact, Jennifer noted something else. He did smell to high heavens, but there was no suggestion of alcohol in the miasma coming from him. Could she have been mistaken?

"You're late. What about that?'' she added defensively. Anything to deflect his attention from her false accusation. "Don't you dare come in all huffy about me being here when you know full well that Beverly's in the hospital.'' How dare he act as if she was in the wrong.

Rich started to say something, then he must have realized what she'd just said. He closed his mouth and jerked back as though he'd been slapped. "Beverly's in the hospital?'' He looked around the empty room. "Something's happened with one of the kids. What's wrong?''

"The kids are fine. They're both in bed.'' Jennifer started to explain about Beverly, but stopped herself. "You didn't know? You really don't know?'' That was a horse of a different color. Jennifer swallowed. Maybe, she could give him a little slack. "Her water broke. She's been in labor since midmorning.''

Rich muttered something pungent. How the hell could everything have fallen apart like this? he asked himself. He thought he'd had everything all worked out.

Shaking his head, he sank to a chair. The weight of the long day seemed to press down against him. He'd never felt so damned tired. He didn't know what to do. He couldn't think.

He scrubbed at his tired eyes and dragged his hands slowly down his face. He rubbed his eyes again. He was so damned tired that every bone in his body ached.

"Look, Jennifer," he muttered, dropping his boots. "I'm beat. My day started at 2:00 a.m. and it hasn't slowed down. I am not going to argue with you. I'm going to take a shower. Maybe then I can think straight."

She looked as if she was going to protest, then she sucked in a breath. "Okay. I guess I owe you that. I didn't know you were stuck out on the range all afternoon."

Maybe he should have said thanks, but he needed that shower. He left her standing beside the playpen.

RICH TURNED OFF the reviving shower and stepped out of the tub. There was no way a shower could make up for hours of missed sleep, but at least now, he could think clearly.

What the hell had happened?

He'd thought he had everything all worked out, and then this....

Thank God for Jennifer.

There were several other reasons Rich might thank the Creator for her, but right now his only reasons were that the kids had had somebody there for them.

He hadn't actually stopped to think about it before

now, but those kids had been through a lot, and he was damned glad that they hadn't been dumped with yet another stranger. They'd been troupers through all this. Too bad he hadn't been able to rise above the occasion as well.

Somebody knocked.

"Yeah?"

"I'm sorry to bother you," Jennifer said through the thin door. "But Caitlyn's having a bathroom emergency. She threw up. Could you hurry?"

"Sure. Be right out," he muttered. All he had to do was finish drying and... Oh, hell. He was so used to living alone that he'd forgotten to bring anything to change into. He looked at the pile of filthy clothing he'd stripped out of.

It was bad enough he'd have to touch them to get them into the laundry bag.

He fastened his damp towel securely around his waist and drew a deep breath. Then he yanked open the door.

Caitlyn skittered past him, her emergency apparently real. Jennifer stood there. Staring at him.

Then Rich remembered he was standing there in nothing but a towel. The thought spurred him to action. "If you'll excuse me, I'll get dressed."

That must have done it, because Jennifer's mouth snapped shut, and she gasped as if she hadn't been breathing. "Sure. Go."

Was this what it was like to live with a woman? he wondered as he shut the bedroom door behind him.

Jennifer stared at the closed door as if she could conjure up Rich's image again just by doing so. She had thought he'd looked good bare-chested, but wearing only a towel was enough to make her drool.

She swallowed. Apparently, it had made her salivate. Something deep inside her stirred and ached....

No, now was not the time for her sexual drive to wake up after being asleep for so long. She shook her head. Compared to this feeling, nothing she'd experienced in the past could even compare. Was this delicious, impossible-to-ignore feeling why women stood by their men, in spite of their faults?

"Jen-a-fer," Caitlyn whined, her tone plaintive. "My tummy hurts real bad."

Jennifer shook herself out of it. She was not here for herself, she was here for the children. Not for Rich. Only the children.

"I'm sorry, sweetie. I'm coming." What had she been thinking? Leaving that little one to suffer all alone?

Caitlyn emerged from the bathroom, looking weak and pale. Her wan expression seemed more frightening than the tired and flushed one from earlier.

"I threw up again," she whined and pressed herself against Jennifer's leg. "I don't like it. I want my mommy." In the space of an hour the cheerful girl who seemed to take everything in stride had turned clingy and whiny. Was that the way it was when kids were sick?

"I'm so sorry, sweetie. I'll do everything I can to make you feel better." Had what Jennifer cooked for supper been the cause of that? She wiped Caitlyn's face with a cool cloth. "Are you feeling any better now?"

"I think so," Caitlyn said, but she shook her head at the same time.

"Do you want to brush your teeth?" Jennifer didn't know about Caitlyn, but she sure would.

"Okay."

Jennifer took Caitlyn's hand and led her back into the bathroom. Her skin felt papery and hot.

The child's fever ushered in a whole new set of problems. Caitlyn was sick. What if Carter got it, too?

There was no way Rich would be able to cope with both children feverish and ill. Her only expert—if she could call Beverly an expert—was in the hospital giving birth, and she sure couldn't count on Rich to be any help. He was probably even more clueless than she was.

At least, she had a vague idea about what to do with stomach viruses—if that's what it was.

"Is everything all right in there?" Rich called.

"I think so." Jennifer wondered how much to tell him, then realized he was the uncle, he'd have to know. "It looks like Caitlyn has a touch of a stomach bug. She's feverish, and she's throwing up."

Rich pushed open the bathroom door. Concern was etched on his strong face. "What do we do? Should we call a doctor? Take her to the emergency room?"

If Jennifer hadn't already started to fall in love with him, she would have done so now. She stopped that thought in its tracks. She couldn't be thinking that. Whoa. When had all those sexual, warm-fuzzies turned to love?

She shook her head and hoped that Rich interpreted the gesture as the answer to his questions. "No," she said finally. "Not yet, anyway. I know what to do for a stomach bug, and a doctor wouldn't tell you anything different.''

"Are you sure? Don't they need antibiotics or something?''

Jennifer liked it that he looked uncertain. "No. Antibiotics won't help.'' Maybe he wasn't the hard case she'd first assumed him to be. He did really seem to care about the children. She smiled, more at the thought than to be reassuring, but she hoped Rich would see it that way. "I wouldn't worry too much unless the condition persists. I have to warn you, though, if she's got it, then there's a chance Carter will. And I wouldn't be surprised if you get it, too.''

His shoulders slumped and he seemed to sag. "I'm gonna get it, too?''

"It's a good possibility. But right now, you seem to be fine.'' Oh, he seemed more than fine in his T-shirt and those sinfully snug, gray sweatpants. Come to think about it, she'd never seen him when he hadn't looked fine.

"What do we do?''

Jennifer drew in a deep breath and let it out slowly. "Well, first we change the sheets on the bed.''

"I can do that.'' He pivoted and went into the room.

Then what? Jennifer didn't have the slightest idea how to proceed. Caitlyn still clung to her like a leech.

Rich returned from the bedroom with an armload of soiled bedding. "Now what?''

"I guess we need to make sure we have plenty of supplies. They're going to need lots of liquids to keep from getting dehydrated. And maybe some children's acetaminophen to keep the fever down. Do you have plenty of juices on hand?''

Rich shrugged. "I'll check," he said tiredly. "I have to put these sheets in the kitchen anyway."

Jennifer escorted Caitlyn back to the bed and tucked her in. "I know your tummy still hurts," she said brushing the child's damp hair with her fingers. "I'm going to leave this bucket right here beside you, so if you feel sick again, you can use it."

"Okay," Caitlyn said, her voice weak and tired.

"I'll leave the door cracked so you can see, but try to go to sleep for now."

"'Kay," Caitlyn murmured, sounding drowsy already.

Congratulating herself for handling it so well, Jennifer tiptoed out.

"Bad news," Rich said, coming from the kitchen.

Jennifer stopped short. "Bad news?" Panic drowned her feeling of well-being. "Please don't say you're sick, too."

"No." Rich looked confused. "I didn't mean to scare you. I just checked the kitchen. We have milk and some soda, but that's all. You said juices, right?"

"Well, liquids," Jennifer clarified. "The soda will do, but not the milk. Just how much soda do you have?"

"A full jug of cola and another half or so."

"That'll hold us for now, but you'd better run out and get some juice before it gets too late." She thought a minute. "I'll make a list."

Anything to keep her from looking at Rich.

She knew he was comfortable in his sweats, but in spite of the distraction of Caitlyn's illness, to Jennifer, he might as well have been nude. What was wrong with her that she couldn't look at the man without thinking of sweat-slick bodies twined together and rumpled sheets? She felt heat rise, unbidden, to her face.

"You look flushed," Rich said. "Are you getting it?"

Rich's observation only caused her to blush harder. "I don't think so. It just seems a little warm in here." She looked around for some way to back up her statement. She fanned at her face. "All that steam from the bathroom and all," she finished lamely.

Rich shrugged. "I guess." He blew out a long breath. "Did you make the list?"

"Yeah. Here." She handed it to him, careful not to let his fingers touch hers.

"Thanks," he said. He lingered by the door as if he couldn't decide whether to turn the knob. "I mean it," he said. "Not just for the list, but...for everything."

"It's okay," she whispered. What else could she say? In spite of it all, she was coming to love those children. Almost as much as their uncle.

"I won't be long," he said, turning the knob. Then he stopped. "God, I'm taking so much for granted. I didn't even ask you." He paused. "Can you stay?"

Chapter Ten

At least, he'd asked.

Not that he'd needed to.

Jennifer nodded, her throat suddenly too tight to speak.

Not so much because he had asked, but because of what she'd been thinking. How had she gone from trying so hard to avoid the man, to...what?

Staying with his children?

Correction. Niece and nephew.

"I'll be back as soon as I can," Rich said. Then he closed the door behind him, and Jennifer felt surprisingly alone. Bereft.

How had things changed so quickly?

She wasn't old enough to worry about her biological clock ticking away, but she couldn't help wondering how it would be to have children of her own. But why now?

That was simple. She'd enjoyed playing mommy with Caitlyn and Carter.

That's why the urge had struck her. Even if she couldn't follow through on it.

Jennifer chuckled. She still had to have another part of the equation. She might be able to raise a child on her own, but it still took two to make one. And, Rich notwithstanding, she still had no likely candidates.

She might have decided that Rich Larsen was a pretty attractive prospect, but so far, he'd done little to show the feeling was mutual. Well, not much, anyway.

He'd kissed her like he meant it the other day after the wedding, and just seeing him in that towel earlier had rendered her senseless and all but drooling.

No—she shook her head. To him, she was just another baby-sitter. That's all she could afford to think about.

He appreciated her help with the kids, but he'd done nothing more than express his gratitude.

Jennifer sighed. For now, that was fine.

RICH RETURNED from the store to find the living room dim and quiet. He flipped on the light and discovered Carter sleeping in his crib next to the dark television set. Jennifer was nowhere to be seen. Rich turned the light back off and stashed his purchases in the kitchen. Then he followed the sound of running water to the bathroom.

Jennifer knelt by the tub and was sponging Caitlyn off. Rich backed up, suddenly embarrassed to be watching.

Jennifer turned around. "You're back."

"Yeah. I got everything on the list. What's with the bath? Wasn't she in bed when I left?"

"Caitlyn was sick again. I thought she'd feel better if I cleaned her up." Jennifer nodded toward the bedroom. "I pulled off the sheets, but I haven't replaced them yet. Can you do it while we finish up here?''

''Yeah. No problem.''

Kids were so much work, Rich thought as he scooped up the soiled linens and dumped them on the kitchen floor. He grabbed the remaining set of sheets from the hall closet and quickly made up the bed. Thank goodness for fitted sheets. He might have learned to make a bed tight enough to bounce a quarter off it in basic training, but this was much easier.

''All done,'' Rich said as Jennifer ushered Caitlyn back to bed. He watched as she tucked the little girl in and planted a gentle kiss on her forehead.

''Sleep tight,'' Jennifer said.

''Don' make the bedbugs bite,'' Caitlyn murmured in response.

They tiptoed out.

Rich nodded toward the baby sleeping in the crib in the darkened living room. ''What's with the sleeping quarters?''

''Preventive measures,'' Jennifer said. ''I hope.'' She gestured toward the kitchen. ''I thought, since Carter hasn't been showing the same symptoms, he might not have been exposed at the same time. Maybe, if we keep him away from Caitlyn, he won't get it.''

''Sounds like a long shot,'' Rich said, but he admired her thinking. He probably wouldn't have thought about it.

''It is,'' Jennifer said, sighing. ''But I had to try.'' She looked up at Rich. ''Do you have any idea where Caitlyn could have picked it up?''

''Beats me. I took them to the park both Sunday and Monday. I suppose they could have bumped into somebody at the wedding reception or at day care before they even came here. I don't know what the incubation period is.''

"Me either,'' Jennifer said. "But the good news is that it usually runs its course in about twenty-four hours.''

"Two down and twenty-two to go,'' Rich said dryly.

Jennifer smiled, the gesture lighting up her eyes. "I think the worst is over with Caitlyn. I don't think she has anything left to throw up. Now you just have to keep her hydrated until she starts to feel her old self again.''

"That sounds eas—''

The phone in the living room rang.

Rich jerked toward the phone. "Who could that be?''

"Maybe it's Nick with news about the baby.''

Then he remembered. "Caitlyn didn't call her mother, did she?''

"Oh, no.'' Jennifer shook her head. "With all the excitement, we forgot.''

Rich yanked up the phone. It was Sherry. "Yeah.'' He listened a minute. "It's okay. Caitlyn's got a little stomach bug, and in all the commotion we just forgot.''

He listened while Sherry gave him much-needed mother advice. He nodded, even though she couldn't see him. "Really, Sherry. She's fine. We've got it under control.''

Jennifer had to smile as she watched and listened to the one-sided conversation.

"Yeah. Jennifer's here.'' He nodded as he listened. "No, Beverly went into labor.''

Rich held the phone out toward Jennifer. "She wants to talk to you."

She took the phone. "Hi, Sherry. Everything's fine," she said before the woman could ask a question. Then she listened. "Yes, just your garden variety stomach bug. I'm sorry we worried you, but we had our hands full."

She felt herself blushing as Rich's intense gaze leveled on her while Sherry inquired after Beverly. Jennifer turned away so she couldn't see Rich watching her, though she could still feel him looking. "No news, so far. It's a first child. I guess it takes longer, or so they say. Nick promised he'd call me as soon as the baby's born." Jennifer laughed. "Of course, he probably doesn't know I'm still here. For all I know, there's a message on my answering machine at home right now."

Sherry rattled off a batch of instructions, and Jennifer was relieved to know she'd instinctively done the right thing. "Yeah, we can handle it. Everything's under control. We'll let Caitlyn call you tomorrow night. I'm sure she'll be back to normal by then.

"You want to talk to Rich again?" She turned back toward Rich.

He held out his hand for the phone.

"Okay. Bye." Jennifer hung up.

"She didn't want to talk to me?"

"Said she'll call tomorrow if you don't call her first," Jennifer said. "Do you have everything under control for now?"

Rich nodded. "They're asleep. Go home." He drew in a deep breath. "I guess I'll call the captain and beg off duty for tomorrow."

Jennifer raised her hands, palm out. "No, don't do that. Al said things are light at the agency right now. I can take the time off easier than you. I'll just bring the laptop with me, and maybe I can get some stuff done while the kids are napping."

It was a good thing she had a very understanding partner, Jennifer thought. When she'd called earlier to explain why she hadn't returned from lunch, Al had told her to take all the time she needed. Whether she wanted to or not, she couldn't help thinking. But, Al was right. Business was slow. He didn't need her in the office as much as Rich needed her here.

Rich looked as if he could kiss her, and Jennifer couldn't help wishing he would, but it wasn't the time. They had two sick kids in the apartment, if Carter's teeth counted. Her needs—no, their hormones—could wait.

"You sure?"

"Yes, I'm sure, Rich. Stop asking me, or I'm likely to change my mind." She reached out to pat him on the cheek, but Rich grabbed her hand and dragged her into his arms.

"Thank you again," he said as he pulled her close.

Jennifer felt his hot breath on her cheek while hers seemed to stop. She tried to breathe and finally took in a shallow breath. Rich lowered his head toward her face, and Jennifer knew what was coming next.

She should have pushed Rich away. She should never have gotten herself in the situation to begin with. She should have run as far and as fast as she could, but she was helpless to stop him. She wanted him to kiss her as much as she wanted to breathe.

She wanted him to do more than kiss her.

It was a good thing she was going home, Jennifer

thought as Rich's lips met hers. She didn't know how much longer she would be able to resist him. And she didn't care, Jennifer thought as a kaleidoscope of emotions swirled around her head. Her knees went limp as cooked spaghetti, and she sagged against him eager to feel his hard body pressed against her. His kisses were drugging, addictive, and if she didn't get a handle on her feelings, she was going to find herself in too deep.

She felt as though she were sinking into a sea of delicious sensations. She was in over her head.

And she didn't care.

Finally, she dragged her lips away from his. It was late. She had to go. But, she didn't want to leave. She stood there for a long moment, her head resting against his chin. Then, drawing a deep breath, she stepped back. "I—I really have to go," she said, her voice breathy, her heart beating like a maniacal tom-tom.

"Yeah. It's time for bed," Rich said. "I mean...I had a late night last night and I gotta get up early for PT tomorrow." He stepped back, increasing the distance between them, and Jennifer felt vaguely bereft.

"Yes," she whispered, backing closer to the door. "I'll see you in the morning." Then she grabbed the knob and resolutely turned it. "I have to go."

Then she turned and hurried out.

RICH CLOSED the door behind Jennifer and wondered, not for the first time, what was going on between them. Every time he kissed her, he felt like he could take on the problems of the world and win. And every time one of those kisses ended, he felt lost. He rubbed his mouth with the back of his hand. Damn, he could still feel her there.

He heaved a deep sigh. He hadn't wanted to get involved with a woman. At least, not with the type of woman who was so obviously the marrying kind. But the thought of not having Jennifer in his life was daunting.

On the other hand, the thought of having someone depend on him for everything was. He'd barely gotten to the point where he felt responsible for himself. He'd had no good role models, no examples of the right way to do it. What was he doing thinking about what he was thinking?

Maybe it was just because he was so tired. For all practical purposes, he'd been up since just after midnight, working on twenty hours now. If he didn't get some shut-eye, no telling what kind of delirious thoughts he'd be thinking.

Yeah, that's it, he convinced himself as he headed toward Ski's room to sleep. It was just the exhaustion talking.

He thought about the pile of stinking laundry on the kitchen floor, but he'd have to go downstairs to the laundry room to wash it. He couldn't leave the kids alone, so that was out. The only sensible thing to do was to go to bed. Get some sleep.

If the kids would let him.

If Jennifer would let him.

At least he'd removed the distracting poster off Ski's wall. Of course, the poster wasn't the worst of his problems. His damned fertile, horny imagination was.

Every time he lay down and closed his eyes, images of Jennifer lying beside him filled his head.

Now that he'd seen the poster, he could imagine how she'd look, naked and rosy in his bed. Since he'd kissed her, he almost knew how she'd feel. He'd seen her with her hair tangled and mussed, and wrapped around his fingers. The only thing he hadn't been able to do in reality was to put it all together. With him. In his bed.

He groaned. He'd never wanted a woman as much as her, and damned if he knew what to do about it.

Rich sighed and turned and tiptoed over to the crib where Carter lay sleeping. He had to see to the kids before he could meet his own need for sleep. He'd found the tooth stuff that Jennifer had gotten for him. If Carter did wake up tonight, maybe he could rub some on his gums and get him right back to sleep. At least, this time he was sort of prepared.

The phone rang, and Rich stumbled getting to it. Both of the kids were asleep, and he intended to keep it that way so he could join them as soon as he got whomever off the line.

It was Nick.

"A girl? No kidding? And you said you thought you were going to have a little soccer player." He listened a little longer while Nick went on and on about his new daughter.

Finally, he glanced at his watch and managed an interjection. "Congratulations, man." He placed the receiver back onto the cradle.

He yawned and stretched and yawned again as he looked around. Damn, he was tired. In spite of the clutter around the small apartment, there was no way he was going to stop to clean it up. He had an appointment with the sandman.

He just hoped he'd be alert enough to hear either of the kids if they needed him.

Rationalizing that he would be no good to them at all if he didn't crash, he gave up the ghost. He left Caitlyn's door ajar and his open. Maybe if he got a good nap first, he'd still be able to function if one of them did wake up.

Now, if he could just stop thinking about Jennifer and get to sleep.

THE ANSWERING MACHINE was blinking frantically, and the phone was ringing when Jennifer finally got home. She'd stopped off at the store to get a few things she thought she'd need for the next day that she hadn't remembered to tell Rich about. Sherry had reminded her of them during their brief chat on the phone.

Hoping there wasn't another crisis with Caitlyn, she set her bag down and reached for the shrilling phone. She didn't need to be called back to Rich's apartment. She had to spend the rest of the evening finishing up the work she should have done this afternoon.

The answering machine clicked on before she picked up the receiver, and she had to fiddle with the buttons to get it to shut off. Breathlessly, she spoke. "Is Caitlyn all right?"

"I'm sure Caitlyn is fine. It's me," an unexpected voice answered. Nick.

Jennifer's muscles went limp with relief, and she sagged against the sofa. Then she drew in a quick breath. What if something had gone wrong with Beverly's delivery? She had gone into labor almost a month early. She sank onto the cushions and listened to the news. "Nicole Marie? It's a beautiful name. When can I see her?"

Jennifer listened as Nick described his new daughter, and was relieved to discover the newborn was healthy. "Well, I'm afraid I'll be tied up with Rich's niece and nephew all day tomorrow, but I'll try to come by tomorrow night. I can't wait to see both of them." She hung up and leaned back against the cushions. "My friend Beverly is a mother," she whispered in awe.

A strong sense of longing settled over her. She hadn't even seen the baby, and already she knew she wanted one of her own.

"I SHOULD'VE paid the extra bucks for the unit with the washer and dryer inside," Rich muttered as he stepped around the pile of soiled sheets in the kitchen. Most of the time using the coin-operated washers in the complex's laundry room wasn't a big deal, but when you had two little kids you couldn't leave alone and you couldn't take with you, it was a big problem.

He'd definitely have to figure out how to get some washing done tonight.

At least, he'd been able to sleep. Most of the night.

Caitlyn had slept right through, and Carter had only wakened once. And all Rich had done was rub some of that tooth stuff on his gums, and he'd settled right down. If only he'd had that stuff the night before.

Rich grinned. He'd discovered something else last night when he'd been learning about the miracle of teething ointment. As he'd massaged the baby's lower gums, he'd felt something sharp. Closer inspection had shown the snag to be a tooth. Carter had cut his first tooth. And he'd been the one to find it. Him. Uncle Sarge.

It was enough to make a guy feel ten feet tall. No wonder Nick had sounded so happy last night.

One of these days he—Rich stopped himself. Had he actually been thinking about being a father himself? Not that long ago, he hadn't been able to think of himself as a responsible adult, much less a father. Or a husband.

He wondered what had precipitated the change.

Someone knocked gently on the door, and Rich had no more time for self-analysis.

He yanked open the door. "Hi," he said.

Jennifer, dressed in another one of those prim, schoolteacher dresses, brushed past him. Even in that virginal outfit, she still made his blood heat and his groin tighten. Rich took a deep breath and caught the scent of her slightly floral perfume. Not the best way to keep from thinking about what he shouldn't be thinking.

She was carrying a large paper sack and, what he presumed was, the laptop computer she'd mentioned last night. She set her burdens on the table and turned to face him. "How did the kids sleep?" She paused. "More important, how did you?"

Rich managed a lopsided smile. Jennifer might have asked about the kids first, but her concern for him touched him. How long had it been since anyone had actually cared?

"We made it through. Carter woke once, but I put some tooth goop on his gums, and he went right back to sleep. Caitlyn hasn't budged since I put her down." He grinned. "I went in to check on her a couple of times to make sure she was breathing. Silly, huh?''

"Not so silly. Human, maybe. So you think you'll survive?" Jennifer smiled, but it turned into a yawn she couldn't quite disguise.

"Ready for whatever," he said, spreading his arms in an expansive gesture. He just hoped that whatever would hold off until things settled down to a little more like normal.

"Guess what?" he added, suddenly remembering.

"I can't imagine," Jennifer said dryly as she started removing things from the bag.

"Carter has a tooth. Lower right. Sharp little sucker." He grinned.

"Well, Uncle Rich. You must be very proud." Jennifer started to reach for him, but stopped, and pulled her hand back.

After last night's explosive kiss, she must be a little leery, Rich supposed. "Yeah, I am," he said. "You'd think I had something to do with it."

Jennifer smiled a half smile that made him think that she was looking at something far away.

"Well. I gotta go." He picked up his gym bag and started for the door. Then he stopped. "Do you think you can hang around tonight?"

Jennifer stopped unpacking the groceries. Her hand was half in, half out of the sack, and she looked at him. Was he asking her for a date?

She shook her head slightly, more for herself than for Rich's benefit. "Why?"

"I've got to be able to get some of this dirty stuff into the wash," he said, then heaved a heavy sigh. "I never realized what logistics were involved in doing simple things like a load of wash when you have kids to take care of." Rich paused. "I'll stop for pizza?" he said looking hopeful, the statement more of a question than anything. "That way we can eat while the stuff is chugging away."

"You don't have to bribe me with pizza," Jennifer said, smiling. "But, I have to admit it's a tempting offer. Pizza is one thing that just isn't much fun for one. Sure, I'll stay."

How long could it take to do a couple of loads of laundry? Two hours? A two-hour fix for her Rich addiction. And if she could get the kids settled, with the pizza, it would seem almost like a date.

Reality returned and Jennifer shrugged away her silly thoughts. All Rich wanted her here for was to help with the kids.

"Go on, Sergeant Larsen. You'll be late for PT. I've got things under control, and I'll have everything sorted and ready to go to the laundry room by the time you get home."

Rich offered a quick salute, of appreciation, Jennifer supposed, then he hurried out.

She could do this, Jennifer told herself as she listened to the sound of Rich's footsteps hurrying down the stairs. Watching these two kids was child's play. She'd help Rich out, get a little work done for Al and have everything ready to go so she wouldn't have to stay in Rich's distracting presence longer than she had to.

Yeah, she could do this. No sweat.

Chapter Eleven

Compared to Wednesday, work on Thursday had hummed along like a fine-tuned machine. Rich looked around his work area with satisfaction. He was ready to go. Early, he figured since he hadn't heard "Retreat" yet from the speaker outside. He glanced at his watch. Anytime now.

Just a minute or so to go, and he was off the clock.

Considering his day yesterday, he probably could be excused for leaving early, but he wouldn't do that. He owed Uncle Sam a full day every day, and he would give it. A few minutes wouldn't make that much difference in the long run.

Finally the sound of the bugle, muffled by the walls, wafted into the room. Rich came to attention. Even though he wasn't present at the flag-lowering ceremony, he always gave it the respect that was due.

It was a simple thing, but important.

The air force had been his family for ten years, the only thing he'd felt like he belonged to until he'd found Sherry again, and found her family, and found Jennifer. He would treat the flag with every respect.

The country it represented had treated him well.

As the last sustained note drifted away, Rich drew a deep breath and reached for the phone.

A heavy hand fell on his shoulder, and Rich looked up to see Captain Thibodeaux at his elbow. "Yes, sir?" he said, hoping the C.O.'s appearance didn't signal extra duty.

He had something to go home for. Someone to go home to. He didn't want to hang around here.

"I just wanted to commend you for putting in your time in spite of Beverly Wilson's unexpected delivery. You know, if you need to take the time off, it's no problem." The captain smiled, and Rich believed him.

But he shook his head. "It's okay, Cap'n," he said. "I've got it covered. One of Beverly's friends stepped in. Jennifer Bishop."

"Nice lady. Her ex was a good combat controller, but he—" Thibodeaux stopped.

Rich hadn't known that Jennifer had been married to another combat control operator. Hell, he hadn't even known she'd been married before. The fact that her ex had been in the squadron explained a lot, like how she happened to know Beverly and Nick. And, it explained why Jennifer seemed to keep pushing him away in spite of the sparks that had been flying between them. A relationship with a special tactics combat control operator was especially hard on a woman. Or so he'd heard.

"Yeah, she is," Rich said, meaning it. "If you don't have anything pressing for me to do, I'd like to get on, sir. I promised Jennifer I'd get home in time for her to go and see Beverly and the baby."

He didn't mention the piles of laundry he had to do. He figured the captain had enough on his mind not to be bothered with all sorts of domestic stuff. He had a wife and kid. He knew the score.

"Go on, then," the captain said. "And don't hesitate to ask for more time or help if you need it. The military family pulls together."

"Yes, sir," Rich said. He'd been dismissed, and considering what he and Thibodeaux had just discussed, he figured he'd best go. He didn't want to give the impression that he was avoiding his responsibilities.

He could pick up the pizza on the way.

WHAT HAD MADE her think that today would be a snap, Jennifer didn't know. But, she had obviously been badly mistaken. And it didn't help that she'd not slept well.

She hadn't had anyone to keep her awake as Rich had the night before, but her dreams had been restless and all about Rich. She'd wakened far too early to feel refreshed, and now her early morning was beginning to catch up with her.

Jennifer yawned and pushed herself up from the couch where she'd sunk after the last battle with Caitlyn. Why she'd expected the child to be a model patient, she didn't know, but Caitlyn had been irritable and cross. Between trying to keep her happy and Carter entertained and dry, Jennifer had had her hands full all day.

And what a long day it had been. She'd stayed up late finishing the computer search she'd been supposed to do in the office, and then she'd had a hard time sleeping. Her mind had raced a mile a minute thinking about Beverly and the new baby, and Rich, and... Dreams were one thing. She was living in the real world.

Jennifer's fatigue this afternoon gave her some sense of how Rich must have felt last night when he'd stumbled in so late and she'd so unfairly accused him of stopping off at the Club to drink before coming home. She supposed she owed him an apology, but she wouldn't bring it up if he didn't. It was embarrassing enough to think about.

"PIZZA MAN IS HERE," Rich announced, grinning at Jennifer who was sitting in the middle of piles of clothing on the living room sofa.

Jennifer jerked to attention, her expression confused. She looked at him as if she hadn't quite figured out who he was and how he'd gotten there.

"Jennifer, you all right?"

She shook her head as if trying to clear it of cobwebs. "Yeah," she said slowly. "Weird. Did I nod off?"

Rich shrugged. "Beats me. Did the kids wear you out?"

Jennifer still seemed befuddled, and Rich had a flash of how she would look as she woke up in the morning, all sleepy-eyed and drowsy. He felt a tightening in his groin, but he forced the thought away.

"No, they were fine. I just... I stayed up too late last night, and now it's catching up with me." She managed a wan smile. "I don't function so well when my schedule is changed."

"Been there, done that," Rich said wryly. Just the day before. And he had been trained to respond at a moment's notice. Just not to teething infants. He looked around. "Where are the kids?"

Jennifer smiled wearily. "Both in bed, and I think they're out for the night. Caitlyn's feeling better, she ate soup for dinner, but she was tired and ready for bed when I tucked Carter in."

Rich raised a silent cheer. He'd have a few minutes alone with Jennifer before they got down to the real reason he'd bribed her with pizza. He'd even picked up a bottle of wine. He placed the box and the wine on the table.

"Nick stopped by the squadron today and brought these." Rich pulled out a couple of pink bubble gum, new-father cigars. "Showed us some Polaroids, too."

That got Jennifer's attention. "Aw, I wish I could have seen them."

Rich shrugged. "It looked like any other baby. To me they all look like Yoda." He patted the pizza box and pulled out a chair. "But as soon as you eat you can go see her in person and come to your own conclusion."

Jennifer went into the kitchen and returned with plates and glasses for the wine. "I'm sure she doesn't look like Yoda," she said as she set the plates on the table. "I doubt her ears are quite that pointed," she added dryly.

Rich shrugged. "Couldn't prove it by me." At the sight of Jennifer's censuring frown, he shrugged and added, "It could've been a bad picture."

Since Jennifer was going to the hospital shortly, she only sipped a little of the wine, but she enjoyed sharing the pizza with Rich. She sat across from him at the tiny kitchen table, and they chatted about things of little consequence, but she could see that

Rich had something on his mind. Maybe, she should have left it at that, but he seemed troubled by something and maybe she could help.

"Something bothering you? Is it the kids?"

Rich looked up, startled. "What makes you think that?"

"I don't know," Jennifer shrugged. "Nothing. Everything. I've gotten to know you in the last few days and you seem more, I don't know, introspective? What is it? Can I help?"

Rich drew in a deep breath. "The captain wasn't gossiping or anything, but he let slip today that you had been married to a combat controller. I never knew Duke Bishop, but I hear he was a damned good operator."

"Oh, he was an operator, all right. He lived for it. It was when things were slow that he couldn't stand it. He wasn't satisfied to be at home with me." Jennifer couldn't believe she was telling him this, but she had gone this far, she might as well finish. "He loved the ops, he loved the excitement, but he couldn't stand it when things settled down after an exercise or an operation. Pretty soon he'd be pacing around like a caged lion and he had to go out and let off steam.

"He started skydiving on the weekends, and that seemed to help for a while. Then it wasn't enough. He'd go out drinking with skydiving buddies, and that wasn't enough." She twisted her paper napkin into a tight roll. "Soon, he was staying out all night. Still, he was okay with me. When things were good, they were great. Then he started coming home smelling like women and cheap perfume. I tried to ignore it, but one day I found lipstick on his T-shirt." She shrugged. "That was it."

Rich sucked in a deep breath and bit back a curse. He needed to let her finish. He wanted to kill the man for hurting her. No, he wanted to make her forget all about that SOB who was too stupid to know what he'd turned his back on.

"He almost seemed relieved when I told him to get out." Jennifer looked off, her eyes looking into the past.

"Funny," she said, shaking her head almost in disbelief. She began to nervously twist her napkin, alternately winding and unwinding it. "I had such a crush on him in high school, but he never gave me the time of day. We had a class together, but he was a few years older than me and I wasn't worth his time then. He joined the air force right out of high school, so I didn't see him for a couple of years." She smiled sadly.

"Then he came back for homecoming all dressed up in his uniform with his medals and ribbons and red beret looking like the conquering hero. He swept me off my feet." She laughed humorlessly. "Apparently, I was easily impressed, but I was seventeen going on eighteen, and I thought I was in love. I could hardly wait till I graduated and we could be married. If I only—"

Rich swallowed and moistened his lips. "I wish I could say something that would make it better, but dammit, I don't want to say anything that might justify what Bishop did." He reached for her hand and the tattered napkin, but Jennifer drew back and straightened in her chair, suddenly alert.

"Oh, no!" she said, switching gears. She looked

down at the shredded remains of her napkin as if she'd never seen it before, then looked up at Rich. "We didn't do the laundry."

"That's okay," Rich said. "I can do it later."

"No. I have to go. You won't have anybody here to watch the kids."

"Damn," Rich muttered. "I keep forgetting." He thought a minute. "Look. I can go down to the laundry room and get it started, then you can go to the hospital while it's washing.

"I know you'd probably rather not have to come back, but I'm desperate. In spite of all those clothes Rebecca packed, pretty soon the kids will be down to nothing."

Jennifer grinned, and patted Rich on the cheek, then she pulled her hand back quickly at the disconcerting jolt of electricity that seemed to arc from his skin to her fingers. She closed her hand, and rested it in her lap. "Poor things will have to sit around the house wearing barrels," she joked to cover her reaction. She blew a strand of hair away from her face. "Okay. You go run and get things started, and I'll get this mess cleaned up."

Rich grabbed up the piles of laundry and noticed that Jennifer was watching him, a skeptical look on her face. "I do know not to wash the dark stuff together with the others," Rich said. He started toward the door. "I'll just put these in and you can go."

"No hurry," Jennifer said, out of habit. But once Rich had gone, she realized that she'd meant it. In spite of everything, she'd enjoyed the feeling of belonging to a family this afternoon. And she'd enjoyed Rich's company. She felt like a weight was lifted after opening up to Rich about her relationship with Duke.

Maybe, once all this was over, they could be friends.

The trouble was, she thought, as she cleaned up the remains of the pizza, friendship wasn't all that she wanted from Rich Larsen.

THE THOUGHT of Beverly's baby may have brought warm and fuzzy thoughts into Jennifer's mind, but seeing the tiny infant had multiplied them tenfold.

She couldn't wait to have one of her own. She wished she'd been able to hold the baby, but considering Caitlyn's bout with the flu bug, she'd only looked at Nicole Marie though the glass observation window at the nursery. She'd get a chance to see her close-up soon enough.

Jennifer stood in the doorway to Beverly's room. If she'd thought about it, she probably shouldn't have come to see Beverly at all. Nick sat on the edge of her bed, and they both had their backs to the door. Jennifer rapped quickly on the jamb. "Hey, Mommy and Daddy. How do you feel?"

They both turned and grinned, though Nick's smile looked brighter than Beverly's.

"Like a million bucks," Nick said.

"I'd deduct about $999,999 and $.50," Bev said wearily. She nodded toward a chair. "Come in. Sit."

Jennifer shook her head. "I probably shouldn't have come at all. Caitlyn seems to have had a stomach bug, but she's nearly over it now." She smiled. "I looked at little Nikki through the observation window, though. She's the prettiest one there."

"Of course, she is," Nick agreed. "I can't wait to get her home."

Beverly leaned back against the pillows. She looked tired, though happy. "Well, if they want to let me stay here a couple more days, I won't object. I was not prepared for how hard it is."

A nurse bustled past Jennifer. "It's harder on you when the baby comes early. Your body wasn't finished getting ready. In a day or so, you'll feel better." She handed Beverly a paper cup containing a pill and then poured her some water from a pitcher on the bedside table.

"I'll take your word for it," Beverly said, accepting the glass of water. She swallowed the pill and washed it down. "It was worth it, though." She smiled, a faraway look in her eyes.

The expression of love on Beverly's face was enough to make Jennifer cry. Would she ever feel that way? Or had she wasted her one chance at happiness on Duke Bishop?

She blinked at the moisture that unexpectedly blurred her vision and swallowed a lump in her throat. "I can see you're tired," Jennifer said. "How 'bout I let you rest, and I'll see you when you and Nikki get home."

"I'll hold you to it," Beverly said through a yawn. She patted her husband on the hand. "You go home, too, hubby. Tomorrow's going to be a big day."

"Roger that," Nick said. "Tomorrow I get to learn what it's like to be a daddy for real."

Jennifer had to smile as she watched him kiss his wife. She wondered if he knew just what he was getting into? And she wondered, if everybody got to do what she and Rich were doing before marriage, would anybody have a child?

She waved to Beverly and turned away. Nick might not know about how rough it is, but he'd soon find out. And, considering her trial by fire had not prevented her from thinking about having one of her own, she didn't think it would have daunted either Beverly or Nick.

"DAMN," RICH MUTTERED as he looked at the five dryers whirling away. His four loads of laundry were done, but there wasn't a single dryer free. Why there were six dryers to eight washers made little sense to him, and to make matters worse, one of the dryers had an out-of-order sign taped to it. He checked the timers on all the machines. From the looks of it, they'd just been activated.

He dreaded going back upstairs and telling Jennifer that she'd have to stay even longer. Though she'd seemed excited about seeing the baby, she really looked beat.

Rich waited around for a couple more minutes in hopes that somebody would come and empty one of the dryers, but no such luck. He drew in a deep breath, set the timer on his watch to remind him in fifteen minutes, and headed upstairs.

The living room was dark, and Jennifer wasn't there, but Rich heard voices from the bedroom. He tiptoed to the half-closed door and listened.

Caitlyn must have wakened, for Jennifer was reading her a bedtime story. The voices he'd heard were really just one, but Jennifer was acting out all the characters, giving each a voice and a personality of his own. What a wonderful mother she'd make!

Eyelids drifting downward, then fluttering back up, Caitlyn listened with rapt attention. She was obviously fighting sleep to hear the end.

He couldn't wait until he and Jennifer had their own kids to read to. Whoa! The thought whammed him like a round from a Howitzer. No, he told himself. Surely, he didn't mean children belonging to him and Jennifer jointly, but each having their own.

They'd never really had a date, unless you counted tonight and the wedding. It was a far cry to suddenly start thinking about children with her.

But, once that notion had entered his brain, Rich had a hard time letting it go. Would it be so bad to have what Nick and Beverly seemed to have?

No. He shook his head. He couldn't do that. There was too much of his father in him. He was sure that Rick Larsen had expected to be a good father, but look what had happened to him. No, there was no way he was going to put any child through what he'd been through.

No way in hell.

"And they all lived happily ever after," Jennifer read. She closed the book and sighed. "Wasn't that a nice story, Caitlyn?"

Caitlyn didn't respond, and Jennifer looked down at her and smiled. "Goodnight, sweetie," she said, then kissed her on top of her curly red head and carefully slipped away.

She put the book on the bedside table and tiptoed toward the door. She must have just noticed him standing there, Rich realized, because she stopped short as she reached for the light switch. Her breath caught.

"I didn't see you there," she said, recovering.

"I didn't want to disturb the performance," Rich said. "Where did you learn to read stories like that?"

"My mom always read stories to me," Jennifer said, switching off the light. "It was a given." She stepped out and shut the door behind her.

Maybe his mother had read to him like that when he was a kid, but Rich didn't remember. He remembered the fights, and the arguments, and the days when his dad was too drunk to stand. Maybe Mom wanted to do things like that, but his father had kept her too busy defending herself.

He wondered why she'd stayed all that time.

"Did you get the stuff in the dryers?"

Jennifer's question jerked him back. "You're not gonna like this," he said.

"Try me. Did you turn everything dingy gray?"

Rich rolled his eyes. "No, I did not turn everything gray, but the dryers were all in use."

Jennifer shrugged philosophically. "It happens. Did you check to see when they'd be done?"

Proud that he'd had the foresight, Rich grinned. He tapped the face of his watch. "Yep, set the timer to remind me to go back and check." As if to verify his statement, it beeped. "That's my cue." He headed for the door. "Cross your fingers that the other guy is keeping track, too."

"Fingers duly crossed, sir," Jennifer said, raising her hands to show him.

"Thanks," he said. "Be right back. I hope."

JENNIFER GLANCED at the clock on the VCR. Rich had been gone for an awfully long time. Was he planning to stay in the laundry room until all the washing was dry?

She leaned back against the couch cushions. Now that she'd had a chance to sit down, the fatigue she'd been fighting all day returned with vengeance. She yawned and stretched and leaned back. Maybe if she just closed her eyes, she could rest. What could it hurt if she slept for a few minutes?

FINALLY, the washing was spinning in the dryers. Whoever had left the stuff in the dryer hadn't come down to get it. After waiting almost thirty minutes, Rich had done the most expedient thing he could think of. He'd taken the dry clothes out and placed them on the folding table.

Rich looked around. There was still no sign of the owner of the clothes, and Rich hated the idea of leaving them piled in a heap. So he'd folded the towels and sheets, but left the woman's intimate things alone. He wondered if he knew the owner of the stuff, then shook away the notion. Why waste his time thinking about her?

He had a woman of his own to go back to. Sort of.

He checked the timers on the machines and, again, set his watch. Maybe that other woman had time to wait. He didn't. Jennifer had to go home.

Not that he would mind if she stayed all night. Hell, he wouldn't mind if she stayed forever.

No, he reminded himself as he trudged upstairs. It was stupid to go there. He was not the kind of man who would make it over the long haul. He might want to, but there was nothing he could do about it. It was in his genes.

And you couldn't argue with heredity, he told himself as he let himself into the apartment.

Jennifer was curled up on the couch sleeping like a baby. He chuckled, and thought how much she looked like Caitlyn.

He started to wake her, but shrugged. No, she could wait for the laundry to dry asleep as well as she could awake, and obviously, she needed the rest.

He went to the kitchen and turned on the light. Two slices of pizza left in the fridge earlier were calling to him, and he could think of worse ways to kill time.

The pizza was good, even warmed up, and by the time he'd eaten and cleaned up, it was time to retrieve the wash.

Baskets laden with fresh-smelling laundry, Rich let himself back in. Jennifer was still asleep, and he hated to wake her, but he had to.

He put the basket down and knelt beside her. "Jennifer, I'm done, you can go home."

She muttered something, but didn't rouse.

Rich touched her on the shoulder. "Jennifer. You have to wake up now."

"Lea' me 'lone," she murmured, clumsily brushing his hand away. "Tired." She rolled toward the back of the couch.

Rich drew in a deep shuddering sigh. Now what? He knew he should wake her, he knew he should send her home, but he couldn't.

He lifted her gently into his arms and carried her into Ski's room. To the bed.

Chapter Twelve

Rich had intended to be a gentleman and sleep on the couch, but after only a few minutes that seemed like hours on the five-foot sofa, his six-foot-plus frame felt twisted like a pretzel. He'd tried the floor, but the carpeting had less padding than the sleeping bag stowed away in the equipment locker at the squadron. He'd slept in worse conditions, but then he'd had the luxury of a bedroll between him and the hard ground. And he'd been dead tired.

He hadn't been distracted by lustful thoughts about a woman sleeping just a room away.

Linking his fingers behind his head, he lay back and stared at the patterns of light sneaking in through the cracks between the venetian blinds. The lights weren't as distracting as the posters had been, but with his only choices the floor and the tiny couch, he wasn't likely to sleep.

He had to get up in the morning, do PT, and show up ready and able for duty. Rich willed himself to sleep.

As if that would work.

After what seemed like hours spent trying to make himself comfortable, he gave it up.

There was plenty of room in Ski's bed, and he'd just lie down long enough to get some shut-eye. He'd roll out of bed before Jennifer even knew he was there. He needed a comfortable place to sleep. That was all, he convinced himself.

He tiptoed to the bedroom door and looked inside.

Jennifer was curled up in a ball right in the middle of the queen-size bed. She appeared to be sleeping so soundly that a grenade could go off next to her, and she wouldn't hear a thing. If only Rich had that kind of exhaustion to sedate him into unconsciousness.

There was plenty of room on either side, and he just needed to get some *Z's*. Nothing more.

He positioned himself carefully beside her on top of the covers. He wasn't cold, just tired. Jennifer was doing him a huge favor, and no way was he going to take advantage.

He lay there, hugging his side of the bed, hardly daring to breathe. Eventually, he willed his tense muscles to relax. This was going to work, he told himself.

Then with a whimpering sigh, Jennifer shifted positions.

Rolling over in her soft, dark cocoon of slumber, Jennifer encountered an obstacle. A warm, comfortable obstacle that seemed to fit itself to her. The sensation was not unpleasant, and she snuggled closer. It was warm and soothing against her, and Jennifer melted into its embrace and succumbed again to healing sleep.

She dreamed of strong arms holding her, of warm breath on her chilly skin, and whispered words of love. If only it were true, she thought from the depths of her subconscious. True or not, she could enjoy the dream. She might have no control over what happened in real life, but in sleep she could have whatever she wanted. True love, happiness, children.

Anything.

She could have anything, but she wanted Rich.

How real this dream seemed! Jennifer could almost smell Rich's aftershave mingled with the warm, man-scent that was uniquely his. How wonderful it was to lay protected in the shelter of his embrace.

Jennifer drew in a deep, satisfied breath. Halfway between waking and sleep, she rolled to her back and stretched like a lazy cat in front of a blazing fireplace. "I could lie like this forever," she murmured.

She heard a rumble in response. Had she spoken aloud?

She turned toward the sound, and rolled to her side and pillowed her head on one bent arm so she could see. What did she almost see in the dim light between her and the window?

"Are you all right, Jennifer?" He moved and rolled toward her.

Perhaps, if she hadn't been caught between her dreams and the real world, this might have alarmed her. In her fuzzy state, it seemed perfectly natural.

"Rich, you're here," she murmured, her body tingling with delight as his warm hand settled on her hip, and branded her with its heat.

He didn't answer right away, and Jennifer thought she had succumbed to wishful thinking. Maybe she was still asleep, and she had dreamed it.

"Yeah," he answered finally, his voice husky and thick with sleep. "You okay with it?"

Jennifer shivered as she realized it wasn't a dream.

"You drifted off while I was downstairs in the laundry room. I couldn't wake you, so I put you in Ski's bed," he answered softly.

Had she asked the question out loud? Or had Rich just read her mind?

Jennifer roused from her sleep-drugged state and looked around. She was fully dressed and tucked snugly under the covers. Rich lay on top, still wearing his BDU pants and the olive-drab T-shirt stretched tightly across his considerable chest. Except that his arm was draped protectively over her hip, his hand resting lightly at the small of her back, he had made no untoward advances.

She couldn't help wishing he had. Though she and Duke had been separated for over a year, and had been officially divorced for months, she still kept her birth control prescription filled. Not because she had been sleeping around, but because of what it did for her complexion.

Still, since she was taking them...

Why not...?

She shouldn't be thinking about that. Getting any more deeply involved with Rich Larsen would be a giant mistake, she told herself.

"Go to sleep, Jennifer," Rich whispered. Then he drew his hand away and rolled to face the window.

Jennifer heaved a frustrated sigh. Now, she was wide awake, and the only thing she could think about was making love to Rich. Why was he being such a gentleman?

She rolled to face the window and found him silhouetted against the light coming through the broken blinds. She turned over to face the wall. How was she going to sleep? She punched her pillow, and wriggled around, trying to make herself comfortable like a puppy in the hay.

As comfortable as she could possibly get, considering the circumstances, Jennifer squeezed her eyes shut and tried to count sheep. But the only image that materialized behind her closed lids was Rich's face. No fluffy lambs, bleating ewes or proud rams, just Rich. Jennifer squeezed her eyes shut and rubbed them till she saw flashes of light, but Rich reappeared as soon as she let up.

She was not going to sleep at all if this continued all night. She had to face it. She wanted Rich. As a lover and a friend.

Rich had never indicated that he didn't want her. In fact, his kisses had told her what neither of them had been willing, or able, to admit. Jennifer drew in a long, deep breath. "Rich?"

"Yes," he murmured in response.

"I can't sleep. Will you hold me?"

Rich hardly dared to breathe. He was afraid that if he touched her again, he wouldn't be able to stop with just touching.

Finally, Rich expelled a long, slow breath. He had never taken an unwilling partner in his life, and it was the last thing he wanted to do now.

"Just hold me. That's all," she said in a breathy whisper.

Rich reached over to hold her, to draw her into his arms. His muscles, his loins were coiled so tightly he feared he might explode. He pressed her against his chest, her back to him to hold temptation at bay.

As if that would work.

All that did was make him want her more. He breathed in the soft scent of her hair, the subtle fragrance that was more likely soap than perfume. He buried his face in the curve of her neck and combed the long silky strands with his fingers, combed them away until he'd bared her velvety, smooth skin.

He brushed his lips against her and felt a tremor run through her as he tasted her warm, slightly salty skin.

She moaned and turned to face him.

Without asking or receiving permission, he took her mouth, pressing his tongue between her lips. He tasted and savored and explored until he could bear no more. He drew away, but she whimpered in protest and drew him back. She pressed him closer. Wordlessly, she begged for more.

And Rich gave her what she needed.

When he thought he might burst from unsatisfied hunger, she pushed him away. Feeling like he'd been doused with a bucket of ice water, Rich waited to see what she would do.

She surprised him.

Jennifer sat up, reached behind her, and began to unbutton the long row of buttons that closed her dress.

Rich reached tentatively to help her, then drew his hand back. "You're sure?"

"I don't know where this will lead," she murmured. "But for now, this is what I want."

Maybe that should have been enough, but although Rich's body ached for Jennifer, his heart seemed to want more. Still, he was young and healthy, and it had been a long, long time since he'd been offered such temptation.

He gave her one more chance to back out. "I don't

have any protection," he whispered though he was already reaching to release the button on his pants.

"It's all right. I never stopped taking the Pill," she said.

Why the hell was he trying to talk her out of it? Here he had a willing woman in his bed, and he was trying to discourage her?

Jennifer pulled the dress over her head and tossed it aside. It whispered to the floor, and Rich, though the light was dim, finally saw the perfect body he'd only suspected lay beneath those demure clothes. She unfastened her bra to reveal the full breasts it covered. One glance confirmed his notion that she was as good as the calendar girl who'd taunted him a few nights ago.

No, she was better.

Jennifer was real.

Rich sat up and faced the window. He didn't know why, but he felt strange having her watch him as he undressed even if it was the middle of the night and the only light came sneaking in from outside the window. He pulled the shirt over his head and tossed it to the floor. As he stripped out of his remaining clothing, he felt her eyes on him, and a jolt of anticipation shuddered through him. They'd barely kissed, and his need was standing straight and tall at attention.

"Rich Larsen, ready for duty," he quipped as he caught sight of her sitting amid the tangled covers, her legs curled to one side, her naked breasts tempting him.

He reached for her and she for him.

Any doubts he might have had evaporated into the night as their fingers touched. It was as if they were destined to be one. Even if his mind was still uncertain, his body knew what to do. And so did hers.

Rich traced a path along her silky skin from her fingertips, up her arm and to her chin. She trembled, and he could feel her skin roughen with gooseflesh as he moved upward. He caught her chin in his hand, tipped it, and took her mouth with his.

She melted to him, whimpering as he thrust his tongue deeper. He tasted her, explored her and made her his own.

Rich drew back and feasted on her with his eyes, now accustomed to the dim light. Her breasts were full, perfect. He touched them with his fingertips, then cupped them with his hands.

He had to taste, had to know. He tested a puckered nipple with the tip of his tongue and almost went over the edge.

After that, their heated bodies took the lead.

They joined and separated and joined again, performing the ageless dance. Rich felt complete when he connected with her, and he sensed that Jennifer felt the same.

Somewhere in his mind, he sang, *I love you, I love you, I love you,* over and over again. He wanted to say it out loud, he wanted Jennifer to know, but he held back. Let his feelings remain unspoken for now. He was showing her in every possible way that he belonged to her and she to him.

Why did they need words?

Jennifer arched against him and moaned, soft and low and shuddering, then fell limp against the sheets. This was what it was all about, he realized as he filled her. This was it.

LANGUID, WARM AND SATED, Jennifer lay in the dark and considered what she had done. Shouldn't she feel guilty? She stretched her deliciously weak muscles and moaned with satisfaction. Never had she felt so loved, so cherished. How wonderful to be held and stroked and loved in a man's arms. How wonderful it was to feel wanted.

Jennifer closed her eyes and tried to sleep. She'd had trouble enough before, surely it would be just as difficult now.

Maybe it was the exhaustion of her endless day, or maybe it was satisfaction from their lovemaking that did it. Whatever the cause, sleep overtook her quickly, and she sank into deep and dreamless slumber.

SOMETHING SOFT and delicate fluttered against his ear, and Rich tried to brush it away. The butterfly lifted off, hovered, then lit again. Again, he tried to shrug if off, but it proved tenacious. This time it seemed to crawl into his ear.

Awareness finally crept into Rich's sleep-drugged brain. A butterfly hadn't roused him. Someone was teasing his ear. Jennifer?

He opened one eye, then slammed it shut against the brittle morning light.

Why was it so bright in here? Had he forgotten to turn off the light before he went to bed? And why hadn't the clock radio wakened him?

"Uncle Witch, you are being such a lazy bones."

Instantly, his mind cleared.

Rich launched his lids upward though fingers of brilliant morning light stabbed at his gritty eyes. "Caitlyn?" he rasped. He rubbed at his eyes and looked again. Caitlyn stood beside the bed, peering into his bleary eyes.

He started to say something, started to ask her what she was doing staring so solemnly at him, when he remembered that he was not alone in the bed. He also realized that he was wearing nothing but the bedclothes.

What had he done?

"What are you doing up so early?" he asked, his voice gravelly and thick, as he maneuvered himself to an upright position, a difficult task, considering he had to keep himself covered in all the right places. Or the wrong places, he supposed.

"It isn't early," Caitlyn announced. "*Sesame Street* is already over."

He squinted at the clock. After nine. Why had he slept so late?

He glanced over his shoulder to the mound of covers that was Jennifer. That was why. His groin tightened at the memory of what had gone on in this bed in the wee hours of the morning.

Now what? He was naked. He had a naked woman in his bed, and he had a very inquisitive four-year-old standing in front of him with a censuring look on her face. He let out a long, low breath and scratched his chest. He yawned and stretched while he figured out what to do.

"Sorry, Caitlyn," he finally muttered. "Why don't you let me dress, then I'll be out to fix you some cereal."

She just stood there.

Hadn't he just told her to leave so he could dress?

No, he realized, he had not. He guessed kids were too literal-minded to understand any subtleties. He cleared his throat. "Caitlyn, I need you to go out in the living room while I get dressed."

"I watch Mommy get dressed."

"I'm not your mommy," he growled impatiently. Then, seeing Caitlyn's face pucker as though she were about to cry, he softened his tone. "I need to have some privacy. I'm not used to having little girls watch me dress."

Caitlyn heaved an aggrieved sigh. "All wight. Carter is getting lonely anyway." She started to turn, but stopped, and placed her hands on narrow hips. "But hurry up. We're getting really hungry."

She minced out, and Rich drew in a deep, calming breath. Well, it was supposed to calm, but having Jennifer buried in the covers next to him made serenity impossible.

He reached over to touch her, but yanked his hand back at the spark that sizzled between them when, in spite of the layers of intervening linen, his hand contacted her hip. "Jennifer. We overslept. Big time." He paused and drew in another deep breath as he watched her stretch and yawn and smile a pleased-with-herself sort of smile. Was that smile for him?

He cleared his throat and shook thoughts of an encore from his mind. "And Caitlyn has been in here asking for her breakfast.

"I'll get dressed first, then you can get up once I'm out of the way." He paused again, reluctant to leave it this way, but he didn't know what to say or how to say it. "I slept through PT. I've gotta go."

It wasn't exactly the kind of parting he would have planned, but what could he do? He was damned if he stayed, and damned if he didn't. And right now, he had Caitlyn's sensitivities to consider.

Jennifer was an adult. She would understand.

He grabbed his discarded clothes and dressed quickly. He had to get out of here before Caitlyn came back. Tonight would be soon enough to square it with Jennifer. Caitlyn wouldn't understand. Rich hurried out, pausing only long enough to close the door softly behind him.

Jennifer lay in the empty bed for a long time, wondering what to do. This wasn't how she'd imagined waking up after a wonderful lovemaking experience like the night before.

She lay in the man-scented sheets and breathed in the musty scent of their lovemaking. She ached deep inside, and she knew she wanted it to have never ended. Tendrils of love and longing wound their way through her from her tender center all the way to her heart. She was in love with Rich Larsen.

If only she knew he was in love with her.

She lay still in the bed and listened while Rich shaved. She heard the buzz of the electric shaver and tried to think of him bristling with stubble, not the two of them, naked together, making love. She shook the erotic thought away. She was going to have a hard enough time facing the children and they had no idea what had transpired in this room, in this bed, without reliving it again in her mind.

It was a good thing Rich had to hurry out to the base. She wasn't ready to face him.

Not until she'd figured it all out. Not till she'd worked it all through.

The bed was warm and cozy, and she'd gotten less sleep than she really needed. Jennifer breathed a deep, long breath and her body became weak. Whatever her best intentions were, her boneless limbs seemed to have other things on their minds.

She drifted back to sleep.

Pounding on the door woke her.

Not pounding really, just a gentle tapping, but it was enough.

"Jennifer? Are you up? I'm leaving."

She rolled to one side and pushed herself to a sitting position. Clutching the mussed sheets to her in case he came in, she cleared her throat. "I'm up," she lied. "You go on. I'll just be a minute."

"Okay," he said.

Jennifer listened as he walked away. She listened until she heard the sound of the door opening and she heard Rich pull it firmly closed.

Why did she feel so empty?

Only a few hours ago, she had lain, warm and naked, in the arms of the man she loved. Now, she was alone.

How many times did men have to leave her before she figured it out?

Then it came to her. She was useful in bed. Nothing else.

There had been no promises.

But then, she'd asked for none. What could he possibly be thinking about her now?

She'd come to take care of his sister's children, and she'd ended up in his bed.

What kind of a woman did that make her?

Jennifer slowly pushed the bedding aside. She slipped into her discarded undergarments and picked up the dress from the floor. After being slept in, and then tossed to the floor, the wrinkles in it were there to stay.

Her mind raced as she tried to smooth the rumpled dress. What would she tell Caitlyn?

Thankfully Carter was too young to know what was going on, but how would she explain to Caitlyn why she had spent the night at her uncle's house? In her uncle's bed. In her uncle's arms.

She sank back onto the soft mattress and tried to button up her dress. No matter what she did, no matter how she tried to explain it to Caitlyn, she still couldn't explain it to herself.

Last night it had seemed so right.

Last night she had figured it all out.

Now, in the light of day, she wasn't so sure.

Even if Caitlyn didn't care what had gone on in this room, in this bed, she did. She had asked for no promises and received none.

Now, she wished she had.

If only he'd voiced what she'd thought—no, hoped—he felt. If only she'd heard those three little words of love from him.

She covered her face with her hands.

What had she done?

Chapter Thirteen

What had he done? Rich asked himself a thousand times as he drove to work. Why hadn't he left well enough alone?

It was bad enough to lie awake and wonder what Jennifer was like. It was another to now know and not have her.

Why can't you have her? a voice from somewhere deep inside him asked?

Because of Rick Larsen, another replied.

Rich drew in a deep, ragged sigh as he waited to be waved in at the gate to the base. Why did what his father had done to him and his family still torment Rich after so many years? The man had been dead for more than a decade.

The gate guard waved him in, and Rich urged his truck forward. Why couldn't things just be simple?

He knew that he wouldn't get a hassle from the captain about missing PT, but he was certain to get a ration of razzing from the team. He shrugged. He was a special operations combat controller, he could handle whatever they dished out.

That he couldn't handle two small kids and one medium-size woman bothered him more.

Rich parked at the squadron and paused to look into the rearview mirror to make sure he'd pass inspection. He jammed the red beret on his head, making sure the flash in front was positioned right and sighed.

At least some of his problems would be over in the morning. Tomorrow Rebecca would be coming to pick up the kids, and the only other problem he'd have to deal with would be Jennifer Bishop.

Compared to this, Kosovo and Bosnia seemed like a cakewalk.

IN SPITE of her distraction, Jennifer got the children fed and settled at play. Now that Caitlyn was feeling better, her sunny, helpful disposition had returned, and even Carter had recovered from his teething woes. Wouldn't his mother be surprised to see his sharp, little tooth?

Jennifer sighed and yawned and looked down at the wrinkled dress. Wrinkles were bad enough, but Caitlyn had spilled grape juice all over the front, and if she didn't get it out now, it would set.

Surely, there would be a robe or something in Rich's closet that she could wear until the dress was dry. She already knew there was an iron and ironing board in the kitchen. And Rich wouldn't be home until five o'clock.

Yes, that was a terrific idea.

She could hand wash it in the bathroom sink using dishwashing liquid. Then she could hang it on a hanger and it would drip dry in the tub.

Yes, of course.

She glanced in the closet of the room where she'd slept, then quickly closed the door. She recognized several of the loud, Hawaiian shirts hanging inside. They belonged to Ski Warsinski. She'd seen him in shirts of that type at several squadron functions. How could she forget that Rich had taken Ski's room while the kids were here?

Glancing in to see that the kids were entertained, she hurried into the other room and flung open the closet door.

Rich's selection of clothing was scant compared to Ski's and much less gaudy. But there was nothing that resembled a robe.

She looked again.

Rich had plenty of uniform shirts and one or two broadcloth dress shirts. Jennifer reached for one, then her gaze landed on the pleated white shirt he had worn to Rebecca's wedding.

Had it only been a week since they'd attended that family event?

Jennifer couldn't help herself. She reached for the shirt and brought it up to her nose. It hadn't been washed since he'd worn it, and the faint scent of Rich's aftershave still clung to the fabric. She breathed it in and was overtaken by the image of the man, not in the dress uniform, but naked and aroused in bed.

Quickly, she let go.

That was something she was trying to forget. She had to. It was something that could never happen again.

Instead, she selected a light blue, broadcloth shirt and pulled it off the hanger. She held it to her. The shirt was huge, but then, so was Rich, and the tails would reach nearly to her knees. If she rolled up the sleeves, it would be fine, and it would cover her.

Surely, Rich wouldn't mind if she wore his shirt. And if he did object, she'd take it home and have it laundered.

"HEY, LARSEN. You're gonna insult me if you don't hoist at least one to celebrate," Tank Mullins said. He'd just been promoted to chief master sergeant, the highest enlisted grade. Mullins had brought in a couple of cases of beer and bags of chips and had the bounty spread out on one of the long packing tables in the parachute shop.

Rich would have enjoyed drinking a cool one to toast Tank's promotion, but he had obligations. "Sorry, Tank. I owe you one. Gotta get home to my kids." My kids. He liked the sound of it, though it wasn't technically true.

"Whatsa matter, Larsen, you getting soft on us?" one of the other guys hooted. He'd obviously already knocked back several. Runt Hagarty was one of the few men on the team Rich had never warmed up to, and he circled Rich like a bantam rooster sizing up a rival. "Hoo-ie, I don't see no apron, but somebody sure got you tied up with them strings."

"Knock it off, Hagarty. Larsen's doing his sister a big favor. Takes a real man to take on two kids he didn't even know before last week." Captain Thibodeaux stood in the doorway, a sweating can of beer in one hand, his red beret in the other.

Hagarty snapped to attention, and Thibodeaux dismissed him with a jerk of his head.

Rich didn't know what to do. Should he go home, or stay just to show Hagarty that he was no wimp? Then Rich considered the source. Hagarty was one of the weakest links on the team. One of the guys that still hadn't learned there was more to the job than posturing and swagger. He didn't have to impress that jerk, Rich decided.

"At least, I got something to go home to," Rich said. He pivoted and strode out of the packing shed. He nodded to the captain. "Later," he said.

As he climbed into the truck and started the engine, the irony of the situation struck him. Sure, he had someone to go home to tonight, but then what? Tomorrow, Rebecca would come and take the kids away.

It might have taken most of the week for him to get up to speed, but now that he had, he was going to miss those kids. He checked behind him and backed out of the lot. Hell, he was going to miss their baby-sitter, too.

Of course, Jennifer was still around town. Maybe they could continue to see each other.

Rich hadn't dated much in his ten-year military career. He liked women, but every time he started to get close, he'd find some reason to end it. Even dead, Rick Larsen still screwed up his life. But this time, maybe it would take.

Jennifer Bishop was worth fighting for.

"Darn it. Still damp." Jennifer fingered the front of her dress and tried to gauge the length of time it would take to dry.

More time than she could afford.

It was almost five. Rich could come in at any minute, and the last thing she wanted was for him to find her wearing little else but his blue dress shirt.

She looked at the dark, damp areas on her dress

and shrugged. Her only choice was to iron it. She sighed and went to get the ironing board.

Caitlyn was watching television, and Carter was happily gumming on one of the frozen teething rings. He appeared to be cutting the mate to the lower incisor and the cold ring was apparently soothing. Anything that kept him happy was fine with her. She glanced at Caitlyn again. She just hoped the little girl hadn't established a habit her mother would object to. Jennifer had no idea what kind or how much television her mother would endorse.

At least, *Reading Rainbow* was educational.

Jennifer started to work. She concentrated so hard that Rich had stepped through the door before the sound of his key in the lock registered.

She gasped and nearly dropped the iron.

"What are you doing here?"

Rich looked at her as if she had two heads. "I live here." Then he looked at her as if she were a canteen full of water, and he'd been stranded in the Mojave Desert.

"I borrowed your shirt," she said lamely. "I needed to iron my dress. I hope you don't mind."

He'd rather see her out of the shirt, Rich couldn't help thinking, but he understood how Jennifer might be uncomfortable wearing that slept-in dress. "No problem."

"I didn't expect you home this early. Usually the guys hang around the shop and…socialize." She looked down and seemed to be concentrating on ironing far more than Rich thought necessary.

"Socialize is not exactly the way I'd describe it," he said, his tone dry. He shrugged. "I can take or leave a free beer. Even though Senior Master Sergeant Mullins made Chief, I had a reason to come home, so I left it. I'll buy Tank a six-pack next week.'' Rich peeled out of the heavy BDU shirt and hung it over a chair.

Jennifer looked up, her eyes bright. ''Tank Mullins was always nice to me,'' she said. ''When everything was falling to pieces with Duke, Tank and his wife, Dottie, did everything they could to make it easier. Too bad Duke didn't cooperate. I'm glad Tank got the promotion. Maybe I'll send him a card.''

''I bet he'd like that.'' Rich could not believe that he was making polite conversation when the object of his desire was standing there wearing only his shirt.

She looked a damned sight better in it than he did. And the opening at the side seams of his shirt fell at just the right place to show off legs that would have made a Rockette proud. Rich chuckled. And to think the first time he saw her he'd thought she looked like a Sunday school teacher.

He'd learned otherwise last night.

Last night. That was something they'd have to talk about.

He could tell by the way she was looking everywhere but at him that last night was on her mind, too. He cleared his throat. ''About last night...'' he said.

She didn't respond, but her slight intake of breath demonstrated that she had heard and understood. Did she think he was going to give her the brush-off?

''Look, I know we were sort of impulsive abou—''

She cut him off with an upraised hand. ''Not in

front of the k-i-d-s," she said. "We'll talk about it later."

"Okay. When?"

"Geez, Rich. Do you think you could let me get dressed?" she said, her tone harried, exasperated.

He raised his hands in a conciliatory gesture. "Sure. Anything you want."

"Hey, kids," he said with false joviality to disguise his disappointment at her reaction. "Did you have a good time with Jennifer today?"

Jennifer tried to ignore Rich and the kids. After all, he was on his best behavior today. Just because he'd skipped the beer bust and come right home didn't mean that he'd do it every time. After all, he was responsible for his sister's kids today. Tomorrow they'd be gone.

She smiled as she watched the way he teased Caitlyn's attention away from the television set. And she almost laughed when he swung Carter up out of the playpen and raised him, giggling and squirming, high above his head.

Rich was a natural father.

Too bad he didn't want to be one with her.

Where had that thought come from?

Jennifer tried to distract herself from that thought by using reason.

He had rushed home early because of the kids, not her, she reminded herself. And just the fact that he seemed to want to talk about last night sent a chill of dread shuddering through her. Was he going to reject her? Give her the old, thanks, but-no-thanks routine? She knew she'd been right about him.

Come next week when the kids were back with Rebecca he could go back to being one of the guys.

It was okay, she told herself. She didn't need a guy like him anyway. She'd sworn off military men. She was looking for a nice, safe accountant. Remember?

She repeated the phrase, I don't need him, I don't need him, I don't need him, over and over again like a mantra as she finished pressing the dress dry.

"Ouch!" Darn, she hadn't been watching what she was doing, and she'd burned her finger. She stuck the wounded digit into her mouth to ease the hurt.

Rich looked over his shoulder at her. "That's not the way to do it," he said. "You need to run cold water on it. Or better yet, use ice."

Jennifer rolled her eyes. "I know what to do, Rich. It isn't a serious burn. I'll live."

"O-ka-ay," he said and turned back to the children.

She could have predicted that. He just wanted to play hero by giving first aid. Didn't he know that making silly conversation with two small children made him more of a hero to her than any other macho deed he could do?

The dress was finally dry except for the gathers at the dropped waist. Jennifer sighed. She couldn't iron it forever. She had to take off Rich's shirt and put her own dress back on. Then she had to go home.

She sighed again.

"You all right, Jennifer?"

"I'm fine. Just tired," she lied. She turned off the iron and unplugged it. She waved the garment in the air as she walked to remove any heat left by the iron. Then she entered the room where everything had happened, closed the door and, with a teary sigh, she took off Rich's shirt.

HOW LONG does it take for a woman to get dressed? Rich couldn't help thinking as he bounced Carter on his knee and waited for Jennifer.

He and Jennifer had something to settle. Something that, to Rich, couldn't wait.

He had to make certain that she understood that last night had not been a one-night stand.

At least, not to him.

Rich stopped bouncing, but Carter didn't. He moved his plump little body as if he wanted the ride to keep going. Rich obliged. He didn't have anything else to do.

He couldn't help laughing at the way Carter seemed to enjoy riding his knee. Kids were such simple creatures. Adults were so complex. When, during their development into adults, did everything get so complicated?

The door to Ski's bedroom opened, and Jennifer came out, holding the blue shirt folded over her arm.

"I'll take this home and launder it for you," she said.

"Not necessary," Rich protested. "It's permanent press. I can handle it."

"You shouldn't have to. I wore it." She looked down at it, scraped at a spot, then brushed the residue way. "Carter got strained peas on it." She sighed, long and deep. "I'm tired. I don't want to argue about it. I just want to go home." She turned toward the door.

"Jennifer."

She stopped.

"We still have to talk about last night."

She seemed to sag, but she said nothing for a long moment. She sighed again, the shift of her shoulders demonstrating the depth of the sigh. "There's nothing to say."

Rich put Carter back into the playpen and reached for Jennifer. Though the baby started to whimper, he ignored him. "You may not have anything to say, but I do."

She shrugged off his touch, but she still didn't look at him. "All right," she said slowly, resignedly. "In the kitchen." She draped the shirt over a chair, then turned toward the children and announced. "Your Uncle Rich and I are going to get your supper started." The tone was falsely bright, and Rich wondered what she expected from him.

"Come on," she said. The set of her shoulders was determined, but she didn't face him. He couldn't help wondering why. Jennifer brushed past and hurried to the kitchen.

She was staring into the cupboards as if the kids' supper menu was a monumental decision. She selected a can, put it on the counter, and reached for a pot in the dish drainer. She still hadn't looked his way.

Tired of the cold shoulder, Rich stopped her before she could open the can. She reacted to his touch as if she'd been burned, but she finally stopped looking away. She turned to him, her eyes bright.

"About last night..." she said.

"Look, Jennifer. I'm cool about last night. Maybe we took it a little too far, too soon, but—"

She stopped him with a wave of her hand. "It's all right, Rich. You don't have to feel that you owe me anything. We're both adults. I'm on the Pill. What happened happened. You're off the hook. I know how you special tactics guys are. No commitment." She shrugged. "I was married to one of you, remember? Been there, done that, got the heartbreak. I don't need to go through it again."

She turned back to the soup can.

"Damn it, Jennifer. Look at me," he said harshly.

"No." She kept her face averted. "I helped you out with your sister's kids. It was just the situation. Nothing more. It's over." She brushed past him and into the living room.

"Jennifer. I am nothing like your ex," he snapped.

"Aren't you?" She grabbed the shirt off the back of the chair, snatched up her bag, then yanked open the front door. "I'll wash your shirt and see that you get it back. I was glad to be able to help," she said, her voice strained. "But it's over. Don't call me." Then she stepped outside and closed the door firmly behind her.

Rich stood there wondering what had just happened, her logic was full of holes, but he hadn't been able to come up with a decent rebuttal. The finality of her action shocked him. And maybe he was like her ex. He had lost his temper when she'd told him they were through.

He'd intended to tell Jennifer that even though the kids had brought them together, he still wanted to see her. How had it gone so wrong?

Sure, he wasn't that experienced with women, but had he been so besotted that he'd confused compassion for love?

He didn't think so.

He slammed his hand against the wall. Damn Duke Bishop for hurting her like that. Damn himself for not knowing what to do.

The sound of his fist hitting the plaster must have frightened the kids, for Carter wailed and even Caitlyn started to whimper. Rich shook his throbbing hand and tried to compose himself. For now, his biggest concern was caring for these children. Thank God, he hadn't damaged the wall. The damage to his knuckles was bad enough.

He'd have plenty of time to work it out with Jennifer when things returned to normal.

Rich inhaled and let his breath out slowly. His hand hurt like hell, but not nearly as much as his heart. Maybe it was for the best. Hell, he'd just punched a wall because he hadn't gotten his way. A wall!

What if it had been one of the kids?

God, maybe he really had inherited that violent streak from his father.

What was wrong with him that he couldn't seem to have a normal life like everybody else?

He thought of the brother-in-law he'd never gotten the chance to meet. He thought of Sherry struggling to recover so she could take care of her kids.

Would his life ever be normal?

TEARS BURNED Jennifer's eyes and blurred her vision, but she managed to hold them at bay until she made the short drive home. Saying goodbye to Rich was the hardest thing she'd ever done. But she'd had to.

She pulled in to the carport and sat in the car,

engine idling, unable to make herself go inside. If she went inside, that would make the end final.

But she'd had to be the one to end it, and she'd been right to do it, she told herself. She'd fought so hard to rebuild her self-esteem and dignity after her disastrous marriage to Duke, and she couldn't let another relationship with another man just like him destroy the rest of her self-respect.

She blinked at the tears. She wouldn't cry. She would not cry. A man was a silly reason to weep.

She wouldn't be an appendage again. She would not be there for the convenience of a man who had no respect for her wants and needs. She'd had that, didn't like it, and didn't want it again.

Jennifer turned off the engine, reached for Rich's shirt on the back seat, and got out of the car.

It was over.

It had been nice playing house with Rich. It had been a silly dream pretending that he was the daddy and she was the mommy of those two great kids, but it was over. Reality was that she was a single woman who had to support herself.

She unlocked the door and stepped inside.

The house was dark and damp and stuffy and no childish voices called out to greet her. This was her reality.

She was a single woman, and she lived alone. The only living things that depended on her were a house full of potted plants. Some comfort they were.

Jennifer closed the door.

If she had done the right thing, why then did she feel so bad?

She drew in a deep breath.

Reality stinks.

RICH LOOKED around his empty apartment and wondered how he was going to stand the silence. Rebecca and her new husband had come for the kids. They'd been gone for only a few minutes, but the house already seemed too empty.

He'd become accustomed to Caitlyn's constant chatter and silly television shows and Carter's babbling. Hell, he'd even miss the diapers.

He looked around. The place seemed like a tomb that robbers had found, looted and deserted.

Rich shook his head. He had to stop this fool way of thinking. Ski would be back anytime now and the place would be jumping again.

The place would be loud with Ski's music and... Rich laughed. Hell, it would be loud with Ski's Hawaiian shirts. With Ski around, there was no way he could ever be bored.

Funny, he thought as he searched for one sign that the kids had ever been there, that Jennifer had been there, just having some noise wasn't the same as...

As what?

Having a family?

Rich shook his head. How did he expect to handle having a family? He had no experience in that. He'd never even been involved in a functional one unless he counted his short time with the Parkers. He admired Sherry so much for having the guts to try, but look at what happened to her.

She had gambled and lost. She had expected to spend the rest of her life with Mike, and just when everything had seemed perfect, Mike was gone, taken in the blink of an eye. How could she stand having everything and then losing it?

Somebody had said it was better to have loved and lost than never to have loved at all, but he disagreed, considering the way he felt right now. Then Rich reminded himself that Jennifer wasn't gone forever like Mike.

She was just across town and fighting the same kind of demons as him. If he put his mind to it, he could win her back.

Yeah, he could win her. Hell, he was a special tactics combat controller. He could attack anything and come out victorious if he set his mind to it. Jennifer was just a small woman. He shouldn't have any trouble winning her.

Of course, Jennifer Bishop wasn't a hostile drop zone. This campaign was going to take special tactics, indeed.

Chapter Fourteen

Jennifer opened her birth control pill compact and started to press out her daily dose. She stopped and looked carefully at the semicircle of pills designated for the rest of the month. She looked again. It couldn't be. How had she managed to skip three days?

She never missed a pill!

She always took one after supper while she watched the six o'clock news.

She shook her head. How, indeed?

With all the excitement in the last few days she had missed her regular routine. She had been late getting home on Wednesday because of Rich. On Thursday, she hadn't come home at all. And last night she'd been so upset that she'd taken a long, soaking bath, then gone straight to bed. Not that she'd been able to sleep for reliving the—

She stopped herself from thinking about it any further. Whatever the reason, she hadn't taken her pills.

What if she were pregnant?

No, she wouldn't think about it. People missed pills from time to time. The directions even explained what to do if you did. She'd only made love that one night with Rich. It would be fine.

Jennifer pressed out the pill for Wednesday and popped it into her mouth. Better late than never.

She still had another week's worth of pills to take. The chances of her being pregnant were slim.

Jennifer closed her eyes and sighed. Rich was a carefree, single guy. He wasn't interested in being a father. Those combat controllers were all the same. Considering that he would have dumped her if she hadn't beaten him to the punch, she knew he wasn't interested in anything permanent.

She'd just have to learn to forget him.

Then she thought about the way he'd made her come alive when he kissed her. And come apart when they'd made love. She was going to have to work pretty hard to forget that.

As if she could.

IT HAD BEEN WEEKS since he'd seen Jennifer, and Rich was no closer to reaching her than he had been the last time he saw her. Rich spent Saturday afternoon washing the week's laundry and thinking about Jennifer. He didn't want to honor her request that they not see each other. He wanted to see her again, and he wanted to know why she wouldn't see him. No way was she the kind of woman to settle for a one-night stand. What they'd had that night had been too right.

Of course, it had everything to do with that jerk she'd been married to. It didn't take a shrink to figure that one out. What he was going to do about it was another question. He'd tried to leave her alone. He'd tried, but staying away was too damned hard.

Letting her come to her senses wasn't working. She was as stubborn a woman as he'd ever seen. He liked that about her, in spite of their current problems. Although, right now, that stubbornness was the biggest stumbling block he faced in getting her back. Not that he'd really had her.

He'd tried calling, but she never answered. He'd even called the office, but he always got that guy, Al. Didn't take a rocket scientist to know she was avoiding him. Probably had Al screening the calls.

Jennifer had already told him that all she did was hunt stuff up on the computer. It wasn't as if she was out on a stakeout or anything. She was dodging him, all right.

Since he'd last seen her, it just seemed as though his world was not as bright without her in it. All the colors seemed shades of gray.

Rich tried everything to divert his thoughts from Jennifer, but nothing worked. He'd spent extra time at the base gym, and he'd run enough miles to qualify for the Iron Man Triathalon. The only thing he was running from was the truth.

He was in love with Jennifer. And since they'd made love, nothing was the same.

Funny how he'd started thinking about things in terms of that date. For the rest of his life—no matter what happened with Jennifer—he'd remember things that way. He'd chronicle his life as before Jennifer and after.

He smiled to himself as he opened the washing machine and started to remove the contents.

A woman at the driers looked up and smiled at him. Did she think his smile had been intended for her? She was tall and model thin, with one of those slender bodies that had once attracted him. "Hi," she said. "I'll be done in a minute." She grabbed a handful of dry clothing and put it on the folding table. "If I don't smooth them out right away everything gets wrinkled and then I have to iron." She made a face.

Rich looked at the cutely wrinkled nose and wondered if that was a come-on and if he should pick up on it. Maybe six weeks ago he would have, but...

He was still hung up on Jennifer. And probably always would be.

He continued unloading his machine, dropping the sheets and towels into the basket so he could carry them all to the dryer in one pass. A flash of pastel caught his eye.

It must have caught hers, too. "You have children?" She sounded disappointed.

He fingered the blanket that Rebecca had missed when she'd stripped his apartment of all evidence that the kids had been there. He started to correct the woman, to explain that he'd only been baby-sitting, but why?

She wasn't the type for him. He liked his women real. Give him one prickly, sexy investigator in schoolmarm clothes any day.

He smiled. "Yeah. Carter," he said huskily. "He's ten months old."

"Bet he's cute like his dad." Why was she still flirting? And why didn't he care?

"Yeah. Looks just like his father," Rich agreed. He did look like Mike, and he was cute. He just wasn't his.

The woman flashed a toothy, photogenic grin and picked up her basket. "See ya."

"Yeah, sure." Rich put the load of wash into the machine she'd just emptied. Had she actually come on to him? If she had, he couldn't have cared less.

He fed the machine the required amount of change, turned it on, and watched as the stuff began to swirl around in the hot air. Once, he would have been on cloud nine that a woman like that had spoken to him, much less flirted.

Why hadn't he taken the bait?

In a word: Jennifer.

In spite of the way she told him not to see her again, in spite of the unreturned phone calls, in spite of his fear of getting involved, he still wanted her. And every day they weren't together seemed emptier than the last.

It might have taken him a long time to realize what he wanted out of life, but now that he had, he was going to move heaven and earth to make it happen.

THANK GOODNESS for Caller ID, Jennifer thought as she stopped watering her plants and listened to the phone ring. She'd had it installed when she and Duke separated. She'd considered taking it out, but now she was glad she hadn't. She glanced at the tiny screen. It was Rich.

She put the watering can down and tugged the lapels of Rich's blue shirt tighter around her. Sure, she'd promised to wash it and return it, but she couldn't let it go. She might not have Rich, but she had something of his.

Maybe that's why she kept it. Had she secretly been hoping he'd come for it? And her?

It was bad enough thinking about Rich Larsen night and day without having to talk to him and prolong the agony. It was bad enough seeing him every night in her dreams. She released her grip on the shirt. Maybe she should return it.

What a mess she was! One minute she was pushing him away, the next wishing he'd come. After all, the only reason he was calling was probably because she hadn't returned his shirt.

She held her breath as the phone rang for the third time. One more ring and the answering machine would pick up. She'd get to listen to his voice, at least. Maybe she was sick for wanting to hear him, but…it had been so long. Hearing his voice as long as she didn't have to answer back was wonderful, exquisite torture.

Jennifer sighed.

She had to admit that Al was getting a little weary of covering for her, but Al was a good guy, and he understood. At least, he said he did. Maybe, if they didn't have voice mail at the office, he wouldn't. Still, she owed him.

The ringing stopped abruptly before the machine could pick up. Relieved and disappointed at the same time, she went back to work. She had to finish watering the plants and get ready for tonight. It was Halloween already.

It was hard to believe that October was over. Where had the time gone?

And then there was the home pregnancy test in the bathroom she hadn't had the nerve to use.

It had been six weeks since she'd seen Rich, and she'd hoped he'd give up by now. Beverly had tried to tell her that it meant Rich was serious, but Jennifer disagreed. It just meant he didn't like losing.

She was a challenge to him. Nothing more. If

she'd give him the time of day, he'd get bored and go away. And considering the phone calls had come less and less often and he hadn't even bothered to leave a message this time, maybe he was finally giving up.

Jennifer sighed. Considering the test she was procrastinating about, maybe she shouldn't be thinking this was a victory.

Maybe it was a false alarm, she told herself. There were plenty of perfectly good reasons why a healthy, young woman might miss her period.

"Darn it, Rich," she muttered as she refilled her watering can. "Why can't you just quit? Do you have to keep torturing me?"

Tomorrow morning she would do it. She would go through with the pregnancy test. Tomorrow she would find out for sure.

RICH PUT DOWN the receiver and drew in a long, gusty sigh. This win-Jennifer-back campaign was proving to take longer than he'd expected. Maybe he should give up. He was man enough to know that a one-sided love affair was destined to failure. But was this thing one-sided?

His gut told him no.

But what the hell did he know about this sort of thing?

He reached to pick up the phone again, but before he could close his fingers over the instrument, it rang. Was this Jennifer calling him back? He knew she had Caller ID; she'd mentioned it once. He knew that she had to know that he was the one who'd been calling her even if he did hang up without leaving a message on her machine.

Maybe she'd changed her mind.

He snatched up the phone. "Jennif—" He stopped in midword. It was someone from the squadron.

Duty called. Jennifer would have to wait.

He had to dress, get his gear together and be at the base right now. He didn't know whether this was a drill or the real thing, but whichever it was, he'd have to push Jennifer Bishop into the back of his mind and get to the business he knew best.

JENNIFER WATCHED the scene unfolding on the evening news with growing horror. Americans were besieged in a small religious compound right in the middle of war-torn Santino in Central America. The protestors chanting slogans had been frightening enough, but when shots had been fired and the minister in charge had reported a bomb threat that had proved to be chillingly real, the danger had been deemed serious enough to send in troops.

She didn't know whether the media had done the naming or the military, but the rescue mission was being called Operation Sunday School. And she didn't need a crystal ball to know where those troops were probably coming from.

Jennifer had been through this several times before, but the difference was that as the wife of a combat controller she'd been in on the wives' grapevine: the unofficial link with what was going on. Now that she was divorced from Duke, she had no pipeline at all. What news was released was strictly on a need-to-know basis, and though she needed to know, the United States Air Force didn't think so.

The silence from Hurlburt Air Force Base was nothing short of deafening.

She hadn't had a call from Rich Larsen in days. And it didn't take a detective to figure out that since the calls had stopped at almost precisely the time the situation in Santino had escalated, Silver Team, Rich's unit, was involved. And so was Rich.

All she could do was watch and hope and pray. Pray that the mission would be accomplished, pray that the men involved would return, and that one man in particular would come home safe. To her.

Jennifer grabbed the remote control and jabbed it off. As if removing the horrible pictures from the screen would do anything toward resolving the situation. Though she could no longer see the terrifying images, the incident was still going on. And somewhere in the middle of it all was the man she loved.

And he might not ever know.

Why hadn't she answered his calls? Why hadn't she opened herself up to him and told him how much he meant to her?

Why hadn't she told him about the new life growing inside her?

Even if he didn't want her, he had the right to know that he was going to be a father.

She did the only thing she could think of. She grabbed up the phone and, in spite of the fact that it was already after normal duty hours, she dialed the squadron.

The phone rang and rang, but Jennifer persisted. Someone was there. Had to be. If only a low-ranking admin clerk to answer the phone. And that admin clerk would surely know a great deal more than she did.

Finally after enough rings that she'd stopped counting, a man answered.

Jennifer didn't catch the name, but she plowed ahead before she lost her nerve. "May I speak to TSgt. Larsen, please," she asked, masking her panic with forced politeness.

"TSgt. Larsen is TDY," the voice answered.

"May I ask where he is and when he'll be back?" Jennifer pressed, her voice quaking, her mind certain she already knew.

"I'm sorry, ma'am, I am not at liberty to release that information," the disembodied voice told her.

In other words, Jennifer thought, *If I tell you, I'd have to kill you.* It was the standard response she'd gotten from Duke whenever classified information was concerned.

"Thank you," Jennifer murmured, but she slammed the receiver down. *For nothing,* she didn't say. The man might not have told her anything, but he'd given her what she needed to know. Rich was there. The father of her unborn child was in harm's way.

Her eyes burned with unshed tears, but she wouldn't cry, not yet. She had one more call to make. She swallowed a lump in her throat the size of a watermelon and punched autodial. Beverly would have news. Beverly would tell her what she needed to know.

Beverly didn't answer.

Then she remembered. Beverly and Nick had gone home to Minnesota to show off baby Nicole to their families. At least Nick would be safe.

Jennifer put down the phone and turned the television back on and tuned in the all-news channel. If she couldn't learn anything from official sources, maybe she could glean something from the cable news reports.

Her eyes streaming with tears, she watched as the fate of her child's father seemed to be unfolding on the screen before her.

She'd done what she thought was right for her, for her wounded heart, but had she? All she'd done was drive Rich away. And now that she knew she loved him and knew that she was carrying his child, he was gone.

RICH LARSEN climbed down the ladder from the C-130 transport plane, exhausted, grimy, but triumphant. Score another one for the good guys, he couldn't help thinking. And score one for him.

He'd managed to go almost a week without thinking about Jennifer Bishop. Then his jubilation faltered. Till now. He'd been back on home soil ten seconds, and she had already barged right back into the front of his mind.

So much for Plan A. He'd figured that participating in Operation Sunday School would help him get his thinking back into perspective. That it would take his mind off Jennifer. Fat chance.

She might have been out of his thoughts while he was busy saving that one corner of the world, but now that he was back, there she was, in glorious living color, in his daydreams. He was going to have to do something about it. He was going to have to shift to Plan B.

Too bad he didn't have a Plan B. He'd been so certain that Plan A would work, he hadn't bothered to make one.

He shrugged. Maybe he didn't have a new plan,

but he did have time to think about it. As soon as his equipment was stowed, as soon as he and the team had been debriefed, he was on leave. Two glorious weeks of leave.

Two weeks to help Sherry get settled back into the little house on Smith Street. Two weeks to play with Caitlyn and Carter. Two weeks to figure out just how to make Jennifer Bishop his.

Forever.

JENNIFER LISTENED as the phone rang and rang and rang. Then it connected. She knew better than to speak, she'd been through this, at least a dozen times before. She'd only get the answering machine. She'd called the minute she'd heard that the team was back, and when no one had answered, she'd even left a message.

As the phone stopped ringing and went into answer mode, she listened to the beeps before the message came on. There were ten. At least. And probably a good half of them were from her. Why hadn't Rich returned her calls?

There were two reasons she could think of for Rich not calling her, and she didn't like either. One was that Rich didn't want to talk to her. The other was that Rich was one of the few casualties produced by the operation. Though the media had reported that casualties were light, they hadn't reported who, pending notification of next of kin.

God, should she call Sherry?

No, no, she couldn't think of that. She wouldn't. Surely, if something had happened to Rich she'd have heard by now. Nick would have been called back from Minnesota and Beverly would have called her. That meant that the first possibility was probably the real one.

Rich didn't want to talk to her.

RICH SAT on the couch and waited while Sherry checked on Carter, not yet awake from his nap. He resisted the urge to help and watched as she slowly walked across the room. She'd made so much progress. No longer limited by the wheelchair, she moved around with the help of two sturdy canes.

"What do you think, big brother? Am I ready to run a marathon?" Sherry lowered herself to sit beside him.

Two pink scars marred her forehead where the halo had been attached. Otherwise, it would have been hard to tell the ordeal she'd been through. Her face was flushed with excitement, or maybe the exertion, but whatever the reason, she seemed well pleased with herself.

"Give yourself a week or two to train, and you'll be in there." Rich grinned. He liked seeing the sister he remembered from when they were kids. Even her sense of humor had returned. He chuckled to himself. He'd always been the serious one.

"Seriously, Bro," Sherry said. "I should be almost good as new in time for Thanksgiving."

"Yeah." Rich wondered what she could feel thankful for. She'd lost her husband. Hell, she had to depend on him and Rebecca for almost everything.

"I can see that question in your eyes, Rich," Sherry said. "I have much to be grateful for. I have my kids. The doctor tells me I'll be able to do almost everything I could before..." She grinned. "Except, maybe, skydiving."

"You skydive?"

Sherry laughed. "Fooled you! Of course I didn't skydive, but I could have." She grinned again. "I don't consider not being able to do it much of a loss.

"Seriously. I won't be able to do much heavy lifting, so I guess a career in weightlifting is out, too." She reached over, took his hand and squeezed. "You know what I have to be most thankful for?"

Rich shook his head. Sherry's hand felt so warm and reassuring, but he couldn't imagine why she'd give thanks.

"You," she said simply. "I was angry with you for so long, and I didn't even try to find you until…until Mike talked me into it. And then you came looking for me right when I needed you most. How's that for fate?" Sherry took in a deep, slow breath, then exhaled. "Yes, I miss Mike desperately, and I always will. But I also have my memories. And our children." She drew Rich's hand up to her face and pressed a kiss to the back of his hand. Then she let go.

Overwhelmed at what Sherry had just said, Rich stroked her cheek. Something hot blurred his vision, and he looked away. He blinked to clear his eyes, but they just filled again. After having no one to care about him for so long, Sherry's sentiments touched him deeply. How should he respond to something like that?

He sucked in a deep breath and held it. Then he let it out. "How did you do it?" he finally asked, his voice tight, his face averted. "How did you get the nerve to try?"

"Try what?"

"To have the whole nine yards. You know, a family. After what we had—our parents—weren't you afraid?''

Sherry pulled him around to face her. ''Afraid of what? That history would repeat itself?''

''Yeah,'' Rich answered thickly. He shrugged and sighed. ''Maybe you could risk it. You don't look like...him.''

''Are you really worried about that?''

''Well, yeah. God, Sherry, all I have to do is look in the mirror.''

''Rich, Daddy was a sick man. I didn't know it then, but after I studied it in school, I figured it out. He suffered from Post Traumatic Stress Disorder from Vietnam, and that made him drink. PTSD made him scared and dredged up all those bad feelings he hadn't been able to deal with. He drank for courage, but it made him mean. He drank to forget. Only sometimes he forgot everything else, too. He couldn't help it.''

She paused and took a breath. ''PTSD is not something that can be passed on like blue eyes or the color of your hair. It happened to Daddy because he wasn't prepared for Vietnam. War did that to him, not heredity.''

''Yeah, but I play war every day,'' he responded tiredly. ''I could find myself in the same situation.''

''Have you, so far? Rich, you just came back from an awful situation, did it turn you to drink?'' Sherry shook her head. ''What happened to Daddy was a tragedy. They took a young man, a farm boy out of rural Florida, showed him how to use a rifle, yanked him up out of the States one day, and dropped him down into a rice paddy the next. He wasn't prepared for it. They do it differently now.''

She looked at him. "You should know. Don't they give you all sorts of training?"

Rich breathed deeply. "Yeah, I suppose they do." He'd been through all kinds of testing and training before he'd been formally accepted into his elite unit. He'd spent almost as much time in classes as he had on the obstacle course. Maybe he was more prepared.

He held Sherry's hand and looked down into pale blue eyes that were so much like his own. "How did you get so smart? Do you think…?"

"Oh, Rich." Sherry shook her head and smiled. "I only had to see you dancing with Caitlyn at Rebecca's wedding." She paused. "Carter took to you like…" She didn't finish, but Rich knew what she was trying to say.

"Don't let our sorry childhood keep you from making your own happy ending." She smiled again. "Don't deny yourself one of the greatest pleasures of life because of our bad luck. You're a natural daddy, Rich. You deserve it all."

Rich couldn't have felt happier if he'd won the Florida State Lottery. Sherry had told him that he could do it, and if she thought so, maybe he could. Now, all he had to do was convince Jennifer.

Chapter Fifteen

Rich hung up the phone, then turned to Sherry who was playing peekaboo with Carter. Though she tired easily, she was getting around well, and Rich was beginning to feel like a fifth wheel under foot in her house. So, he'd herded her and the kids into her minivan and taken them for a ride and ended up at his apartment. It might have seemed silly to anyone else, but he enjoyed being able to entertain her in his apartment. It was a simple pleasure he'd never thought he'd have.

He loved being with the kids again, and he'd enjoyed getting the chance to know his sister as a fully developed adult. He glanced at Caitlyn, quietly playing with a sticker book, and smiled. He hadn't ruined her with the steady diet of videotapes and children's television.

''She wouldn't talk to me,'' Rich said as he paced the room and tried to figure out what to do next. ''You heard it. She wouldn't answer. I know she was there. I know she was.'' Sherry was planning a huge Thanksgiving dinner, and she'd asked him to invite Jennifer.

Considering he'd spent the better part of the week

trying to come up with a workable Plan B, Sherry's dinner party seemed like the best way to break the ice.

If only Jennifer would answer the phone.

"Why didn't you leave a message?" Sherry challenged.

Rich shrugged. "I guess I wanted to speak to her directly. Hell, I want to speak to her face-to-face, but I doubt she'd let me get close enough to hear what I have to say. So, now what do I do?"

Sherry didn't respond, but Rich could see her thinking. He snapped his fingers in front of her face. "Hey, Sis. Are you there?"

"Hush," she hissed, waving him away. "I'm thinking." She closed her eyes, then grinned. "I've got it," she announced after a long minute.

"What?"

"You have to play hard to get."

He looked at her beaming face and couldn't help frowning. "Huh?"

"You know, absence makes the heart grow fonder?"

"Yeah. So?"

"Just trust me, big brother. I know what I'm doing." She covered her face with her hands and then moved them quickly away. Carter chuckled in the husky, throaty voice that Rich loved to hear. "From today on, I want you to pretend you never met Jennifer Bishop and leave everything up to me. No phone calls, no letters, nothing."

"What's that going to accomplish?"

"Trust me, big brother. It'll work."

Rich had to admit to himself that his campaign

hadn't been working, but he sure didn't like it that Sherry was keeping him out of the loop.

"Don't worry, Uncle Witch," Caitlyn said, looking up from her stickers. "Mom and I will make Jen'fer come. And then I can get to wear my weddy dwess again."

"Huh?" What did the dress have to do with anything?

"I said she could wear it for special occasions, and a big, family Thanksgiving dinner qualifies," Sherry explained, looking over Carter's fuzzy head at Rich's frown.

"Well, let's go," he said shrugging. "If we don't get moving, Carter'll fall asleep in the car again."

Rich liked his interpretation better, he thought as he hustled everybody out the door. If Jennifer would come, maybe Caitlyn would get to be a flower girl again.

THE WEATHER seemed more like spring than late November, and Jennifer was hot and sticky as she took the pumpkin pie out of the oven. She was having a hard time working herself up into a festive mood, and being uncomfortable didn't help. She'd offered to bring something to Sherry's, and she wasn't going to back out just because the weather had turned decidedly un-November-like, even for Florida.

Jennifer wasn't sure she should have accepted Sherry's invitation to Thanksgiving dinner, but she'd really had no other choice except to be rude and refuse. And Sherry had assured her that inviting the people who had helped out while she was laid up had been her idea, not Rich's. She couldn't help wishing that it had been Rich's idea. That would mean he still cared.

Rich had been avoiding her, or so it seemed. Though Nick had assured her that Rich had been part of Operation Sunday School, and the invitation from Sherry had eased her fears that Rich had been a casualty in the mission, she'd still been unsuccessful in getting in touch with Rich by phone. The one time she'd gotten an answer at Rich's apartment she had spoken to Ski and he'd sounded pretty evasive. Finally, she'd given up.

Obviously, the invitation had been all Sherry's idea and not Rich's.

After pestering her to death all that time, it irked her to no end that he'd suddenly decided to play coy. Or had he finally lost interest as she'd known he would?

Even if he wasn't interested in her anymore, he had a right to know he was going to be a father. And if she couldn't get him on the phone, then she'd have to ambush him at Sherry's.

Jennifer wasn't naive enough to think that he'd want to be a part of the baby's life. Or hers. But she wasn't going to keep it from him.

What he did from that point on was up to him.

Jennifer looked in the mirror and sighed. Maybe, on the outside it didn't show, but she felt very pregnant. Her breasts were tender and felt even more generous than they already were. And the last thing she wanted to do today was drive all the way to Pensacola and behave as if everything was peachy when she felt like a fallen woman.

She stepped back and gave herself the once-over

in the full-length mirror. At least she didn't look like one.

No way would Rich suspect.

But she would tell him.

By midnight, she'd know whether she was going to go through this alone.

By the time the clock struck twelve, she'd either be a princess with a Prince Charming, or she'd be prepared to swell up like a pumpkin all by herself.

RICH PEERED OUT the living room window with the eagerness of a child waiting for Santa. "Are you sure she said she'd come, Sherry?"

Sherry laughed. "Didn't Mama always tell us that 'the watched pot doesn't boil'? She's going to be here. Now, sit down before I find something for you to do."

"I'm not watching a pot," Rich replied irritably. "I'm going out of my gourd." He turned away from the window. "Give me something to do. I'll pluck the turkey, chop wood. Anything to keep from twiddling my thumbs and waiting."

"You must be in love," Sherry muttered.

"That's no secret. Except to Jennifer. I don't know why I let you talk me into playing hard to get. She probably thinks I hate her." Not calling her for the past few weeks had been the hardest thing he'd ever done.

"Well, today will be your chance to set her straight. Just make sure you don't blow it." Sherry opened a drawer in the china cabinet. "Stop pacing, Rich. You're making me a wreck." Sherry gestured toward the open drawer. "The silverware is in here. Set the table."

"But—"

"You've been driving me crazy all day. You said you wanted something to do, so go set the table. I have to baste the turkey."

Rich wasn't sure about this plan of Sherry's, but at least Jennifer had agreed to come. He just hoped she wouldn't back out at the last minute.

JENNIFER PULLED UP in front of the house in the quiet Pensacola neighborhood and came to a halt behind Rich's black pickup truck. Relief surged through her. He's here.

Taking a moment to compose herself, she looked at the little house. The lawn had been cut, and a row of potted chrysanthemums brightened the tiny front porch. What a difference from that first time when she and Rich had seen it looking so sad and neglected! It looked lived in now.

Of course, Sherry's husband was gone, but she was so blessed to have his children. In spite of her tension, Jennifer smiled.

Those brave, yellow mums seemed to promise that everything would be all right. They almost shouted that life would go on, no matter what.

Jennifer looked at the row of cheerful flowers, and she had to think that she and Rich would work it out.

She turned the key, and the engine rumbled down. She looked down at the dark grease she couldn't get out of the ridges of her fingertips, and hoped what she remembered about cars was right. At one time, she'd regretted taking auto shop because she'd met Duke there, but if her plan worked out today, that class would have been worth it.

In case she didn't get a chance to talk to Rich,

she'd made sure she'd get time alone with him on the way home.

Taking in a deep breath for courage, Jennifer pushed open the car door and stepped outside.

The front door to the house flew open, and Caitlyn, wearing the yellow organza flower girl dress, came running. "I been waiting for you," she announced as she skidded to a halt at the curb. "Look, Mommy said I could wear my weddy dwess 'cause it's a special 'casion." She pirouetted. "Don't I look beautiful?"

Leave it to Caitlyn to ease the tension. Jennifer gathered her close and squeezed her in a bear hug. "Oh, I have missed you, you sweet thing. And you are the prettiest girl in the world." She smiled. "I can't wait to get my hands on that cute little brother of yours and hug him, too."

Hoping to catch a glimpse of Rich, Jennifer looked over Caitlyn's head toward the house. She knew he was there. The truck hadn't driven itself, but she didn't see him. Her eyes misted, but she blinked back the moisture. He was probably helping Sherry keep Carter amused. "Why don't you take my pocket book so I can bring in the pie?" She handed it to Caitlyn who scampered ahead.

Now that she was here, Jennifer couldn't help thinking everything would work out. If Sherry could pull herself together, so could she. She opened the passenger side door and picked up the cardboard box containing the pie.

"Come on, Jen'fer. Hurry up. We're all hungry," Caitlyn called from the front door.

Jennifer hurried, not because of what Caitlyn said, but because of her own agenda.

She was greeted with the rich aroma of turkey and

spices and yeasty bread. Her heart lifted. The festive mood she hadn't been able to find earlier appeared. She spotted Rich, belly down on the floor, playing with Carter, and her spirits soared higher.

Then Rich got up and left the room.

That hurt worse than not finding him waiting for her, but she wasn't going to jump to conclusions. He probably had something to do for Sherry.

Jennifer pasted a bright smile on her face and carried the pie into the kitchen where Sherry was cooking, surrounded by clouds of aromatic steam. Rich wasn't there.

Determined not to let the slight get to her, Jennifer chatted with Sherry about nothing in particular. By the time she'd exhausted all the safe topics, Rich came in through the back door, a greasy rag in his hands.

He must have been surprised to see her there, for he stopped short. He smiled, and the room seemed to fill with light. "Glad you could come," he said. Then he went to the sink and washed his hands as if she weren't there.

He turned to Sherry. "Let's get this show on the road. I'm starved."

SITTING THROUGH dinner and making polite conversation as if his life didn't depend on it was a damned sight harder than storming a radar site on some god-forsaken island, Rich couldn't help thinking. And trying to avoid Jennifer had been even harder, considering how small Sherry's house was.

He'd wanted to corner Jennifer somewhere and tell her he loved her and demand that she marry him, but he wanted to do it with some finesse. He wanted to make it a little romantic. He didn't want an audience.

And if he could just hold out for another hour, he'd be able to complete Operation Jennifer.

Jennifer sat across from him and just next to Sherry. Feeling her eyes on him had made avoiding her all the harder for Rich. Why was Sherry insisting that he continue this stupid charade? It was one thing not to call, but something else to ignore the woman he loved when he was sitting across the table from her.

Having Jennifer so close had all but ruined his appetite. Though his stomach was in knots, he forced himself to eat. As long as he kept his eyes on his plate it wasn't too hard.

Finally the endless meal was over.

"Would you like some pumpkin pie, Rich?" Sherry passed a piece to Tom. "Jennifer made it."

"I don't like pies made out of jack-o'-lanterns," Caitlyn announced. "Just give me some whipped cream."

Sherry looked sternly at her daughter. "Caitlyn," she said, her expression disapproving. "Jennifer made this just for us. It's rude not to try it."

Funny how his appetite had just picked up. Rich started to say he'd eat Caitlyn's, but she interrupted.

"I said I would try the whipped cream. That's p'lite, wight?"

Jennifer struggled to conceal a smile. Even Sherry's mouth twitched.

"I tell you what, Caitlyn. You and I can share a piece. I don't really like whipped cream that much." Rich glanced at Sherry. "Will that work?"

Sherry laughed. "Sure, Uncle Rich. Undo all the hard work I've done to keep this child from growing up a heathen." She sliced the pie, heaped on a generous portion of whipped cream, and gave it to Jennifer to pass to Rich.

This was the closest he'd come to her all day, though he'd seen the simmering glances that she had been sending his way when she thought no one was looking. Covert tactics were his specialty; he'd noticed. Those looks were all that had kept him going.

Making sure their fingers touched, he took the pie from Jennifer, and he felt the sizzle of awareness arcing through them. The current was too strong to be one way.

He glanced at the grandfather clock above Sherry's head. It was almost four o'clock. Soon it would be dark, and once darkness fell, he could resume working on Operation Jennifer.

"Hey, Uncle Witch. You're holding my whipped cream." Caitlyn stood at his elbow, her hands on her hips.

How long had he and Jennifer been holding hands in the guise of passing a piece of pie? It didn't matter to Rich how long he hovered there, it didn't matter if everyone knew how he felt about Jennifer as long as Jennifer knew.

Reluctantly, he took the plate and placed it in front of him, lifted Caitlyn to his lap and indulgently watched as his niece scraped all the topping off his dessert.

He didn't care about pie. If everything worked out, dessert, for him, would come later.

REBBECA AND TOM were the first to leave. Newlyweds, they couldn't wait to be alone, Jennifer supposed.

Carter had already been put to bed, and Caitlyn

and Rich were sprawled on the floor playing a cut-throat game of Chutes and Ladders. Why she had ever thought that he wouldn't be good father—correction, husband—material was beyond her. And if her ESP was working as well as she thought it was, he had come to believe it, too.

She'd stayed later than she'd planned, but she tired easily now, and there was still that long drive home to Fort Walton Beach. At least, if her plan worked, she wouldn't be going alone.

Jennifer went to the kitchen to collect her empty pie plate then returned to the family group in the living room. Her heart swelled as she looked at Rich playing with Caitlyn. Someday that scene would be hers.

"Bye, Caitlyn," Jennifer called as she found her purse on the coat tree. She hugged Sherry and turned.

"Aren't you gonna say goodbye to me," Rich said, looking up from the game.

Oops. Jennifer smiled and covered her mistake. "Sorry, I thought you were too busy with your game to notice."

"Oh, I always notice," Rich said, and Jennifer flushed with joy.

She almost didn't know how to respond to that. She turned to Sherry one more time. "Thank you for inviting me. I had a wonderful time."

Jennifer stepped out into the night, cooler now that the sun had gone down, and took a deep breath of the evening air. Then she hurried to her car.

It was time to get on with the rest of The Plan.

RICH WASN'T SURPRISED when Jennifer came back to the door, breathlessly explaining that her car wouldn't start. He hadn't heard the engine over Caitlyn's gloating cries as she won another game.

"What's wrong?" he asked as he pushed himself up off the floor and wiped his sweating hands on his jeans.

Jennifer shrugged. "I don't know what's wrong. It just won't start."

Rich turned to the coat tree and grabbed his jacket. "I guess I could take a look."

"I'd really appreciate it," Jennifer said and stepped back outside.

Rich turned to Sherry and winked. Operation Jennifer was underway. He followed her outside.

She already had the hood up, but it didn't look like she'd done anything. "I'm not sure I know what to look for," Jennifer said.

Rich aimed a light on the engine, letting the beam play over the parts for effect. He knew what was wrong.

"I don't see anything. Maybe, you just flooded it. You said you had a good battery?"

Jennifer drew in a deep breath, looked toward the sky, and crossed her fingers. "It's the one that came with the car. It's been slow to start in the mornings, but it got me all the way here just fine." She hated playing dumb, but if her plan worked, it was worth it. "Can you fix it?"

Rich stepped back. "Sure, I can fix it. But not tonight. I don't have the right equipment here."

Jennifer managed a crestfallen expression, though she was cheering inside. "Oh, no. You mean, I'm stranded."

Rich took in a deep breath, then let it out. "No. It just happens I'm going the same way."

THE FIFTY-ONE-point-seven miles between Sherry's and Jennifer's houses might as well have been a thousand. Finally, they passed the gate in front of Hurlburt Air Force Base. Just a few more minutes and they could talk.

Rich drew in a deep, relieved breath. If he had to wait much longer, he just might explode.

"I really appreciate you going out of your way to bring me home," Jennifer said.

"No problem," he said tersely. He had so much to say, but sitting in a cramped four-wheel-drive pickup wasn't the place to say it.

"Turn here," Jennifer said. "I forgot that you'd never been to my house before."

He had, but he wouldn't tell her that. On one particularly torturous night he'd driven down her street with the intention of beating her door down, tossing her over his shoulder and carrying her to the nearest justice of the peace. Only a man walking his dog kept him from it.

"Now what?" It was damned hard playing like he hadn't been here, but he had to make this look good.

"Make a left here, and it's the third house on the right."

Rich pulled up in front of the neat little rancher. She'd left the carport light on, and it beckoned him. He drew in a deep breath, then exhaled slowly.

"Would you like to come in?"

Rich glanced across the seat. Jennifer held that pie plate as if it were a shield. What if he'd read her wrong?

He swallowed. "Sure. Maybe you could offer me a cup of coffee?"

Her eyes lit up like an airport search light. "That's the least I could do. Come on in." She pushed open the door and scrambled down.

Rich caught her by the elbow as she pushed open the back door. "Jennifer, I have a confession to make."

She didn't shrug him off, and she let him hold her arm as she stepped inside and flipped on the light. She turned to face him. Her expression was eager, hopeful. "Yes?" Her voice was breathless.

Rich closed the door behind them, and they stood face-to-face in front of it. "I don't want any coffee."

She swallowed. "Is that it?"

"What?"

"Your confession. You don't want coffee?" She gnawed uncertainly at her lower lip, and Rich wanted so much to kiss it.

"No," he said, then swallowed. "There was nothing wrong with your car." He reached into his jacket pocket and produced a handful of greasy wires loosely wrapped in paper towels. "I sabotaged it so you'd ride home with me."

The look on her face was priceless. "I don't be— You didn— I—" She stopped trying to talk and went into another room. When she turned on the light, Rich could see it was the kitchen.

He followed, wondering what she was thinking. Please don't let her be mad, he prayed silently.

Jennifer reached into a drawer, then handed him a cellophane-wrapped four-pack of chewable antacid tablets. One roll was missing. "I have a confession of my own," she said. "I killed the battery by neutralizing the acid. I wanted us to be alone." She paused, took a deep breath, exhaled, then went on. "We have to talk."

Rich laid his greasy bundle on the counter. He took Jennifer's hands and covered them with his. "I was a little slow coming to it, but I guess it's better late than never. I love you, and I want—"

She stopped him with her fingers to his lips. He kissed them, and took her into his arms. "I wan—"

Jennifer wanted so much to hear the rest, but until he knew the whole story, she wouldn't let him go on. "Rich, if you're going to say what I think you are, you'll make me the happiest woman in the world. But first, you need to know something."

She hated the panic on his face, the wariness in his eyes. "I hope it's good news," she continued. "It is to me, but you might think otherwise...."

He stopped her. "Nothing you can say would be bad unless it's that you don't love me."

She shook her head. "Please, Rich. This is hard for me. Let me get it out."

"All right," he said slowly. "Let me have it." He drew in a deep breath as if he were bracing himself.

"Remember when I fell asleep, and you put me in Ski's bed?"

He nodded.

"And we made love."

He nodded again. "How could I forget?"

"I told you I was on the Pill."

"Yeah."

"I missed a few."

"Yeah, and...?"

"They don't work that well if you don't take them."

Rich stared at her as if she were one of the Seven Wonders. His eyes grew bright, and he turned away.

Had she misread him? Was that a look of dismay? "You mean...? You're...?"

She nodded.

His gaze shifted to her still-flat stomach. "Hoo-ah!" he said softly, an expression of wonder on his face. Then he broke into a wide grin. He opened the back door and shouted into the night. "Hoo-ah!" for anyone to hear.

Then he closed the door and gathered her into his arms. "We're going to have a baby?"

Jennifer smiled and nodded against his broad, solid chest. She felt the beat of his heart against her cheek, and it felt so good to be in his arms.

Rich held her for a long time, then he had to speak. "You know, I wasn't sure I was worthy of a wife, a family, happiness. I was so sure I was just going to turn out like my dad that I was afraid to try."

She brushed her fingers against his lips, but he pushed her hand away. Sherry had told her a little about it at the wedding, but it would be good to hear it from Rich.

"You could probably guess, considering our life in foster care, that Sherry and I didn't have the greatest childhood," he said, pausing as if he didn't know how to go on. He drew a deep breath, let it out, swallowed, then went on. "My dad was a drunk, and when he drank, he wasn't a lot of fun to be around. He beat my mom, he beat us and generally made life miserable for the three of us. Oh, Mom tried, but she was already sick, and Dad was too far gone to help...."

Jennifer wanted to stop him, to keep him from

having to admit all this, but she knew that it would help him to actually say it out loud. Sherry had hinted at some of it, but she sensed there was more. "It's all right, Rich. It wasn't your fault."

"Yeah," he said huskily. "I know that now. But kids are funny. They think everything is centered around them. When stuff is good, it's because of them, and when stuff is bad, it's their fault, too." He stopped and shook his head. "And I had another strike against me. I look like my dad. At least, what he looked like before he got so far gone." He drew in another breath and ran a shaky hand through his hair. "I thought if I looked like him, then I must be destined to be like him, too.

"And I couldn't bear the thought of inflicting that on any other woman, any other kid." He stopped, his voice tight, choked.

"You don't believe that anymore, do you?" Jennifer asked, her voice barely above a whisper.

Rich smiled and shook his head. "No, after spending all that time with the kids, I started to believe, and then I talked to Sherry about it. She set me straight. She's pretty smart for a little sister," he said, his smile quirking wider.

Jennifer took the smile as a good sign and answered it with one of her own. "You're not the only person who had to learn a thing or two. Look at me. I was gun-shy, too. I figured that since my ex-husband was in Special Tactics and an immature jerk, that all combat controllers were. Even when I had the truth right in front of me." She drew in a deep breath. "Can you forgive me for lumping you into the same group as Duke Bishop?"

"I'll forgive you under one condition."

Jennifer's breath caught in her throat. "What's that?" she asked, hardly daring to breathe.

"You have to marry me and let me spend the rest of our lives proving you wrong."

Jennifer smiled. "Is that all?"

Rich looked down at her and grinned. "Seems like plenty to me. I'm sentencing you to life."

"That's a pretty long one," Jennifer said. "But since I love you, I think I can tough it out."

"You do? You really do?"

Jennifer looked up at him. After all this, could he still doubt? "Yes, Rich, I really love you, and I intend to spend the rest of our lives showing you just how much."

Rich pulled his jacket off and tossed it high into the air. "Hoo-ah!" he shouted. "I'm the happiest man in the world."

Jennifer just smiled. No one could be happier than she was at that moment. Then she looked at Rich. No one could be happier than both of them.

HARLEQUIN®

AMERICAN *Romance*®

JUDY CHRISTENBERRY

is back
and so are the citizens of Cactus, Texas!
Harlequin American Romance is proud to
present another **Tots for Texans** story.

STRUCK BY THE TEXAS
MATCHMAKERS
June 2001

Dr. Jeff Hausen came to Cactus, Texas, to get away from the harshness of big-city life. Diane Peters returned to her hometown with a law degree under her belt and the hopes of one day settling in the big city. But when the two met, the sparks flew.... And with *a lot* of help from the Texas matchmakers, wedding bells might soon be ringing!

Available wherever Harlequin books are sold.

HARLEQUIN®

Makes any time special ®

Visit us at www.eHarlequin.com   HARTOTS2

Meet 50 loving dads in

babies
& BACHELORS USA

Take 4 FREE BOOKS,
Plus get a FREE GIFT!

Babies & Bachelors USA is a heartwarming new collection of reissued novels featuring 50 sexy heroes from every state who experience the ups and downs of fatherhood and find time for love all the same. All of the books, hand-picked by our editors, are outstanding romances by some of the world's bestselling authors, including Stella Bagwell, Kristine Rolofson, Judith Arnold and Marie Ferrarella!

Don't delay, order today! Call customer service at
1-800-873-8635.
Or
Clip this page and mail to The Reader Service:

In U.S.A.
P.O. Box 9049
Buffalo, NY
14269-9049

In CANADA
P.O. Box 616
Fort Erie, Ontario
L2A 5X3

YES! Please send me four FREE BOOKS and FREE GIFT along with the next four novels on a 14-day free home preview. If I like the books and decide to keep them, I'll pay just $15.96* U.S. or $18.00* CAN., and there's no charge for shipping and handling. Otherwise, I'll keep the 4 FREE BOOKS and FREE GIFT and return the rest. If I decide to continue, I'll receive six books each month—two of which are always free—until I've received the entire collection. In other words, if I collect all 50 volumes, I will have paid for 32 and received 18 absolutely free!

267 HCK 4537
467 HCK 4538

Name	(Please Print)		
Address		Apt. #	
City	State/Prov.	Zip/Postal Code	

* Terms and prices subject to change without notice.
  Sales Tax applicable in N.Y. Canadian residents will be charged applicable provincial taxes and GST. All orders are subject to approval.

DIRBAB02

© 2000 Harlequin Enterprises Limited

 HARLEQUIN®

makes any time special—online...

eHARLEQUIN.com

your romantic escapes

—Indulgences—

♥ Monthly guides to indulging yourself, such as:
  ★ Tub Time: A guide for bathing beauties
  ★ Magic Massages: A treat for tired feet

—Horoscopes—

♥ Find your daily Passionscope, weekly Lovescopes and Erotiscopes

♥ Try our compatibility game

—Reel Love—

♥ Read all the latest romantic movie reviews

—Royal Romance—

♥ Get the latest scoop on your favorite royal romances

—Romantic Travel—

♥ For the most romantic destinations, hotels and travel activities

All this and more available at
www.eHarlequin.com
on Women.com Networks

HINTE1R

USA Today bestselling author

STELLA CAMERON

and popular American Romance author

MURIEL JENSEN

come together in a special
Harlequin 2-in-1 collection.

Look for

Shadows and *Daddy in Demand*

On sale June 2001

HARLEQUIN®
Makes any time special®

Visit us at www.eHarlequin.com

PHAR

Harlequin truly does make any time special. . . . This year we are celebrating weddings in style!

A Walk Down the Aisle
WEDDING CELEBRATION

To help us celebrate, we want you to tell us how wearing the Harlequin wedding gown will make your wedding day special. As the grand prize, Harlequin will offer one lucky bride the chance to **"Walk Down the Aisle" in the Harlequin wedding gown!**

There's more...

For her honeymoon, she and her groom will spend five nights at the **Hyatt Regency Maui.** As part of this five-night honeymoon at the hotel renowned for its romantic attractions, the couple will enjoy a candlelit dinner for two in Swan Court, a sunset sail on the hotel's catamaran, and duet spa treatments.

MAUI *the Magic Isles*™

A HYATT RESORT AND SPA ®   Maui • Molokai • Lanai

To enter, please write, in, 250 words or less, how wearing the Harlequin wedding gown will make your wedding day special. The entry will be judged based on its emotionally compelling nature, its originality and creativity, and its sincerity. This contest is open to Canadian and U.S. residents only and to those who are 18 years of age and older. There is no purchase necessary to enter. Void where prohibited. See further contest rules attached. Please send your entry to:

Walk Down the Aisle Contest

In Canada
P.O. Box 637
Fort Erie, Ontario
L2A 5X3

In U.S.A.
P.O. Box 9076
3010 Walden Ave.
Buffalo, NY 14269-9076

You can also enter by visiting www.eHarlequin.com
Win the Harlequin wedding gown and the vacation of a lifetime!
The deadline for entries is October 1, 2001.

HARLEQUIN®
Makes any time special ®

PHWDACONT1

HARLEQUIN WALK DOWN THE AISLE TO MAUI CONTEST 1197
OFFICIAL RULES
NO PURCHASE NECESSARY TO ENTER

1. To enter, follow directions published in the offer to which you are responding. Contest begins April 2, 2001, and ends on October 1, 2001. Method of entry may vary. Mailed entries must be postmarked by October 1, 2001, and received by October 8, 2001.

2. Contest may be, at times, presented via the Internet, but will be restricted solely to residents of certain geographic areas that are disclosed on the Web site. To enter via the Internet, if permissible, access the Harlequin Web site (www.eHarlequin.com) and follow the directions displayed online. Online entries must be received by 11:59 p.m. E.S.T. on October 1, 2001.

   In lieu of submitting an entry online, enter by mail by hand-printing (or typing) on an 8½" x 11" plain piece of paper, your name, address (including zip code), Contest number/name and in 250 words or fewer, why winning a Harlequin wedding dress would make your wedding day special. Mail via first-class mail to: Harlequin Walk Down the Aisle Contest 1197, (in the U.S.) P.O. Box 9076, 3010 Walden Avenue, Buffalo, NY 14269-9076, (in Canada) P.O. Box 637, Fort Erie, Ontario L2A 5X3, Canada.

   Limit one entry per person, household address and e-mail address. Online and/or mailed entries received from persons residing in geographic areas in which Internet entry is not permissible will be disqualified.

3. Contests will be judged by a panel of members of the Harlequin editorial, marketing and public relations staff based on the following criteria:

   • Originality and Creativity—50%
   • Emotionally Compelling—25%
   • Sincerity—25%

   In the event of a tie, duplicate prizes will be awarded. Decisions of the judges are final.

4. All entries become the property of Torstar Corp. and will not be returned. No responsibility is assumed for lost, late, illegible, incomplete, inaccurate, nondelivered or misdirected mail or misdirected e-mail, for technical, hardware or software failures of any kind, lost or unavailable network connections, or failed, incomplete, garbled or delayed computer transmission or any human error which may occur in the receipt or processing of the entries in this Contest.

5. Contest open only to residents of the U.S. (except Puerto Rico) and Canada, who are 18 years of age or older, and is void wherever prohibited by law; all applicable laws and regulations apply. Any litigation within the Province of Quebec respecting the conduct or organization of a publicity contest may be submitted to the Régie des alcools, des courses et des jeux for a ruling. Any litigation respecting the awarding of a prize may be submitted to the Régie des alcools, des courses et des jeux only for the purpose of helping the parties reach a settlement. Employees and immediate family members of Torstar Corp. and D. L. Blair, Inc., their affiliates, subsidiaries and all other agencies, entities and persons connected with the use, marketing or conduct of this Contest are not eligible to enter. Taxes on prizes are the sole responsibility of winners. Acceptance of any prize offered constitutes permission to use winner's name, photograph or other likeness for the purposes of advertising, trade and promotion on behalf of Torstar Corp., its affiliates and subsidiaries without further compensation to the winner, unless prohibited by law.

6. Winners will be determined no later than November 15, 2001, and will be notified by mail. Winners will be required to sign and return an Affidavit of Eligibility form within 15 days after winner notification. Noncompliance within that time period may result in disqualification and an alternative winner may be selected. Winners of trip must execute a Release of Liability prior to ticketing and must possess required travel documents (e.g. passport, photo ID) where applicable. Trip must be completed by November 2002. No substitution of prize permitted by winner. Torstar Corp. and D. L. Blair, Inc., their parents, affiliates, and subsidiaries are not responsible for errors in printing or electronic presentation of Contest, entries and/or game pieces. In the event of printing or other errors which may result in unintended prize values or duplication of prizes, all affected game pieces or entries shall be null and void. If for any reason the Internet portion of the Contest is not capable of running as planned, including infection by computer virus, bugs, tampering, unauthorized intervention, fraud, technical failures, or any other causes beyond the control of Torstar Corp. which corrupt or affect the administration, secrecy, fairness, integrity or proper conduct of the Contest, Torstar Corp. reserves the right, at its sole discretion, to disqualify any individual who tampers with the entry process and to cancel, terminate, modify or suspend the Contest or the Internet portion thereof. In the event of a dispute regarding an online entry, the entry will be deemed submitted by the authorized holder of the e-mail account submitted at the time of entry. Authorized account holder is defined as the natural person who is assigned to an e-mail address by an Internet access provider, online service provider or other organization that is responsible for arranging an e-mail address for the domain associated with the submitted e-mail address. **Purchase or acceptance of a product offer does not improve your chances of winning.**

7. Prizes: (1) Grand Prize—A Harlequin wedding dress (approximate retail value: $3,500) and a 5-night/6-day honeymoon trip to Maui, HI, including round-trip air transportation provided by Maui Visitors Bureau from Los Angeles International Airport (winner is responsible for transportation to and from Los Angeles International Airport) and a Harlequin Romance Package, including hotel accomodations (double occupancy) at the Hyatt Regency Maui Resort and Spa, dinner for (2) two at Swan Court, a sunset sail on Kiele V and a spa treatment for the winner (approximate retail value: $4,000); (5) Five runner-up prizes of a $1000 gift certificate to selected retail outlets to be determined by Sponsor (retail value $1000 ea.). Prizes consist of only those items listed as part of the prize. Limit one prize per person. All prizes are valued in U.S. currency.

8. For a list of winners (available after December 17, 2001) send a self-addressed, stamped envelope to: Harlequin Walk Down the Aisle Contest 1197 Winners, P.O. Box 4200 Blair, NE 68009-4200 or you may access the www.eHarlequin.com Web site through January 15, 2002.

Contest sponsored by Torstar Corp., P.O. Box 9042, Buffalo, NY 14269-9042, U.S.A.

PHWDACONT2

Harlequin Romance®
Love affairs that
last a lifetime.

HARLEQUIN® *Presents~*
Seduction and passion
guaranteed.

*Harlequin®
Historical*
Historical
Romantic
Adventure.

HARLEQUIN® *Temptation.*
Sassy, sexy, seductive!

HARLEQUIN® *SuperRomance®*
Emotional,
exciting,
unexpected.

HARLEQUIN®
AMERICAN *Romance®*
Heart, home
& happiness.

HARLEQUIN®
Duets™
Romantic comedy.

HARLEQUIN®
INTRIGUE
Breathtaking
romantic suspense.

Get caught
reading
Harlequin.

HARLEQUIN®
Makes any time special®

Visit us at www.eHarlequin.com

PHGCR